THE LESSON

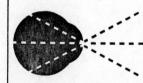

This Large Print Book carries the
Seal of Approval of N.A.V.H.

THE LESSON

SUZANNE WOODS FISHER

THORNDIKE PRESS
A part of Gale, Cengage Learning

GALE
CENGAGE Learning·

Detroit • New York • San Francisco • New Haven, Conn • Waterville, Maine • London

GALE
CENGAGE Learning·

LIBRARY OF CONGRESS CATALOGING-IN-PUBLICATION DATA

Fisher, Suzanne Woods.
   The lesson / by Suzanne Woods Fisher.
      pages ; cm. — (Stoney ridge seasons ; #3) (Thorndike Press large print Christian romance)
   ISBN-13: 978-1-4104-5556-7 (hardcover)
   ISBN-10: 1-4104-5556-4 (hardcover)
   1. Teenage girls—Fiction. 2. Amish—Fiction. 3. Large type books. I. Title.
PS3606.I78L47 2013b
813'.6—dc23
                                              2013001145

Published in 2013 by arrangement with Revell Books, a division of Baker Publishing Group

Printed in Mexico
1 2 3 4 5 6 7 17 16 15 14 13

This story is for my youngest daughter,
Meredith,
who happens to be a full-time teacher
and a part-time detective.

1

The year Mary Kate Lapp turned nineteen started out fine enough. Life seemed full of endless possibilities. But as the year went on, a terrible restlessness began to grow inside of her, like sour yeast in a jar of warm water on a sunny windowsill. There were days when she thought she couldn't stand another moment in this provincial little town, and days when she thought she could never leave.

On a sun-drenched afternoon, M.K. was zooming along on her red scooter past an English farmer's sheep pasture, with a book propped above the handlebars — a habit that her stepmother, Fern, scolded her about relentlessly. She was just about to live happily ever after with the story's handsome hero when a very loud *Bwhoom!* suddenly interrupted her reading.

Most folks would have turned tail and run, but not M.K. She might have considered it, but as usual, curiosity got the best of her. She zoomed back down the street, hopped off her scooter, climbed up on the fence, and there she saw him — an English sheep farmer in overalls, sprawled flat on the ground with a large rifle next to him. The frightened sheep were huddled in the far corner of the pasture. Doozy, M.K.'s big old yellow dog of dubious ancestry, elected to stay behind with the scooter.

M.K. wasn't sure what to do next. Should she see if the sheep farmer was still alive? He didn't look alive. He looked very, very dead. She wouldn't know what to do, anyway — healing bodies was her sister Sadie's department. And what if the murderer were close by? Nosir. She was brave, but you had to draw the line somewhere.

But she could go to the phone shanty by the schoolhouse and make a 911 call for the police. So that's what she did. She waited at the phone shanty until she heard the sirens and saw the revolving lights on top of the sheriff's car. Then she jumped on her scooter and hurried back to the sheep pasture.

The sheriff walked over to ask M.K. if she was the one who had called 911. She had known Sheriff Hoffman all her life. He was a pleasant-looking man with a short haircut, brown going gray around his ears, and a permanent suntan. Tall and impressive in his white uniform shirt and crisp black pants, radio clipped to one hip, gun holster on the other. He questioned M.K. about every detail she could recall — which wasn't much, other than a loud gunshot. She didn't even know the farmer's name. The sheriff took a pen from his back pocket and started taking notes. (What would he write? *Amish witness knows nothing. Absolutely nothing.*) But he did tell her she did the right thing by not disturbing the crime scene. He took her name and address and said he might be contacting her with more questions.

M.K. stuck around, all ears about whatever she could overhear, fascinated by the meager clues the police were trying to piece together. When the county coroner arrived in his big black van, M.K. decided she had gleaned all she could. Besides, the trees were throwing long shadows. The sun would be setting soon and she should get home to let her father and Fern know about the murder. It was alarming news!

She took a shortcut through the town of Stoney Ridge to reach Windmill Farm as fast as she could but was intercepted by her friend Jimmy Fisher. Standing in front of the Sweet Tooth Bakery, he called to her, then ran alongside and grabbed the handle-bars of her scooter to stop her. She practically flew headfirst over the handlebars.

Men! So oblivious.

"I need your help with something important," Jimmy said.

"Can't," M.K. said, pushing his hands off her scooter. "I'm in a big hurry." She started pumping her leg on the ground to build up speed. Doozy puffed and panted alongside her.

"It won't take long!" Jimmy sounded wounded. "What's your big hurry?"

"Can't tell you!" she told him, and she meant it. The sheriff had warned her not to say anything to anyone, with the exception of her family, until they had gathered more information. She felt a prick of guilt and looked back at Jimmy, who had stopped abruptly when she brushed him off. She liked that he was a little bit scared of her, especially because he was older and much too handsome for his own good.

She glanced back and saw him cross the road to head into the Sweet Tooth Bakery where her friend Ruthie worked. Good! Let Ruthie solve Jimmy's problem this time. M.K. was always helping him get out of scrapes and tight spots. That boy had a proclivity for trouble. Always had.

Distracted by the dead body and then by Jimmy Fisher, M.K. made a soaring right turn near the Smuckers' goat farm, and possibly — just possibly — forgot to look both ways before she turned. Her scooter ended up bumping into Alice Smucker, the schoolteacher at Twin Creeks where M.K. had spent eight long years, as Alice was herding goats across the road into an empty pasture.

A tiny collision with a scooter and Alice refused to get to her feet. "I AM CONCUSSED!" she called out.

M.K. was convinced that Alice was prejudiced against her. And she was so dramatic. She insisted M.K. call for an ambulance.

Two 911 calls in one day — it was more excitement than M.K. could bear. She hoped the dispatcher didn't recognize her voice and think she was a crank caller. She wasn't! Nosir.

Naturally, M.K. waited until the ambulance arrived to swoop away with Alice, who was hissing with anger. When M.K. offered to accompany Alice to the hospital — she knew it was the right thing to do, though the offer came with gritted teeth — Alice glared at her.

"You stay away from me, Mary Kate Lapp!" she snapped, before she swooned in a faint.

Alice. So dramatic.

After M.K. rounded up the goats and returned them to the Smuckers' pasture, she arrived at Windmill Farm, her home and final destination. She couldn't wait to tell her father and Fern about the news! She was sorry for the sheep farmer — after all, she wasn't heartless. But finally, something interesting had happened in this town. It was big news — there had never been a murder in Stoney Ridge. And she had been the first one on the scene.

Well, to be accurate — and Fern was constantly telling her not to exaggerate — M.K. wasn't *quite* on the scene. But she did hear the gunshot! She absolutely did.

She knew Fern would be irritated with her for being so late for dinner. Fern was a stickler about . . . well, about most everything. But especially about being late for dinner. The unfortunate incident with Alice Smucker had slowed her down even more. The accident did bother M.K. — she would never intentionally run into anyone. Especially not Alice Smucker. Of all people!

M.K. set the scooter against the barn. She heard her mare, Cayenne, whinny for her, so she went into the barn, filled up the horse's bucket with water, and closed the stall door. She latched it tightly, her mind a whirl of details. It wasn't until she had pulled the latch that she noticed her father's horse and buggy were gone. She peered through the dusty barn window and saw that the house was pitch dark, its windows not showing any soft lampshine. Where could her father and Fern have gone? They were always home at this time of day. Always, always, always.

This day just kept getting stranger.

Guilt pinched the edges of Chris Yoder's conscience. Old Deborah had taught him better manners than to ignore a neighbor's greeting, but he wasn't interested in being neighborly. All that interested him was fixing up his grandfather's house. For now, it was a disaster. It looked as if a good puff of wind would be all that was required to bring the house tumbling down.

Jenny turned around to peer out the buggy window. "I think she was hoping you would stop and say hello, Chris. She's seems like such a nice old lady."

"Can't," Chris said. "Gotta get home." Erma Yutzy was a very nice old lady, and he had done some odd jobs for her, but she liked to talk and he could never find a way to break in and excuse himself. But it wasn't just that he wanted to avoid Erma Yutzy

13

today. He was always in a touchy mood after a trip to town. People were everywhere — on the sidewalks, in the stores, riding bikes, eating ice-cream cones, sipping expensive coffees. As if nothing bad could happen. As if nothing could hurt them or threaten their sense of security.

"This isn't going to work," Jenny whispered. "We're going to get caught."

Chris glanced over at his thirteen-year-old sister. The last few months had taken a toll on her. She had always been a worrier. She worried about everything and everybody. "It's been working for over six weeks now, Jenny. If we were going to have a problem, we would have had it by now. I think we're home free." He didn't entirely believe that, but he knew it was best to ease Jenny's concern.

Jenny's chin jutted forward. "Plunking me in school is the worst idea you've ever had."

"No, it's not," Chris said. "You need schooling. And I need you to not be underfoot."

"I'm going to need new shoes for school." She scowled at him. "We can't afford them."

She had him there. He had no cash to spare, but he had been prepared for lean times. And he wasn't going to let a few dollars stop his sister from getting an educa-

14

tion. Schooling was something he didn't take for granted.

"Think of school as an adventure. Something new." Chris kept the smile on his face and the worry out of his voice.

Jenny leaned her head against the window and closed her eyes.

For a moment he was lost in another time of his life, another season. Was it only two months ago? It seemed like much longer. That was the week that Old Deborah, as close to a grandmother to him as anyone ever would be, passed to her glory.

Hours before she had died, she had covered his hand with hers. "Every now and then, Chris, life throws you something you'd never have chosen in a million years. I know that's how you feel right now."

He looked into her tired brown eyes. "How am I going to do it?"

She smiled. "The Lord taught us to pray, 'Give us *this* day our daily bread.' We're supposed to live one day at a time, not to borrow another day's troubles."

One day at a time. That's how they had been living ever since they arrived in Stoney Ridge two weeks ago, but he hadn't expected things to be this hard. They were scraping by on a wing and a prayer. But there were good things too. They were set-

15

tling into a new home. He had picked up some odd jobs, like mowing Erma Yutzy's lawn, that provided ready cash. Just today he had gotten a tip at the hardware store about a man named Amos Lapp who needed a fellow to help with fieldwork because he had some heart trouble. Wasn't that a sign of God's just-in-time providence?

A whinny from his horse made him smile. Chris had a magnificent Thoroughbred horse, Samson, that he had raised since he was a foal. The stallion was a legacy from Old Deborah, along with the knowledge that a little piece of real estate in Stoney Ridge was waiting, intended for him from his grandfather. It was a start.

He exhaled. One day at a time.

After Jimmy Fisher watched Mary Kate Lapp charge up the road, he started to head to the Sweet Tooth Bakery but changed his mind. He wasn't really in the mood to try to talk to Ruthie today — she often burst into a fit of giggles when she was around him. Plus, it was getting late and he knew his mother would be wondering where he was. Chore time on the chicken-and-egg farm.

He had really wanted to talk to M.K. She would have a good idea about how he

16

should proceed. Much better than Ruthie. M.K., for all her shortcomings, was very reliable about these kinds of things.

Jimmy was in love. At a horse auction in Leola — his favorite pastime — he had noticed an attractive young Amish woman who was selling a two-year-old brindled mare. He couldn't take his eyes off that girl. Shiny auburn hair, snapping green eyes. And tall! He'd always wanted to marry a tall woman. It was a dire disappointment to Jimmy that he wasn't as tall as his brother, Paul. Jimmy wasn't tall at all, but he held himself very straight as if to make the most of what he had. He planned to rectify that genetic flaw for the next generation. Tall was good. It was number five on his list of critical requirements for his future wife.

The brindled mare had fetched a good price, and the young woman was saying goodbye to the horse, tears streaming down her face. Jimmy was touched. Three heartbeats later, he tracked down the auctioneer to find out to whom the mare had belonged. The auctioneer was taking a break behind the large canvas tent while the horse lot was being changed. A stub of a cigar hung from his mouth as he eyed Jimmy. "Why do you want to know?"

"I had an interest in that brindled mare,"

Jimmy said. That was true. It wasn't a lie. He was more interested in the mare's owner than the mare, but he wasn't lying. "Just wondered if they might be breeders or not." Jimmy kicked a rock on the ground with the toe of his boot. "Giving some thought to becoming a breeder myself. Just thought I'd talk to her, ah, him." He cleared his throat, tried to act nonchalant.

The auctioneer threw the cigar stub on the ground and rubbed it out with his shoe. "I thought you Amish knew everybody, anyway."

"A common misperception," Jimmy said. *Along with assuming we look alike and think alike and act alike.* He nearly said that part out loud, but held back, given that he had become so mature lately. Still, it rankled him how the non-Amish lumped the Amish into one-size-fits-all.

Take Jimmy and his brother, Paul. They might share a passing resemblance — both blond, with their father's strong nose and high forehead — but no two brothers could be more different. Paul was thirty now, still unmarried, still at home under his mother's very large thumb. It wasn't that Paul didn't want to marry and start a family of his own; he just couldn't quite decide on a wife. He was always juggling a few girls, attracted to

18

each one but not in love with any of them.

Jimmy had no trouble making decisions, or falling in love. He fell in love, he fell out of love — but at least it was love! He had passion, and emotion, and wasn't afraid to make a commitment like Paul was. Or, at least, he wouldn't be afraid to when he fell in love for the last time. He planned to marry within two years. It was all planned out. And he had just found his missus. Done! Checked off.

The auctioneer took a loud slurp of coffee and tossed the paper cup on the ground. "Her name is Emily Esh. Father is Emanuel Esh. They live near Bart. Father's a darn good horse trader." He handed Jimmy a card: *Domenico Guiseppe Rizzo, purveyor of fine horses.* "This is the guy you need to see if you want to get into pony racing."

Jimmy peered at the card. "Wait. Is that Domino Joe?" He knew Domino Joe. Knew him well. "What makes you think I have an interest in pony racing?"

The auctioneer glanced at his watch and strolled back to the auction block. Over his shoulder, he tossed, "If you're already acquainted with Domino Joe, then why would I think you don't?"

Jimmy frowned and stuffed the card in his pocket. Emily Esh. What a beautiful name.

It had a musical sound . . . what was it M.K. called that kind of thing? Allit, alliter, alliteration. That was it!

Now . . . how to meet Emily Esh? He remembered that M.K. had talked Ruthie into going to a youth gathering in Bart this summer, hoping to meet a more intelligent crop of boys, she had said. "I've known these Stoney Ridge boys forever," she said airily to Jimmy. "And most of them have no idea how to carry on an intelligent conversation. They just want to talk about the latest prank they pulled or about what the best hunting sports are or all about their dogs."

At the time, Jimmy took offense. M.K. was always showing off her big brain, as if it wasn't obvious to everyone that she had a different way of thinking. He had a hunch that she could go to the ends of the earth and she still wouldn't find what she was looking for, because that fellow didn't exist. But now, the Bart youth gathering sounded very intriguing to Jimmy.

He just needed M.K.'s help. He wanted to meet Emily Esh, his future missus.

M.K. waited restlessly for her father and Fern to return home. She went down to the honey cabin, tucked at the far edge of Windmill Farm's property, and wrote on some labels for honey jars, but her hands felt shaky with excitement. She didn't like the way her handwriting ended up looking — like she was nine, not nineteen. Just yesterday, she had finished spinning her most recent supply of honey from her brown bees' honeycombs into long, thin clean jars. She sold her honey at Fern's roadside stand. She wished she had left some chores to do. She swept the floor and straightened up, then went back to the house.

In her bedroom, she spent some time looking for her old detective notebook. She finally found it, tucked deep under her mattress. She opened it to a clean page and wrote SOLVE SHEEP FARMER'S MURDER!!! in bold letters across the top and underlined it three times, breaking the pencil point in the process. She found another pencil and numbered the page from one to ten.

But how?

She pulled out her detective books from the bottom bookshelf and spread them out on her bed.

#1. Look for overlooked clues that the culprit might have left in his haste.
A. Go back to the pasture.

She spent the next ten minutes drumming the pencil against the page as she searched in vain for ideas to proceed. When her head began to ache from thinking too hard, she put her books away and stuffed the notebook back under the mattress.

She thought the house seemed stuffy, so she opened the windows downstairs in the living room and kitchen. A breeze moved into the room, carrying a faint perfume from Fern's rose garden. M.K. sat down, stood up, walked around, sat down again. Her mind was spinning, like dandelions in the wind. She was so antsy that Doozy gave up following her. He curled up in the living room corner and went to sleep. She jumped up and went into the kitchen, knowing just what to do to keep her mind and hands busy.

After her sister Sadie married Gideon Smucker and left home, M.K. was at loose ends — she had finished formal schooling, she was missing the companionship of Sadie and Julia, her married sisters, and she was driving Fern crazy. A serious case of "ants in her pants," Fern diagnosed. M.K. needed something to do, so Fern taught her how to bake bread.

M.K. went into the kitchen and pulled out the flour canister. On the windowsill was a jar filled with a noxious-looking substance, placed where the late afternoon sun would warm it but not too much. She picked up the jar, remembering the first time Fern had shown it to her.

It was the winter after Sadie and Gid's wedding, two years ago. The lower half was a thick gray pillow, looking like something you'd find on the moon. Fern had shaken it up, then opened it. A strong sour smell exploded into the air.

"Phew!" M.K. pinched her nose like a clothespin. "What is that horrible thing?" She leaned closer to inspect it.

"It's my sourdough bread starter," Fern said. "It's been in my family for generations. It came from a carefully tended mother dough that my great-great-great-grandmother brought over from Germany in 1886."

"How could all those grandmothers have kept it alive all that time?"

"Some mysteries are best not to examine too closely," Fern said in her matter-of-fact way. "Starters are sturdier than they appear. But I guard that starter like gold at Fort Knox." She scooped out a hefty measure of foamy pale-yellow-white starter and put it in a bowl. "I refresh it every week so it stays healthy." She turned on the tap, testing the temperature with her fingers. "I add water that's just barely warmer than your fingers." When she got it right she gestured to M.K. "Try it."

M.K. stuck her fingers under the stream. She hardly felt the water. M.K. filled a glass measuring cup and stirred it into the jar of starter. It foamed up.

M.K. jumped back, then stared at it. "Why, it's alive!"

"Exactly."

Danger! M.K. was hooked.

A noise outside jolted her back to the present. She peered out the window, hoping to see a buggy roll up the driveway. But no — it was only a noisy bluejay, gorging himself on black oiled sunflower seeds that filled the blue bird feeder on the porch. M.K. rapped on the window to shoo the greedy bird away.

She took out a large bowl and measured a cup of flour. She used a sturdy wooden spoon and stirred the flour into the heady sponge, filling the air with a sour scent, unique to yeast. She turned the dough out on a layer of fine white flour that she scattered across the surface of the counter. As she began to knead the bread, back and forth, over and under, pushing and pulling, her restlessness began to slip away. Like it always did. She didn't like to admit it, but Fern was right. Her hands needed to be busy.

Two hours later, the loaves were baked and cooling on the counter. They were far more dense than Fern's would have been. M.K. never had the patience to let dough rest as long as it needed. But the kitchen was clean and shiny for Fern's critical inspection just as she walked in. M.K. met her at the door. Over Fern's shoulder, she saw her father near the barn, untacking the horse from the buggy shafts.

"Where have you been?" M.K. asked. "I've been waiting for hours!"

A wall came up, chilled the air. Fern didn't speak immediately. Doozy let go of a soft, joyous woof and his tail wagged slowly, then stopped.

"Where have *you* been?" Fern replied, sharp as a pinch. "You were due at the schoolhouse at six. There was a work frolic to get the schoolhouse ready for school on Monday."

M.K.'s hands flew up to her cheeks. "I forgot! I forgot all about it."

Fern frowned at her. "If you were a bird, you would be a hummingbird. Flitting from place to place. You can't be still."

25

"But there's a reason! Something has happened!"

"So we heard," Amos said in a weary voice as he opened the kitchen door and walked into the room. His weather-tanned face, with its work wrinkles running down his cheeks, looked exasperated. "You ran into Alice Smucker. How did you happen to do that?"

Oh. *Oh!* M.K. had forgotten all about the collision with Alice Smucker. Her mind was wholly preoccupied with the shocking murder. "Well, there's rather a lot of Alice."

Amos raised a warning eyebrow at M.K. "Alice Smucker will be unable to start the school year due to a mild concussion."

"Really? She *actually* has a concussion? The doctor really, truly said that? Because —"

Amos sent M.K. a warning frown, but too late.

"— Alice can be a bit of a hypochondri—"

Amos held up his hand to stop her. "Mary Kate, it doesn't matter whether the doctor said so. That's what Alice Smucker believes she has, and it was because you didn't look where you were going on the scooter and you crashed into the poor woman."

"Dad, it wasn't really that big of a crash. More like a tiny bump."

Amos shook his head. "She has a ferocious headache and can't teach for the foreseeable future."

"That's a shame," M.K. said.

Amos and Fern exchanged a look.

The first ripple of concern fluttered down M.K.'s spine. "What?"

"The members of the school board were at the work frolic," Amos said. "They came to a decision about who can fill in for Alice."

"Well, Gideon, of course. He's done it before. He's a fine teacher. Better than Alice." M.K. hoped Sadie wouldn't mind having Gid gone all day. She had little twins, a boy and a girl, who ran her ragged. At least, they ran M.K. ragged whenever she popped in for a visit. To M.K.'s way of thinking, children ran everybody ragged.

Amos and Fern exchanged another glance, and M.K. sensed something dreadful was coming, like the stillness right before a storm hit. She felt the hair on the back of her neck tingle. "If not Gid, then who? Who?" In the quiet, her question sounded like an owl.

"The school board has decided you will fill in for Alice," Amos said.

"Me? Me?" she said with a squeak. "Teach school? You want me to teach school?" She was outraged! It was just an accident. She hadn't run into Alice on purpose! "No! No, no, no, no, no. I can't do it! Absolutely not!" The very thought terrified her. Stuck in a hot room with twenty-five slow-witted children, all day long? *Boring!* Supremely boring! "Dad, you've got to tell the school board that I just can't do it. Tell them you and Fern need me to help at Windmill Farm." She swept her arms in a wide arc, accidentally knocking over something from the counter onto the floor, where it shattered. She looked down, horrified. It was the jar that held Fern's one-hundred-and-fifty-year-old bread dough starter. She covered her face, then peeked through her fingers to gauge Fern's reaction.

At first, Fern looked stunned. Then her mouth set in a straight line. "Clean up that mess. Then you'd better get ready. The school board wants to meet with you tomorrow, 8 a.m. sharp, at the schoolhouse."

M.K. said nothing. As she scooped shattered glass and tangy-smelling starter into the garbage, she felt that the whole day had taken an unsatisfactory turn. She had encountered a shocking murder, she had been suspected of intentionally running her scooter into Alice Smucker (when all she had been doing was riding her scooter), and now there was this uncomfortable expectation that she would teach school.

Suddenly M.K. was looking ahead, into the terrible future. Her life had been completely rearranged. This was too much. It was all too much!

What a day. The worst of her life.

2

The early morning air was quite sharp, hinting of summer's end. Amos stood by the barn and watched his youngest daughter zip off on her scooter to meet with the school board. Mary Kate had a woebegone look on her face, as if she were heading off to the gallows. He nearly caved, nearly gave her an excuse to tell the school board that she was needed at the farm and couldn't possibly teach school. But then he would have to face his wife with that news and the thought stopped him short.

Besides, he knew Fern was overly blessed with a sixth sense about his children. Last night, she told him that Mary Kate had turned down Ruthie's request for her to go through baptism instructions this fall. For three years now, Ruthie had pleaded with M.K. to join her in the classes and M.K. always said no, that she wasn't ready. This time, Ruthie was going ahead without her.

"That restive spirit has always worried me about M.K.," Fern told Amos. "It's nothing new, though it's getting worse. She slips around rules, she reads books in church, she sticks her nose where it doesn't belong, and now look at this." Out of her apron pocket she pulled a folded piece of paper and thrust it at Amos.

He unfolded the paper. "A passport application?"

"I sent her to the post office to mail a package to Julia and Rome, and look what she came back with."

"Where did you find it?"

"It had slipped under the bench in the buggy."

He folded it and handed it to her. "Put it back where you found it. She'll be looking for it."

Fern slipped it back into her pocket with a sigh. "You're not going to let her know we are aware she is planning to flee the country?"

"She's young," Amos said in M.K.'s defense. His greatest hope in life would be that his children would accept his beliefs and join the church, but he was a believer in free will. He would never insist or put a timetable on that important decision. Time belonged to God. "Younger than most."

"She's nineteen. And I don't think age has anything to do with it."

"Then what do you think her problem is?"

"It's that quick mind of hers. It's got to be kept busy or it gets her into trouble. Teaching school would be challenging for her, Amos. She'll end up learning more than the scholars."

But would the scholars survive her? Amos loved his youngest daughter, but she had a unique way amidst a community that frowned upon uniqueness. How many times had Deacon Abraham taken Amos aside, in his quiet, gentle manner, to suggest ways of redirecting M.K.'s bottomless pit of energy? His daughter always meant well, her intentions were good, but she had a nose for trouble, a knack for being in the wrong place at the wrong time. She thought her real job was to know everyone in Stoney Ridge and everything that was happening. And she was filled with excuses. Nothing was ever her fault. Just like careening into Alice Smucker last night.

Amos wouldn't have said so at the frolic yesterday, with the school board tsk-tsking over Alice's concussion, but he had to agree with M.K. about Alice's hypochondria. Alice was rumored to be absent more days than she was in the schoolhouse teaching.

He'd never known Alice not to have an ailment, magnified to serious proportions.

Even Sadie, his middle daughter, who never said an unkind word about anyone, gave Alice a tea remedy each week to help manage her sensitive digestion. Earlier in the summer, Sadie had confessed to Amos that the remedy was just tea and sugar, nothing more. "Alice just wants someone to listen to her," Sadie said. "Since her father remarried, she's just lonely. Once I figured that out, I realized I was wasting time trying to find remedies for her symptoms. I gave her tea and sugar one time, and she said that was the best cure of all." Sadie lowered her voice. "I didn't tell her it was just tea and sugar."

Amos straightened his straw hat. He had a full day ahead — and a young fellow was coming by to see about cutting hay for him.

Maybe Fern was right. Maybe teaching would challenge M.K. and keep her mind out of trouble — like the trouble she could get into by trying to solve the murder of that poor sheep farmer. "Leave that to the police!" Amos had told M.K. last night. But he could see that she was itching to get involved and solve the crime. She gave him six different scenarios last night, accusing every single surrounding neighbor of the terrible deed. As Fern frequently pointed out, once she latched onto an idea, she was like a fox with an egg in its mouth — all the hollering in the world wouldn't make her drop it.

Maybe Fern was right. Maybe teaching school was the answer for M.K. He hoped so.

"Whoa." Chris Yoder pulled back on the reins, drawing the horse to a halt. He leapt from the buggy seat and hopped down to find the owner of this big farm. A soft meow greeted him. He bent over and scooped up a barn cat that wove between his feet. "Who are you?"

"That's Buzz."

Chris looked up to see a tall, muscular, middle-aged Amish man facing him. "Amos Lapp?"

The man nodded. "Are you the fellow sent to me by the manager of the hardware store? Chris Yoder?"

Chris nodded. "How did a cat get a name like Buzz?"

"I always let my children name the animals. My youngest daughter went through a stage when she was naming every animal names that sounded like sounds."

"Onomatopoeia."

"That's it! That's it exactly!" Amos laughed. "I couldn't come up with that word if my life depended on it."

Chris set Buzz on the ground and reached out a hand to shake Amos's. "I was told at the hardware store that you needed some help with fieldwork. The manager, Bud, said you'd had some heart surgery."

"You heard right," Amos said. "I had some serious surgery awhile back and there are limitations as to what I can do in the fields."

"I've had a lot of experience with growing crops." Chris looked over the fields. He could see that the corn tassles were drying out, which meant the corn was about ready to pick. The third cutting of hay needed to get done before the predicted rainstorm at the end of the week. "Should I get to work on the hay? Or the corn?"

"Not so fast!" Amos grinned. "Though I like the way you think. Can you tell me a little about yourself?"

This was the part Chris dreaded. He kept his gaze on the fields. "What would you like to know?"

"What brings you to Stoney Ridge?"

"I need a job." Chris didn't mean to sound rude, but he didn't want to volunteer anything he didn't need to. The less people knew about him and his little sister, the better.

Amos watched him for a while. A long while. Then, to Chris's relief, all that Amos said was, "Let's give it a day's trial, then." He put his straw hat back on his head. "When you hear the dinner bell clang, come up to the house and join my wife and daughter and me for lunch."

"I brought my own lunch. I'll be fine." That was a lie. His first lie. He didn't have a lunch. But he didn't want to get chummy with Amos Lapp and his family. For now, it was better to keep his distance.

Amos Lapp shrugged. "Suit yourself."

Chris chanced a look at him. "Tools for haying in the barn?"

"Yes. Back room."

Chris nodded. "I'll go get started." He hurried to the barn before Amos Lapp thought of anything more to ask him.

A single brown horse grazed under the shade of an oak tree, and a bright flash of blue and orange darted across the road — a bluebird. It was going to be another hot, humid day. Mary Kate's face felt beet red. A bead of sweat dripped down her back. She slowed the scooter as she rounded the bend in the road that led to the schoolhouse.

The door of the schoolhouse was wide open. The school board members were already there, waiting for her. Her stomach twisted into a tight knot. This was a terrible thing. A terrible, terrible thing.

She set her red scooter against the building, told Doozy to stay, took a deep breath, and walked into the schoolhouse. At the sound of her arrival, the men stopped talking and looked up. Orin Stoltzfus, Wayne Zook, Allen King. She knew each of these men — had known them all her life. Yet right now, she felt like she was being judged and came up lacking. Orin Stoltzfus stood up. He had the most experience on the school board. School board members were voted in and served a three-year term. Each year, an old board member finished his term and a new member was voted in.

Orin gave her a warm smile, showing the gap in his front teeth. "Good morning, Mary Kate. So glad you offered to step in for Alice."

Offered? *Offered?!*

Fern! This is all your doing, she thought for the hundredth time. "Just how long do you think Alice will need some relief?" M.K. planned to drop by Alice's later today with a loaf of freshly baked bread. A peace offering. "A few days?"

The men exchanged glances.

"A week?"

Still no response.

The oatmeal M.K. ate for breakfast shifted and rolled, turning into concrete. "Surely, she couldn't have been badly hurt." Meekly, she added, "Could she?"

Orin exhaled. "No, she's not too terribly hurt. But she seems to sense she might be facing imminent demise."

"Oh, is that all? Alice has been predicting her imminent demise for years!" M.K. looked hopefully at the men. "She's had two feet in the grave for as long as I've known her! Everybody knows Alice is as sound as a dollar. Maybe she needs to be working, to keep her mind busy." M.K. put a finger in the air. "Was mer net im Kopp hot, hot mer in de Fiess." *If your brain doesn't work, your feet must.* "Fern is always telling me that."

Orin scratched his neck. "I'm guessing we'll need you to substitute for two weeks. Maybe three, tops."

M.K. blew out a puff of air. "Okay. Three weeks." She could do this for three weeks. "I just want to warn you. I'm not much of a teacher."

Over her head, Orin and Wayne exchanged a look: *Is she always like this?*

"You like to read," Allen King offered. His

jowls jiggled through his sparse whiskers as he spoke. "Why, you've got your nose in a book all the time! Just last Sunday, the preacher pointed out that you were reading during his sermon. Remember?"

M.K. remembered. She had tried to leave the book in the buggy, but she just couldn't concentrate on a thing until she found out if Robinson Crusoe was eaten by cannibals. She didn't think so, because it would have made a very strange and abrupt ending to the book. But she had to know for sure. So she slipped it under her apron and sat in the far left corner, against the wall. Ruthie covered for her by leaning forward, keeping her out of range of Fern's eagle eyes. She still wasn't sure how Ruthie's father, preaching at the time — and everybody knew he was a long-winded, dry-bone preacher — happened to notice M.K.'s book. He had paused and pointed a long finger at M.K. "Mary Kate Lapp! Put that book away on the Sabbath."

It was mortifying.

Fern confiscated her book and returned it to the library. She gave M.K. a one-minute lecture about how even good things become idols when they distract us from God. Fern was famous for her one-minute lectures.

"Isn't there anyone else who might like to

teach?" M.K. protested weakly.

"Nope," Orin said. "Can't think of any."

"Really? I can think of all kinds of people who would be wonderful teachers: Gideon Smucker, Ruthie Glick, Ethan King, even . . . even . . . Jimmy Fisher!" She nearly choked on the words because, even though she and Jimmy had made their peace over the years, he wasn't the brightest lantern in the barn. But she was desperate! And desperate times called for desperate measures.

"No," Orin repeated, shaking his head. "We are confident you are the one."

All three men looked at her, waiting for her to agree with them. And what could she say? It was her fault that Alice was injured. The families were counting on the start of school. The scholars shouldn't be penalized. She grabbed her elbows. "The thing is, Orin, the thing is, I really don't *want* to be a teacher."

That was putting it mildly. She was absolutely sure she would be bored to death if she were confined to these four walls in this stuffy room. Every day, the same as the day before. Hadn't she put in her time? Eight long years. How much more could she endure from this little schoolhouse?

A general silence met M.K.'s confession.

The men exchanged awkward glances. Orin walked up to her and put a hand on her shoulder. "Mary Kate, being Amish means you care less about what's best for you and more about what's best for the church."

Certainly, the inside of M.K.'s head had gone numb. Against her will, she had been strategically cornered. There was no way to respond to Orin's comment without sounding like she was a fence jumper. And she wasn't a fence jumper. She definitely wasn't. Well, maybe a little. Lately, she'd even been thinking of jumping all the way to Hong Kong. Or maybe Madrid. She couldn't quite decide.

This is all your doing, Fern! she thought for the hundred and first time. Inwardly, M.K. sighed, defeated. Outwardly, she agreed with Orin and spent the next half hour getting a tutorial about how to keep the coal heater from acting up on a cold winter morning. She started to explain that she would only be here for three weeks, gone long before winter, so she didn't need to learn how to feed coal into the stove, but she decided to keep her mouth shut. No one listened to a word she said in this town, anyway.

Orin seemed enraptured with this heater, describing each part with loving detail. *Blah,*

blah, blah. She stopped listening to Orin when he got distracted with a loose seam holding the stovetop pipe in one piece. She had a bad experience with a stovepipe once — courtesy of Jimmy Fisher — and liked to stay clear of them. Finally, Orin ran out of things to inform M.K. about.

And then M.K. and Doozy slunk home.

As soon as his mother had gone to town, Jimmy Fisher made a beeline to Windmill Farm to talk to Mary Kate. No one answered his knock at the farmhouse. He crossed over to the barn to look for Amos but couldn't find him. Then he saw Fern hanging wet laundry on the clothesline. The soapy scent of fresh laundry perfumed the morning air. Jimmy breathed in deeply — it was one of his favorite smells. But he thought twice about meeting up with Fern and scooted behind a tree. Fern thoroughly intimidated him. Thankfully, he spotted Hank Lapp in his buggy shop. The shop was an old carriage barn, with a small apartment up above where Hank lived. Buggies and parts, in various stages of disarray, littered the shop floor.

"JIMMY FISHER!" Hank boomed, when he caught sight of him. "You're a little late for fishing today, boy. I went out before dawn." Hank Lapp's sun-leathered face exploded into a smile.

Being around Hank always reminded Jimmy of the effects of electricity — instantly, a dark room would be filled with dazzling light and a fellow had to blink rapidly to allow his eyes to adjust to the brightness. Jimmy leaned against the buggy Hank was tinkering on. One side of the buggy was dented, as if it had been broadsided by a car. Buggy and car collisions were a frequent occurrence in Lancaster County, and the buggies always took the brunt of it. But, as Hank often said, it meant he would always have plenty of work.

"I didn't come to go fishing, Hank. Wish I had joined you this morning, though. No, I came by to talk to Mary Kate. Is she working at the honey cabin?"

"Naw. She's down at the schoolhouse. Should be back any minute now." He picked up a long piece of cut fiberboard and held it up against the side of the buggy to see if it would fit as a replacement part. "But she'll be in no mood for yikkity yakking." He motioned to Jimmy to hand him a screw. "BLAST. Cut it too short."

Jimmy's gaze shifted to the hay field. He saw someone out there behind Amos's two draft horses, cutting hay, but he could tell that someone wasn't Amos. "Who's that?"

Hank looked out to the field. "Young fellow Amos hired to cut hay."

Jimmy squinted his eyes. "I can't tell who he is. Someone new? Why didn't Amos hire me?"

"Probably cuz you have a knack for disappearing whenever there's a need for hard work."

Jimmy was deeply offended. "That's not true." Maybe it was partially true.

Hank bore down on Jimmy with his good eye. "I hear you've developed a fondness for pony racing these days."

"I just prefer the front end of the horse to the back end. But I could use some extra cash, seeing as how I have a girlfriend."

Hank strode to the workbench and rummaged around for some tools. "Oh? A new flavor of the month?"

"It's not like that this time, Hank. I think I have found my missus."

Hank frowned at one tool, threw it down, picked up another. "Just how long have you been courting your potential missus?"

"Well, see, that's why I need to talk to M.K. I haven't quite met my missus yet."

Hank jerked his head up. A big "HAW!" burst out of him. "You and Paul are cut out of the same cloth! Immer gucka. Nie net am kaufen." *Always looking, never buying.*

Jimmy frowned. Hank Lapp was hardly one to give marital advice. He was a dedicated bachelor. Hank had been mildly courting Jimmy's mother for years now — if you could call it courting. He showed up regularly for Sunday dinner, followed by a long nap in a recliner chair.

Why Jimmy's mother put up with Hank was a mystery. But then, in a way, the casualness of Hank's courting must appeal to her as well. Edith Fisher could remain in complete charge of her life — and her sons — and didn't have to change anything to suit a man. Jimmy loved his mother, but he wasn't blind to her faults. He remembered how henpecked his own father had been. Ironic for a man who had raised chickens and sold eggs for a living.

"Whose buggy is this?" Jimmy said. He recognized his friends' buggies because they had customized the interiors: fuzzy dice hanging down from the rearview mirror, red shag carpet, a boom box. But this buggy looked pretty plain, stark. Clearly, an adult's.

"Bishop's." Hank turned the fiberboard right side up. "WELL, LOOKY THERE! I had it upside down."

"I thought the bishop's accident happened

months ago."

"It did, but it's hunting season, in case you hadn't noticed. I've been needing to spend my time at Blue Lake Pond. Under my watch, many a goose has flapped its last over that lake."

It was always hunting season in Hank Lapp's mind. "Ooooeee! I'll bet Bishop Elmo's breathing down your neck to get it fixed."

Hank glared at Jimmy, and that wasn't a pretty sight. He had one eye that wandered and when he tried to glare, it gave him a frantic, wild-eyed look. Crazy as a loon. "BOY, DON'T YOU HAVE SOMEPLACE YOU NEED TO BE?"

A flash of red down on the road caught Jimmy's eye. It was M.K., zooming along on her scooter. "I do! There's M.K." He started down the hill. Over his shoulder, he tossed, "Talk to you later, Hank."

Mary Kate saw Jimmy Fisher running down the driveway to meet her, and considered turning the scooter around and zooming away. She didn't know what was on his mind, but when he kept turning up like he had been doing lately, it usually meant he needed advice or money or both. She was in no mood to be generous with either.

She hopped off the scooter as the driveway's incline began, and walked the rest of the way. Doozy ran off to chase a jackrabbit. Poor pup. He tried so often to catch one of those long-eared, long-legged jackrabbits and never could. As M.K. met up with Jimmy, she wiped her forehead with her sleeve. Today was going to be a scorcher.

"What?" she said flatly.

Jimmy gave a look of mock offense. "Is that any way to greet your most devoted friend?"

"I'm in no mood for small talk." She kept walking. "What do you want?"

He kept up with her. "Why is everybody so concerned with your mood today?"

She stopped abruptly. "They're not. That's the *whole* problem. No one is concerned about my mood today or any other day." She blew air out of her cheeks. "Jimmy, do you ever feel like you're a horse in a pasture and all you can think about is getting out of the pasture?"

"No. I feel as if I'm a horse in a race, and I'm in the lead by two stretches. That's how I feel."

She rolled her eyes. The ego of Jimmy Fisher was legendary. "I have just been roped into being the next schoolteacher at Twin Creeks."

47

"What?" Jimmy tilted his head, as if he hadn't heard her properly. A beat of silence followed. Then another. "You? Of all people, you?"

And then Jimmy started laughing so hard that M.K. thought he might pass out from a lack of oxygen to the brain. Infuriating! She started marching up the hill.

Jimmy rushed to catch up with her, gasping to get his laughing fit under control. "I can't remember a single week going by that Spinster Smucker didn't end up plunking you in the corner, face against the wall, or making you stay in for recess, or keeping you after school. Not one! Not *one* single week!" He was overcome with another laughing fit and had to bend over at his knees to wheeze for air. He patted his knees for effect.

M.K. was disgusted. But what he said was true — she had constantly been in trouble during her years at Twin Creeks School. And it was never her fault! Never. Maybe a few times. She wasn't sure who was happier on her eighth-grade graduation day: she or Alice Smucker.

A straw hat in the distant field caught her attention. She shielded her eyes. "Who's Dad got cutting hay?"

Jimmy inhaled a couple of deep breaths

and tried to wipe the amused look off his face. "Some new guy your dad hired." He shifted his gaze out to the field. "I don't know why he didn't hire me."

M.K. watched the new hire. From here, he looked young — twenty, twenty-two-ish. She thought she knew everybody in Stoney Ridge. How did someone slip in without her knowledge? She blamed this teaching job. Too upsetting. "Probably because you're always running off to horse auctions."

Jimmy frowned at her. "I am conducting research."

M.K. snorted and started up the hill again. "Research for pony races, you mean."

Jimmy caught up with her again. "I'll ignore that insult because you're having a bad day. But since we're discussing my future, I'd like to ask for your help in a very delicate matter."

M.K. stopped, intrigued. "What do you need help with?"

"I've found the one."

"The one what? A horse?"

"No! A woman. I'm in love." He covered his heart. "A deep, enduring love."

"Really?" That was a very strange thought for M.K. She often wondered what it felt like to be in love. Being in love, she imagined, would make all the colors in the world more vivid, all the stars shine more brightly, all the moments of her life dance and crackle with excitement like flames leaping in a bonfire.

"I met my future bride. Someone whom I am sure you know. After all, you know everybody."

She smiled. Finally, someone appreciated her. "Who is that?"

"Emily Esh."

"Emily Esh? Oh Jimmy, she's . . ." She paused, trying to find the right words to say. It was easy to see why Emily Esh had attracted Jimmy's attention. She had huge, dinner-plate-sized eyes, an enigmatic, slightly-turned-up-at-the-corners smile, and a figure that curved in all the right places.

"What?"

"She's . . ." How to say this? "She's super brainy."

"So?" His face clouded over. "What's your point?"

"It might be hard to impress a girl like Emily. Not to mention that she has plenty of guys fluttering around her."

Jimmy kicked a dirt clod with his boot. "You think I'm not smart enough for her?"

M.K. looked at Jimmy. "You're enough for any girl, Jimmy." That wasn't the problem. She might be a little hard on Jimmy — he was spoiled and impulsive and insensitive and egotistical — but there was a good heart somewhere under that handsome exterior.

"Will you help me, then? Will you arrange an introduction for me with Emily Esh?"

M.K. let out a puff of air.

"Please? I'll do anything."

"Anything?" She raised an eyebrow.

"Anything." He gave her a sly look. "Besides teach at Twin Creeks School."

She narrowed her eyes. "Help me solve the murder of the sheep farmer."

"What murder?"

M.K. closed her eyes, thoroughly exasperated. Did she have to do everything around here? "Yesterday afternoon, a sheep farmer was shot to death in his field. Orin Stoltzfus told me this morning that the police can't find any clues. That means the culprit is still on the loose."

Jimmy looked at her as if she'd lost her mind.

The sound of a clanging dinner bell floated down the hill. M.K. hadn't eaten much for breakfast and she was starving. "That's the deal. As soon as we solve the crime, I will introduce you to Emily Esh." She hurried up the hill. When she got to the

51

top, she heard Jimmy call her name. She spun around.

"OK!" He grinned. "It's a deal!"

The first thing Chris did when he got home from work was to take a shower. Cutting alfalfa hay all day made his entire body feel scratchy and itchy. But he did a good day's work, Amos Lapp had said, and told him to come back tomorrow. And he paid him generously too before he left for the day. Cash. Enough to buy new shoes for his sister to start school in a few days. And maybe enough to splurge on an ice cream cone afterward.

When he told Jenny that they were heading into town tonight to go school shopping, she balked. "We should go back to Ohio, so Mom knows where we are."

"We've been over this, Jenny. If we stayed in Ohio, Child Protective Services would step in and put you in a foster home. And Mom doesn't need to know where we are. All that matters is we know where she is."

Jenny scowled. But then, she was always scowling. Her face was going to be set in a permanent scowl. "She's going to get out soon. Then things will go back to normal."

Normal? What was normal? Their mother was a part-time house cleaner and a full-time drug addict. Old Deborah had been a godsend to them. She was an older Amish woman who became connected to the Ohio Reformatory for Women by fostering prisoners' children — an informal arrangement, outside of Child Protective Services but blessed by them, that suited everyone. Chris and Jenny had been living with Old Deborah, off and on, since Chris was eight and Jenny was one.

Once a month, year in and year out, Old Deborah took them by bus to Marysville to visit their mother. The program Old Deborah participated in wasn't trying to convert children to become Amish. Its goal was to keep incarcerated mothers involved in the lives of their children. Studies showed that there was less recidivism if mothers felt like they were continuing to parent their children. The Marysville warden had created all kinds of programs to enhance the bond with mothers and children. But Chris and Jenny had stayed with Old Deborah longer than they had lived with their mother. They couldn't help but look Amish, act Amish, talk Amish, and mostly, think Amish. For Chris, for the first time, the whole of his life really began to be transformed into something other than what it had ever been, something leaning toward normal.

It rankled their mother. She made sharply pointed comments about the Amish, but what could she really do about it? Old Deborah was raising her children for her. And doing a wonderful job with it too. She was grandmother, counselor, mentor . . . all wrapped into one warm, loving package. She fed them, washed their clothes, combed out Jenny's tangled hair, took them to the dentist or doctor if they needed medical attention. Old Deborah and her church family were loving toward them. Chris had no doubt they wanted them there. Life was stable at Old Deborah's. No one was on edge — waiting for his mother's dip into addiction. Chris knew what to expect each day at Old Deborah's. It was peaceful and safe and good.

On some level, Chris's mother must have known that her children were better off with Old Deborah than with CPS. Or maybe she just liked having the visits. She never registered any formal complaints about the Amish school or Amish church Chris and Jenny attended, though she gave Old Deborah plenty of informal complaints. But when Chris became baptized in the church last fall, she blew her top. It still chilled Chris to think of his mother's outburst, filled with horrible accusations. He just stood there, taking it, not answering back, just like he always had, but he hadn't been back to see her since.

Jenny didn't remember what it was like before Old Deborah's, but Chris did. And he would do everything in his power to make sure he and Jenny never went back to that. After that scene his mother had made about his baptism, Old Deborah quietly took him aside. She told Chris that his grandfather had sent her some legal papers, right before he died. He was leaving a house in trust for Chris and Jenny, and property taxes were paid out of the trust each year. When Chris turned twenty-one, he would inherit the house and land. When Jenny turned twenty-one, half of the house would belong to her. Old Deborah gave Chris a package with all of the legal paperwork, including a key to the house. "There's just one little hitch. Your mother is the executor of this trust." Old Deborah took a deep breath and closed her eyes, scrunching up her wrinkled face. "I might not have shared that piece of knowledge with her."

"What? Mom doesn't know? Why not?" It wasn't in Old Deborah's nature to deceive anyone.

Old Deborah opened her eyes. "Your grandfather put a condition in the will — as long as your mother wasn't using drugs, wasn't in jail, the house could go to her first. That was the condition until you turned twenty-one. Your grandfather asked me to use my judgment about when your mother should be informed about the will. So I kept waiting for the right moment to share it with her. I wanted to make sure she was truly freed from her drug habit . . ."

"But she never has been."

"No, not for long." She offered up a smile, but it didn't travel to her eyes. "Not yet, anyway."

Not ever, Chris thought. His grandfather must have thought so too. Why else would he create such a will? He knew that Grace Mitchell would spend her life skirting in and out of jail or rehab. Or both.

"I think it's time to go back to Stoney Ridge. This winter, you'll be twenty-one. Your mother is . . . indisposed. The house was meant for you and Jenny."

Chris fingered the cold metal key. A simple little door key that unlocked so many memories. "Stoney Ridge? Go back to my grandfather's house?"

"Yes. This is your chance to start a life of your own." She covered his hand with hers. Her hand was so small and fragile compared to his work-roughened one, but it was powerful in its own way. Like the rudder of a ship. "Chris, one thing I have learned over the years — your mother may not be able to be a good mother, but she does love you and your sister. Her problems get in the way of that love. Lord only knows I wish your upbringing had been different, but maybe you had an extraordinary upbringing, because it has made you an extraordinary young man."

He had trusted Old Deborah in every way, and though she was gone, he trusted her judgment even now. After her funeral, the very next morning, before news of Old Deborah's passing had time to spread outside of the Amish community, he had quietly packed their few belongings, and he and Jenny set off for Stoney Ridge in Lancaster County to claim their inheritance. He felt bad that he hadn't said goodbye to the friends who had been so kind to him and Jenny — the Troyers, especially — but the fewer people who knew where they were headed, the better. He didn't want any news of Stoney Ridge to trickle to his mother. Not now. Not until late January, after his birthday.

What a crazy thing he had done! Traveling the back roads of Ohio and Pennsylvania with a horse and buggy. It took weeks!

Many days, they only covered twenty to thirty miles, and on Sundays, they stayed put. It didn't matter how long it took — Chris wasn't going to jeopardize Samson's well-being. And time was one thing he had plenty of.

Finally, the day came when they arrived in Stoney Ridge. The little town hadn't changed much. The Sweet Tooth Bakery was still on the corner of Main Street, across from the post office and the brick bank. They walked down Main Street and he knew, instinctively, to turn right down Stone Leaf Drive, as if he'd never left. When he came to the lane that led to the house, he stopped and took a deep breath.

Jenny looked up at him. "Did you forget where it is? Has it been too long?"

He shook his head. "I didn't forget." From Ohio — a four-week trip. From his childhood — an eternity.

They walked up the lane and turned into a cracked and crumbling concrete driveway that led to the house. The property wasn't large — it was surrounded by farmland.

"Here it is, Jenny."

"Yuck."

"Hello?" he called out softly.

All was quiet. The house was deserted and looked it. The clapboard frame of the house was just the way he remembered it — brownish gray with chipped, flaking paint, the trim painted white. The porch sagged on one side. A clothesline with bleached-out wooden clothespins was looped between the posts, just under the rafters. A memory wisped like a fast-moving cloud through Chris's head. He remembered his mother hanging her underwear there and his grandfather raging at its impropriety. His grandfather cared about things like that. His mother didn't.

Chris walked up to the front door. He tried the doorknob, expecting nothing, but when it turned in his hand, he let out a surprised gasp.

"What?" Jenny rushed to his side.

He pushed the door open, its hinges screaming a protest.

What he saw made him want to back right up and run. "I guess we're home," he whispered.

3

Mary Kate woke early, after a restless night. Today was the first day of school, and she was the schoolteacher. She had absolutely no idea how to teach school. She slipped out of bed and dressed, then went downstairs. Last night, she had made up a batch of wheat bread dough and put it in the refrigerator. It was a special recipe that required a long kneading time.

She took the bowl out of the refrigerator and turned the dough onto a lightly floured surface. She deflated the dough — gently pressing down to let the air out. By gently squeezing out the excess carbon dioxide, the yeast would be more fully distributed throughout the dough. Then she started the kneading process: turn and fold, turn and fold, turn and fold. She knew she would need the task this morning — kneading bread could dispel a good deal of anxiety from even the most nervous heart.

And it did help. By the time her father woke to head outside and feed the livestock, she was almost calm. Almost. "There's coffee started," she said. Her voice sounded thin and wavery.

Amos poured himself a cup and peered at the bread she was kneading. "Wheat. Hmmm. You must be feeling pretty fidgety."

Panic rose up again inside of M.K. "I can't do it, Dad."

Amos put the coffee cup on the counter. "Of course you can. You've never failed yet at anything you tried to do, have you?"

"Well, no, but I have never tried to teach school."

"You've tackled every job that ever came your way. You never shirked, and you always stuck to it till you did what you set out to do. Success gets to be a habit, like anything else a person keeps on doing."

M.K. felt a little better. It was true; she had always kept on trying, she had always had to. Well, now she had to teach school.

"Remember when Sadie ended up with the job of tending chickens? And she just couldn't bring herself to butcher one. You just picked up that ax and —" he made a cutting motion with his hand — "the lights went out on that poor chicken. You must have only been eight or so."

61

"Seven."

"And remember when Jimmy Fisher took his pigeons to school and accidentally released them inside the schoolhouse?"

M.K.'s head snapped up. "That was no accident! He let them go on purpose."

"And you helped capture them."

M.K. grinned. "Alice Smucker hid under her desk."

"Now that is not something you would ever do as a teacher. You're too brave."

She put the bread dough into an oiled bowl to rise. Fern would bake it later this morning. She turned to her father. "Do you really think I'm brave?"

He patted her shoulder. "The bravest girl I know."

At ten minutes to seven, M.K. couldn't put it off any longer. She picked up her Igloo lunch box and left for school.

Jenny couldn't believe her ears. "You mean you want me to lie to everyone and say that my last name is Yoder?"

"It's for the best, Jenny," Chris said. The two of them were eating together at the kitchen table. "This is kind of . . . interesting. I don't believe I've ever had Cream of Wheat that looked like soup before." He lifted his spoon and the Cream of Wheat slipped off like a waterfall.

Jenny may have used a little too much liquid.

She had learned a lot from Old Deborah, but mostly about gardens and herbs and remedies. Old Deborah's healing work took up so much of her time that she didn't cook or bake like most Amish women did. As a result, Jenny had never been much of a cook, but now, she realized, things were going to have to change. She had better figure out how to cook if they were going to eat anything that wasn't from a can or a box. "Old Deborah would never agree to a lie. Using her name as ours is wrong, wrong, wrong."

Chris added raw Cream of Wheat into the bowl until it resembled gray wallpaper paste. He took a taste and gagged. Then he put his spoon down, frowning. "Old Deborah raised us like we were her own. She would understand."

Jenny sighed. She knew her brother well enough to know it was useless to try to reason with him. Stubborn. He was just so stubborn about some things. She picked up her brown lunch bag and walked to the door, dreading what lay ahead.

Three hours later, M.K. rang the bell to

start her first day of school. Calling the cattle to the trough of knowledge was how she had always thought of it. Doozy took up residence on the front steps — as far as M.K. would let him come — and wouldn't budge.

Before M.K. was a sea of polished wood desks. The children tripped over Doozy as they hurried inside the classroom and stared at M.K. She stood, ramrod straight, and faced all of those scholars.

There were so many! So many beady little eyes.

She racked her brain for what came next. Nothing came to mind.

For the first time in her life, her mind was a complete blank. Empty. She thought she might get sick. She might get sick and die, right on the spot. That, she thought, would serve the school board right.

From the back of the room, Jenny sized up the new teacher. She could see this young teacher nervously knot and unknot her hands. You could tell she didn't know where to begin or which way was up. Her voice wobbled as she said "Good morning" to the students. Wobbled.

"Morning, M.K.," said a few students.

A boy with big glasses raised his hand as

high as it could go. "We should probably call you Teacher M.K."

"Yes, of course. Thank you, Danny. Please call me Teacher M.K.," she corrected, but her voice sounded uncertain.

What kind of a name was Emkay?

A big boy leaned over his desk and winked at Jenny. She snapped her head away from him. How rude! Boys were never rude in her old school. But then, there was an abundance of girls in the upper grades. There was only one boy who was her age at her old school, Teddy Beiler, and he was frightened of the girls. Teddy had a permanently startled look on his face.

Then the new teacher tried to take roll and dropped the roll book. Twice. When she dropped it the second time, the big boys in the back of the room quickly changed their seats just to confuse her. And it did. When she straightened up, she looked thoroughly flustered.

"I'll start with the first grade," the teacher said. "Barbara Jean Shrock?"

A little hand shot up. "Here," Barbara Jean said in a thin, piping voice. "But I'm not staying." There was a whistle in Barbara Jean's whisper because she was missing her two front teeth, so *staying* came out as *th-taying.* She sat primly, her purple dress

65

pulled snugly over her small bony knees. The sneakers she wore dangled several inches above the ground. Her tiny hands were neatly folded in her lap.

"Well, let's get through the roll, at least," the teacher said. "Eva Zook?"

Another little girl raised her hand. "Here."

"Now the second grade." This went on for a few more minutes until something happened that interested Jenny. When the teacher reached the sixth grade, she called out, "Danny Riehl?"

"Here," a boy said. It was the same boy who had spoken up earlier. He had a round face and wore big glasses with adhesive tape in the middle. His hair was the color of straw. He was earnest, Jenny thought. An earnest boy.

A tall girl in the back row stood up. "I'm Anna Mae Glick and I need to sit next to Danny Riehl."

The teacher's face shifted to a frown of puzzlement. "Why is that?"

"Because we're going to be married someday," Anna Mae Glick said smugly. "He's already asked me. We're going to get married when I'm twenty and he's eighteen. It's all settled."

Danny, who was sitting a couple of desks in front of Anna Mae, froze. He looked at the teacher in panic. "No, Anna Mae, I didn't say I would marry you," he protested. "I never did."

Anna Mae glared at him. "You did!" she said. "You promised! Don't think you can break your promises like that." She snapped her fingers to demonstrate Danny's broken promises.

"No, I never did," Danny repeated quietly. He looked troubled.

The big boys started snickering. One of them — the one who had winked so rudely at Jenny, said, "Anna Mae, you mean that *nobody* would ever marry you, not in a hundred years."

"You mean that nobody would ever marry you," Anna Mae retorted. "Any girl would take one look at you, Eugene Miller, and be sick."

Yes and no. Eugene Miller did carry with him a strong odor. Pig farmers, Jenny guessed. You didn't want to get downwind of him. And Eugene could be rude, but he wasn't bad looking. He was man-sized and there was a rim of fuzz on his upper lip.

Anna Mae crossed her arms. "M.K., just so you know, Eugene Miller is a nuisance."

Eugene Miller let out a room-shaking guffaw.

"Eugene and I are permanently mad at

each other," Anna Mae added. "Just so you know."

"Anna Mae, you are in the eighth grade," the teacher said, consulting her roll book. "You need to sit with your class."

Anna Mae scowled but sat down in her seat, a few rows behind Danny.

Jenny began to wonder if this teacher was going to ever get the class to an actual subject before the end of this first teaching day.

Peering once more into the roll book, the teacher looked relieved at the prospect of getting roll call back on track. She read Jenny's name but seemed puzzled when Jenny was the one who answered. "Shouldn't you be sitting up front with your own grade?"

"I am sitting with my own grade," Jenny said firmly.

Flustered, the teacher glanced at the roll book again. "How old are you?"

"Thirteen."

"I would have thought ten," Anna Mae said loudly.

Jenny glared at Anna Mae. She crossed that girl off her potential friend list. That was unfortunate because there weren't many girls in the upper grades.

"Are you new to Stoney Ridge?" the teacher said.

Chris had warned Jenny to think twice before she said anything. Anything at all. "Yes," Jenny said, slowly and carefully.

The teacher tilted her head at Jenny, as if she was about to ask something else, but one of the big boys sent a paper airplane sailing across the room. It hit the window and fell to the ground. The teacher went to pick it up. Breathing a little hard, she asked, "Whose is this?"

Of course, no one would admit to it. They all kept their eyes facing forward, even the little ones. Teacher M.K. looked up and down the rows at the children, then threw the airplane into the garbage can. A big boy snickered. Eugene Miller. Jenny thought that boy had a saucy way about him. His face held a big grin as he looked right at the blackboard. And the silly teacher didn't do anything. Not a thing.

At that exact moment, Jenny knew that this young woman would never make it as a teacher. She didn't want to be the boss.

M.K.'s armpits were wet and she felt like throwing up. She stared at the children, who were staring back at her.

Six-year-old Barbara Jean Shrock stood by her desk and tugged on M.K.'s dress. "I'm going home."

"Barbara Jean, you can't go home," M.K. said, feeling a rise of panic. "It's only nine in the morning."

Barbara Jean planted her little feet. "You thaid I jutht needed to get through roll call."

M.K. was ready to go home too. This whole experience, the full hour of it, was turning out just like she had thought it would. *Disastrous.* Each time she thought she had the classroom under control, something would happen that was entirely out of her control. The last something was a mouse. She strongly suspected that Eugene Miller had something to do with that mouse in the classroom, but she couldn't prove it. When she told him to catch it, he said, "You're not the boss of me, M.K. Lapp. I remember when you were in eighth grade and you put a black racer snake in Teacher Alice's bottom desk drawer. She practically had a fatal heart attack, right then and there."

And what could M.K. say to that? It was the truth. In fact, it was the essence of the problem. M.K. had been the worst offender of any pupil — by a long shot. Hadn't she just been reprimanded in church for reading a book? How could she possibly try to act like she was in charge when she was known for being the ringleader of mischief?

She knew these pupils, and they knew her. It was hopeless. And the thing was — she didn't blame them one bit. She should not be standing here as their teacher.

Eugene Miller was in the third grade when M.K. was in eighth. He was a little too smart-mouthed for his own good, even back then. And he was at that troublesome age now, a renowned prankster. He had dark, shaggy hair that hung in his eyes, and he wore a smirk of superiority on his wide mouth as if laughing at the whole world and everyone in it. Clearly, he was the leader of the big boys, and she knew he could easily influence them to make trouble for her.

And then there was that overly petite new girl — Jenny. She looked at M.K. with unconcealed suspicion. As if she knew M.K. had no business teaching.

It dawned on M.K. that she had probably stared at poor Alice Smucker in the same insolent way as Jenny was staring at her. It was the first time she could recall having a sympathetic feeling for Alice Smucker. Ever. The thought amazed her.

Barbara Jean pulled on M.K.'s sleeve again. "Thee you thometime at church."

M.K. had to think fast. If she allowed Barbara Jean to leave, the entire classroom would think up excuses to leave. Had she

71

been in their position, she would be invent-
ing excuses for each of the students and selling them for a nickel during recess. "Barbara Jean, tell me why you want to go
home."

Tears filled Barbara Jean's eyes. "I love
my mom tho much. You don't know how
hard it ith to be away from thomeone you
love *that* much."

M.K. felt tears prick at her eyes. That she
understood! She pulled Barbara Jean into a
hug and whispered, "I miss my mom like
that too." She wiped away Barbara Jean's
tears with her handkerchief. Then she wiped
away her own tears.

Ridiculous. This was getting ridiculous.
Somehow, she had to pick up the pieces of
this class and carry on. "How would you
like to be the teacher's helper and sit at my
desk?"

Barbara Jean gave that some thought.

"If you still want to go home at lunch,
then I'll let you go."

Barbara Jean whispered a *yeth,* so M.K.
led her right up to her desk.

M.K. felt rather proud of herself. She had
actually solved a problem. The feeling
quickly dissipated as she heard a high-
pitched scream from the back of the classroom. Someone had lit a match and tossed

it into the trash can at the back of the room. As M.K. rushed outside with the flaming trash can, she thought she caught a smirk on Eugene Miller's smug face. Why, that boy was another Jimmy Fisher. Worse.

Somehow, she stumbled ahead through the day, one eye on the clock, willing this hour to be over, and then the next and the next.

Chris tried to hold back a smile when he heard Jenny's complaints about the new teacher. He burst out laughing when she described the teacher's looks: bony, wispy haired, wild-eyed, false teeth that wobbled when she talked. His sister had a vivid imagination. "What's her name?" he asked.

"Teacher M.K. That's all I know about her. That and the fact that she has had no teaching experience whatsoever. I'm not even sure she can read. Probably not."

Chris rolled his eyes. "I highly doubt the school board would give the teaching job to a teacher who couldn't read."

"Well, I heard that the real teacher was run over by a crazed lunatic. Just last week. And she's dying as a result. That's a fact. I heard that too."

Chris knew Jenny had impossibly high expectations for teachers and they always fell short. Jenny had yet to find a teacher who challenged her. She was always "bored." But the more he heard about the school day — starting with the fire in the trash can and ending with the disappearance of a little first grade girl, the more he had to agree with Jenny's assessment. This new teacher sounded like she had no ability to control a classroom filled with big boys. No backbone at all. If this was day one, it was going to be a long school year.

He knew what it was like to have good teachers and not-so-good teachers. That was the thing about a one-room schoolhouse. You didn't have much of a choice with your teacher. At least Jenny had a place to be each day, and this hapless teacher was too preoccupied with putting out fires to ask his sister too many questions about her background.

But he did make Jenny promise not to stir up any trouble. The last thing she needed to do was to add to this poor pitiful teacher's problems with the big boys.

Chris had problems of his own on his mind tonight. He stared at the ceiling. The sight of water stains and peeling plaster did little to dispel the cloud of gloom hovering over him.

He was working at Windmill Farm this

morning and got caught in an untimely conversation with Hank Lapp, Amos's uncle. Chris had been cutting hay in the north field and noticed the bit for the large Belgian wasn't fitting properly. The big horse kept tossing her head. When Chris examined the bit, he saw that a piece of it had come undone and was causing discomfort for the horse. That wouldn't do. He headed back to the barn to see if he could either fix the bit or find another one.

As he passed by a buggy, a loud voice called out: "DADGUM!"

Chris stopped to locate the source of the voice.

"BLAST! WHERE DID THAT DAD-GUM THING GO?"

All around the buggy were tools. Chris looked into the shop and thought he had never seen such a mess. Buggy parts and tools littered the floor. Every horizontal surface was filled. A headful of wild white hair popped out from under the buggy and peered up at Chris in surprise. If Chris wasn't mistaken, one of the man's eyes wandered.

"Uh, hello," Chris said to the head. "I'm helping Amos cut hay."

The wild-haired man pulled himself out from under the buggy. "So I heard!" He rose to his feet and thrust an oil-smudged hand at Chris. He pumped Chris's hand up and down. "Hank Lapp. Known far and wide for my buggy repairs."

"Not hardly," came another voice.

Chris whirled around to face another older man with a long white beard.

"When will this buggy be ready, Hank?" the man said. "It's been months now."

"Now, Elmo, what we've got here is a tricky problem," Hank said. "Very hard to fix. Needs just the right part and I can't seem to . . . uh . . . locate the source."

As the two men discussed the buggy, the conversation became more animated, especially on the part of Hank Lapp. Chris decided it would be wise to slip quietly away. On the ground, he noticed a clevis — a little metal pin that held the singletree to the buggy shafts. He bent down and picked it up, then walked to the buggy. He looked up to see if he could interrupt the men, but Hank was waving his arms, talking fast, trying to explain why there was such a delay in fixing this particular buggy. Chris slipped the clevis into place and rose to his feet. Hank abruptly stopped talking. The two men stared at Chris.

"I think I found that part you were looking for." Chris knocked on the singletree that kept the traces from working their way off on their own. "See? It works."

Hank came over to check it out. "LOOK AT THAT! Well, wonders never cease."

Elmo sized up Chris as if he had just noticed he was there. The way he looked at Chris made him nervous. It was like the man was peering into his soul. "And who are you?"

"That's Amos's hired help. New to town." Hank looked over at Chris. "Son, I didn't catch your name."

"Chris Yoder."

"Chris Yoder, this is Bishop Elmo." Hank pulled on the trace holders to make sure they were taut.

The bishop. *The bishop?* Oh, this was not good. Not good at all.

Bishop Elmo, cheerful and bespectacled, took a step closer to Chris. "New to Stoney Ridge?"

"Really new. Just arrived."

"Any relation to Isaac Yoder?"

Chris shook his head.

"Melvin Yoder?"

Chris shook his head more vehemently. He did not want to start down that long road of dissecting family trees. Two thoughts ricocheted through his mind at that moment. One, that Bishop Elmo would ask why he hadn't seen him in church more often once he discovered how long Chris had been here. That could be answered easily — they really just arrived a few weeks ago. A second and far more dangerous question was that the bishop might inquire — no, definitely would inquire, by the way he looked at that moment — as to where Chris had come from. Actually, it was surprising that he'd been able to evade the question so far with Amos Lapp and a few other people he had done odd jobs for, thanks to Bud at the hardware store. Chris quickly searched his brain for something to comment on, hoping it might redirect the conversation.

He held up the bit in his hand. "I left the horses in the field while I fixed this bit. It sure is a hot day. I'd better get back to work." He rushed off to the barn before Bishop Elmo could squeeze in another question.

And still, Elmo managed to call out, "I'll expect to see you in church in two Sundays, Chris Yoder."

Church. A feeling of dread washed over Chris. He would be found out.

Stop it! he told himself fiercely. They'd come this far, hadn't they?

4

M.K. didn't think it was possible for Day Two as a teacher to be worse than Day One, but it was. The school had never been so noisy, including all of M.K.'s eight years as a student. All over the room there was a clatter of books and feet and a rustle of whispering. Whichever way she turned, unruliness and noise swelled up behind her. She didn't think anything could have been more disruptive to a classroom than yesterday's fire in the trash can, until Eugene Miller left during today's noon recess — taking three other eighth grade boys with him. M.K had a horrible feeling that each day, fewer and fewer students would return after lunch. By Friday afternoon, the schoolhouse would be empty.

Six-year-old Barbara Jean had started the exodus yesterday when she disappeared during lunch.

M.K. gave permission for Barbara Jean to

go outside to the girls' room, but then she was gone for so long that M.K. panicked. She raced outside. Where was Barbara Jean? M.K. was hesitant to call out her name. It was unlikely that she'd left the school, wasn't it? But she wasn't in the girls' bathroom, nor the boys'. In just a matter of minutes, she had lost a child. Barbara Jean had gone missing.

Finally, M.K. found Barbara Jean behind the big oak tree, playing with her doll. "Oh, good!" M.K. said, flooded with relief. "I thought I'd lost you!" She was sure Barbara Jean had gone home.

But why should it matter if a few pupils slipped off to go home?

She didn't know why, but it did matter.

Fern had been right about one thing: M.K. was going to have to figure out how to get through this teaching job. For two weeks and three more days.

But how? How?

Amos put the ladder in the wagon. He untied Rosemary's reins from the post and walked her over to Chris, waiting for the horse and wagon by the path that led to the orchards. He had thought Chris would want to head home early this afternoon after he finished cutting hay in that last field, but the boy asked if Amos had something else for him to do. That was easy to answer — work on a farm was never done. Amos had noticed that a variety of early ripening apples were starting to fall from the trees. Another sign of autumn's arrival.

Normally, Amos enjoyed every part and parcel of farming, but picking fruit from trees was one task he was happy to pass off to a younger soul. Up and down that ladder, empty the sack in the wagon, then back up the ladder. Over and over and over. Not easy work for the knees of a fifty-six-year-old man. Yes, he was happy to share that chore.

Amos held the reins out to Chris, but he was preoccupied, staring up at the house. Amos shielded his eyes from the late afternoon sun to see what had caught Chris's attention. M.K. was shelling peas on the porch, and Jimmy Fisher sat sprawled on the steps, his long legs crossed at the ankles, talking to her. Chris startled when he realized that Amos stood behind him and turned abruptly to lead Rosemary up the gentle rise toward the orchards.

Amos walked down the hill and crossed the yard to where Fern was hanging laundry on the clothesline. "Fern, does it seem as if Jimmy Fisher is hanging around an awful

81

lot? More than he used to?"

Fern lifted one of Amos's blue shirts up and hung it upside down so the arms dangled in the wind. "I'll say. That boy is eating me out of house and home."

Amos watched Jimmy throw back his head in laughter at something M.K. said. "I always thought those two would either kill each other or fall in love." He chuckled, pleased. "Guess it's the latter."

Fern gave him a sideways glance. "You think those two would be a good match?"

"Sure. Don't you?" He thought it was a wonderful idea. Being in love with Jimmy might cure M.K. of that restlessness. She wouldn't have time to think about anything else — trying to keep tabs on what Jimmy was up to would keep anybody busy. And M.K. would be good for Jimmy too. He never had a swooning effect on her like he did on all the other girls.

Fern clipped a pair of black trousers to the line. "Was mer net hawwe soll, hett mer's liebscht." *What we are not meant to have, we covet most.* She picked up the empty basket and started toward the house.

Amos puzzled on that for a while. What did that saying have to do with Jimmy and M.K.? Half the time, he had no idea what Fern meant. She spoke in riddles.

■ ■ ■ ■

Day Three. After M.K. dismissed the students for the afternoon, she put her head on her desk. She was a horrible teacher, just like she had known she would be. And she had an entire two weeks and two days looming ahead of her.

Maybe, if she were thought to be a truly terrible teacher, the school board would fire her. Ah, relief! Followed swiftly by mortification. She would have to move away. Far, far away.

Shanghai. Johannesburg. Reykjavik.

Maybe that wouldn't be such a bad thing. Over the last year, she couldn't stop thinking about what the world outside of Stoney Ridge would look like, what it would sound like. What filled her mind were thoughts of breaking free from this Amish life of careful routine. Every day looked like the day before it. Every day looked like the day in front of it.

There were moments, mostly in church, when she had to sit on her hands to stop herself from jumping up and shouting at the preacher, "You already said that! Over and over again! Every two weeks, the same sermon! The same piece of Scripture! Same,

same, same! Let's try something new!" She would love to see the look of surprise and horror on everyone's faces.

Of course, she didn't dare. She would never do such a disrespectful thing. She had been raised to respect her elders.

But, oh, how she would love to do it. Just once!

And then she started to think she might be going crazy. How awful it would be if she really did go berserk one day. She could hear the women clucking about it now . . . "Poor, poor Mary Kate. There was always something a little off-kilter about that girl. One moment, she seemed right as rain. The next moment, a raving madcap."

Deep down, she knew she could never do anything to intentionally hurt her father, or her sisters, or Uncle Hank. Or Fern.

It was a good thing she loved Fern, because that woman was impossible. M.K. knew Fern was behind this teaching job. It had Fern written all over it. Fern had a way of knowing what a person was thinking, without that person ever having to say it aloud. She had no doubt that Fern knew she was toying with the idea of leaving the Amish. Fern always knew.

But teaching a roomful of slow-witted, obstinate children? What a cruel, cruel mantle to place on M.K.

She was pretty sure Fern was savvy to the fact that M.K. had turned Ruthie down about joining this year's baptismal instruction class. She probably knew she had turned Ruthie's pleading down for the third time in a row. Fern knew everything.

Or maybe Ruthie told her. Ruthie just didn't understand. Every year, she begged M.K. to go through baptismal instructions with her, but M.K. just couldn't do it. Not yet.

She knew she would have to decide, at some point. She couldn't walk this line forever — one foot in the church, one foot out. If she left before she was baptized, then she could remain on good terms with her family.

And do what? The practical side of her always took over this internal conversation, and that was saying something because M.K. didn't have a practical bone in her body. She wasn't much of a long-term thinker. It was one of Fern's continual complaints about her. "Act first, think later," Fern said. "That's why you're always in hot water." She was constantly trying to tell M.K. to think "down the road."

So what would it look like, down the road, to leave Stoney Ridge? What would she do?

She wasn't prepared to do much of anything outside of the Amish life. Even if she had a car, she didn't have a driver's license. How could she get a job? She didn't have a high school education. And she certainly didn't want to clean houses for English people for the rest of her life. Cleaning houses and waitressing were the only jobs former Amish girls seemed to get. *No thank you.*

She was a crackerjack beekeeper, though, thanks to her brother-in-law Rome. Maybe she could sell her bees' delicious honey in Paris. That sounded like fun. She knew a Plain girl shouldn't flame those desires to see such worldly places, but she did. She just couldn't help herself.

Oh, but there must be something or someplace or maybe even someone out there with enough excitement to satisfy M.K.'s restive nature. She just knew it was out there. Something was calling to her.

She let out a deep sigh. For now, she was stuck. Stuck for two weeks and two more days. She pulled her small Igloo lunch box out from under her desk (there was no way she was going to leave her lunch in the coatroom where Eugene Miller could slip a frog or snake into it — after all, hadn't she endured Jimmy Fisher's mischief for countless years?) and locked up the schoolhouse.

She wanted to go investigate the murdered sheep farmer's pasture and look for clues. Solving this crime was the only bright spot of her day.

After school let out, Jenny rushed to the corner mailbox with the letter she had written during the school day. She had to get it in the mail before the day's mail was taken out. She knew Chris was over at Windmill Farm, but she still looked over her shoulder as she read it one more time before putting it in the envelope.

Hi Mom,
   Just wanted you to know that Chris and I might not be able to see you for a while. We're together and doing fine. I'm going to school, too.

She chewed on her lip, thinking. Should she have added this last part?

   Probably nobody told you, but Old Deborah passed. I thought you should know. Here is four dollars that I saved up. I'll try to send more. Don't worry about us.

Love,
Jenny

She had wanted to write more. She had wanted to let her mother know that she and Chris were living in Stoney Ridge, that Chris was fixing up their grandfather's old house and planned to start a horse breeding business. Chris had been adamant that their mother not be told where they were. He would be furious if he knew she was writing to her mom. But she felt like a traitor if she didn't. Her mom may not be much of a mother, but she was the only mother Jenny had.

She licked the envelope, put on a stamp, opened the mailbox, and let the letter slide down its big blue throat.

Men! So frustrating.

M.K. was chased away from the crime scene area by the sheriff before she had time to uncover a single clue. Sheriff Hoffman took his sense of duty to ridiculous limits, she thought. He had a gun in his holster on his belt that he liked to pat, to remind her it was there, at the ready. How was she supposed to know that no trespassing included the first witness on the scene?

Sheriff Hoffman had glared at her. "You stay out of this pasture, Mary Kate Lapp. We got your statement. We'll come to you if we have any more questions. And we won't.

You only heard a shot. That's all. That's nothing we don't know. This yellow tape here is meant to keep out riffraff. All riffraff."

Riffraff?! She was *not* riffraff. How insulting. Clearly, the police had no new information. If only they would have let her search the pasture. She was sure she would find a clue to the poor sheep farmer's untimely demise.

M.K. walked over to her red scooter and picked it up. How could she solve this crime when she wasn't even allowed near the crime scene? During school today, when she had the children reading quietly at their desks, she pulled out the most recent issue of her *Crime Solving* magazine. She read about how often a simple footprint could lead a clever sleuth to the perpetrator.

The only footprints she could find, besides those of the dead farmer's, were hoofprints that belonged to sheep. And it was then that Sheriff Hoffman happened to pass by in his patrol car and turned on his noisy siren.

So frustrating!

Maybe she would have to come back after dark, with her father's big flashlight.

She hopped on her scooter and started down the road, deep in thought. She built up speed to crest the hill. Just as she

89

reached the rise, she crouched down on the scooter to improve aerodynamics. She had read about aerodynamics in a book from the library. It had suggested that a rider cut down on any draft by making oneself as sleek and small as possible. She liked to go down this hill with her eyes closed. There weren't many opportunities in the Plain life to let go and go all out. This hill, though, offered a taste of it. Danger *and* risk.

Suddenly, she heard someone yell "Watch out!" then a loud "ooouf" sound as her eyes flew open.

Chris Yoder was heading home from a long day at Windmill Farm. He had ducked through a cornfield filled with drying, green-golden stalks and slipped out to cross the road, when suddenly a flash of a red scooter flew right into him. He yelled, but it was too late. Chris was thrown into the ditch on the side of the road. Headfirst. Into murky, stagnant ditch water.

"I'm so sorry," someone called to him. "Are you hurt? I had my eyes closed and didn't see you."

Even though Chris had landed in water, his head had hit the bottom and he was sure he was seeing stars. He was drenched in smelly ditch water. A big yellow dog peered down at him in the ditch and let out a feeble "Woof." Chris shook himself off and staggered onto solid ground. Life returned to him pretty quick as he sized up his attacker — a young Amish woman with concerned brown eyes. "Why would anybody, anywhere, in their right mind, EVER ride a scooter with their eyes closed?"

The young woman pointed to the hill, flustered. "It's just that it's such a good . . . never mind." She bit her lip. "I said I was sorry."

Chris squeezed murky water out of his sleeve. "You should be."

Now she started getting huffy. "Well, I'm not as sorry as I was a minute ago! Maybe you should look where you're going."

"Maybe you should just LOOK. As in, keep your eyes open."

She started to sputter, as if she was gathering the words to give him a piece of her mind. But then she threw up her hands, muttered something about how this day was a complete disaster, hopped on her scooter, and zoomed away. The big yellow dog trotted placidly behind her.

Chris wiped his face off with his sleeve. Amazing. That girl had the *gall* to be mad at him! The nerve!

But she was cute. Very cute. That he happened to notice.

Stoney Ridge was caught in the grip of an Indian summer. Long, hot days. Long, windless nights.

Late Thursday night, Jimmy Fisher tossed pebbles up at M.K.'s window, but she didn't come down like she usually did. This was their summertime system — he would drop by after being out late with his friends, and she would come down and meet him outside to hear all about it. She thought his friends were hopelessly immature, but she liked hearing about their shenanigans.

Tonight, Jimmy and his friends had climbed the water tank in a neighboring town and dove into the reservoir, forty feet below. Such brave-hearted men. It made him proud to be in the company of these noble fellows. He wondered what M.K. would say about that. He tossed another pebble up at her window. Still nothing. As he looked around in the dark for something more substantial to toss at her window without breaking it and risking Fern's wrath — something he had experienced on occasion and took pains to avoid — a police car pulled up the driveway. Jimmy hid behind the maple tree. His first thought was that Sheriff Hoffman had figured out what he had been doing tonight and had tracked him here. It might have happened once or twice before. But then the car pulled to a stop, the sheriff got out and opened the back door. M.K. bolted out, an angry look on her face.

Wait. What?

Oh, this was too good.

If Jimmy were a more gallant man, he would quietly leave.

But this was too good.

The sheriff banged on the front door. In the quiet of the night, Jimmy could hear a pin drop. He heard M.K. try to convince the sheriff that she could handle things from here, but he didn't pay her any mind. From where Jimmy stood, he could see the front door. He saw a beam of light through the windows as someone made his way to the door. Jimmy heard the click of the door latch opening, and there stood Amos in his pin-striped nightshirt, with Fern in her bathrobe, right behind him. Their eyes went wide as they took in the sheriff standing beside M.K., who looked very small.

"I can explain everything!" M.K. started.

The sheriff interrupted. "Sorry to bother you in the middle of the night, Amos. But I believe this young lady belongs to you."

Amos looked bewildered. Fern looked like

she always looked, as if she had expected a moment such as this. "What has she done now?" Fern asked in a weary voice.

"I found her disturbing a crime scene," Sheriff Hoffman said.

"That is not true!" M.K. said.

Fern shook her head. "Was she trying to get in that poor farmer's sheep pasture again?"

The sheriff handed Amos, who still seemed stunned, a large flashlight. "Sure was."

"I wasn't disturbing anything," M.K. said. "I was looking for clues."

"I keep telling you, we don't need any help solving crimes," the sheriff said. He sounded thoroughly exasperated. He turned and headed to his car, then spun around. "You stay out of that pasture, Mary Kate Lapp."

Jimmy slipped behind the tree again. The front door closed and the sheriff drove away. He waited awhile to make sure no one would see him and quietly strolled home.

Oh, *this* was too good.

5

M.K. couldn't stop yawning. She didn't even mind that Eugene Miller and his cronies had left after lunch again. It was easier to get through the afternoon's work without them. She hoped the boys were smart enough to stay out of sight until after half past three, though she doubted it. She almost fell asleep as second grader Timmy King puzzled over subtraction problems at the board. The warm air in the room, the gentle buzz of a bee on the windowsill. "Nicely done, Timmy," she said. She glanced at the clock. Two and a half hours to go. She read out loud for a while, but no one seemed to hear. She thought about dismissing everyone early because it was so hot.

Could she do that? Why not? She was the teacher.

She put down the book. "Let's try again on Monday." Barbara Jean, the youngest of

95

everyone, clapped her hands, making M.K. laugh. Just as M.K. stood and opened her mouth to say, "School's out! Go on home!" the school door opened wide. In walked Eugene Miller, Josiah Zook, Davy Stoltzfus, and his brother Marvin.

And Fern. In walked Fern.

The boys took their seats. "These boys seemed to have gotten lost after lunch," Fern announced, as if she was on a mission to find them. "So I helped them locate the schoolhouse. They won't be getting lost anymore."

A few snickers circled the room. Fern went to a chair in the back and sat down. M.K. knew that look on Fern's face. It was the look that said she was going to be staying for a while. For the next two and a half hours.

M.K.'s heart sank. She turned to the third graders. "Rise, please, and bring your readers."

Tick. Tick. Tick. The clock inched forward, painfully slow. Finally, it was half past three and the class was dismissed. Fern waited.

"Where did you find the boys?" M.K. asked.

"Hank found them fishing at Blue Lake Pond. He's been worried that all the rainbow trout will be gone by the end of September with those four spending their afternoons fishing, so he ran them off and I happened upon them."

M.K. closed up the cloakroom and locked up the front door. "Why do you have the buggy?"

"We're not going home." Fern pointed to the buggy. "Hop in. We've got someplace we need to be."

"Fern, it's Friday! My first free afternoon —"

"Nothing is as important as this."

M.K. knew not to push it. The ride home from the sheriff must have been a shock to her dad and Fern. It was ridiculous, really. All a simple misunderstanding. She had gone out to see if there might be another clue, something the police missed. There was a problem and it needed solving. Hadn't she learned in life to just solve the problem herself?

And suddenly she was under threat of arrest. Again! How was she supposed to know that the police were patrolling the area? Why hadn't they been patrolling when the murder occurred? She would have liked to ask Sheriff Hoffman such a bold question, but of course she didn't dare.

Fern slapped the reins on Cayenne's rear

end and the buggy lurched forward. "Is that the way you've been teaching?"

"What do you mean?"

"Was today a typical afternoon? Class by class comes up and reads out loud?"

"That's the way Alice Smucker ran the classroom."

Fern was silent, so silent that finally M.K. couldn't hold back another minute. "I told you that I wouldn't be a good teacher! Dad said I've never failed at anything I've tried to do, but this —"

"Well, see, that's the problem right there."

"What is?"

"Tried. You've never failed at anything you've *tried.*"

"I'm failing at this!"

There was a silence, then Fern's voice, sounding soft and hard at the same time. "You haven't *tried* to teach. You're just babysitting. Not even that. The trouble with you, Mary Kate, is you can't see a day ahead."

That was not a new observation.

"You're spending most of your time thinking about solving that sheep farmer's death. You think about it more than the police do."

That was somewhat of an exaggeration, but the sheep farmer murder was taking up a great deal of M.K.'s thoughts. Somebody had to solve the crime before Stoney Ridge was riddled with murders! "I'm teaching the same way Alice Smucker did. Everything's the same. Every single thing."

Fern looked at her as if she might be addlebrained. "You spent eight long years complaining about the time in Twin Creeks School. Seems like a smart girl like you should be able to figure out what's wrong with that logic."

It seemed that way to M.K. too, but she couldn't quite figure out what Fern was getting at. She scrunched up her face as if she was thinking hard, and she was. "How do I know how to teach any different? Alice Smucker was the only teacher I've ever had."

"No, she wasn't."

Fern thought she knew everything, but she didn't. "Oh yes she was!" Then M.K. clapped her hands over her mouth. "Oh, no! She wasn't." M.K. had completely forgotten about Gideon Smucker's brief tenure. He had filled in for his sister, Alice, after there was an unfortunate collision with a runaway sled (a sled that happened to be carrying M.K., but that was beside the point). "But it was easier for Gid. He was a man. The big boys obeyed him. It's always easier for men."

"Why do you think the children obeyed Gid?"

"Probably because Eugene Miller hadn't moved to Stoney Ridge yet."

Fern rolled her eyes.

"Eugene is a bandersnatch, Fern. The very worst of the bandersnatches! He makes Jimmy Fisher seem like any teacher's dream. Eugene makes vulgar noises whenever I turn my back. Yesterday, he put a book up on the doorjamb so that when I walked in, the book fell on my head. And there he was at his desk, with a sweet-as-pie smile pasted on his face. He's just a school yard bully — always making outlandish suggestions and daring his friends to join him. Eugene Miller pushes a person to the limit of politeness. The very limit."

This very morning, she had slipped outside to fill her thermos with water from the pump. When she returned to the classroom, she found that Eugene had drawn a caricature of her on the chalkboard. Never mind that it was actually a rather amusing likeness — he had made a fool of M.K.

"Did the children obey Alice?"

M.K. sighed. "I suppose. She made everything a mind-numbing routine, so the boys used school to catch up on their sleep." Boring. School had been incredibly boring. But

M.K. was starting to feel a mild twinge of guilt as she complained about Alice's teaching. It was a new feeling for her. At least the boys didn't disappear during lunch under Alice's tutelage. "Teaching isn't that easy, Fern." She gave herself an A+ for trying.

"No, I'm sure it isn't, if someone were actually trying to teach."

M.K. was insulted. She was trying! Sort of. Now and then.

"Wann epper mol nix meh drumgebt, is es schlimm." *When you don't care, you are in a sorry state.*

M.K. tried not to flinch. Fern's sayings were worse than a beesting, and she knew all about beestings.

"How long do you plan on wallowing in self-pity?"

"Fine." She let out a sigh. "I'm done wallowing. No more wallowing. Really."

"Good."

M.K. waited, sensing from Fern's change in tone something was coming. "Where are we going?"

"To visit Erma Yutzy."

M.K.'s heart sank a notch lower. Any more bad news today and it would be in her stomach. "I don't like talking to old people. They make me uncomfortable."

Fern released a long-suffering sigh. "What

101

a thing to say."

"I'm sorry, but the way they look at me with their watery eyes makes me uneasy. And their skin is like wrinkled crepe paper. Old people can be odd too. Some as odd as a cat with feathers. I never know what to say to them." She could tell by the way Fern was clutching the reins that she was running out of patience. "You can't deny that, Fern. Just last month, Mose Weaver came to church in his pajamas."

"Mose Weaver is having a few forgetfulness problems."

"Well, how old is Erma Yutzy, anyway?"

"She's turning one hundred next month."

One hundred years old?! M.K. was intrigued. What would it be like to have one hundred years of stored memories jammed in your head? It boggled her mind. "Why today? Maybe we should wait for her birthday."

"Can't. Erma's too busy planning her party."

Planning her party? Who would still be alive to attend? Fern stopped the horse in front of Erma's house. M.K. hopped out and waited for Fern to join her.

Fern didn't budge. "I'll be back in an hour or two."

An hour or two? Fern was leaving M.K.

alone with this ancient lady for an hour or two? "Fern! What am I supposed to talk about with her?"

Fern simply pursed her lips as if the why of it was too obvious to say.

She slapped the horse's reins and trotted out the driveway. Over her shoulder, she tossed, "Did I happen to mention that Erma was a teacher?"

Oh. *Oh.*

Fern! So overinvolved.

Amos had hired some hardworking hands on his farm, but he had never seen anyone work as diligently as Chris Yoder. It was as if Chris had something to prove — though Amos didn't get the feeling that he was showing off. It was more like the boy had something to prove to himself.

The boy? Really, Chris Yoder was a young man. Amos reviewed what he had come to learn about Chris Yoder: he had a tremendous work ethic, even for an Amish man. He had a kind touch with animals, which Amos admired. Chris hurried off at quitting time, as if he was expected somewhere else. Or maybe someone was expecting him.

That was about all Amos could gather about Chris Yoder. He was as closemouthed as they came, responding to Amos's questions in one- or two-syllable answers. He wouldn't join the family for dinner. Instead, he spent his lunch hour sweeping out the barn or binding hay.

Fern had been too preoccupied with M.K. this week to think twice about Chris, though she did ask about him once. "Who in the world is this hired hand and why doesn't he come to the house and introduce himself, be sociable?" Amos answered by saying he was just the quiet type. That satisfied Fern for now, but he knew that when she did get him in her sights, Chris would sing like a canary, without even realizing he had been questioned by a skilled practitioner. Until then, Amos could wait.

There was something about Chris Yoder that appealed to Amos. He was carrying some kind of a burden, and he was too young or too proud to realize that all he needed to do was to ask for help.

Chris knew that Jenny didn't like going home to an empty house, so he worked through his lunch hour to finish up the day's work. He needed to earn a full day's wage, but he didn't want her to have to be home alone very long. As he walked down the lane from Windmill Farm, he braced himself for a litany of complaints about school: the feebleminded teacher, the tragic shortage of girls in her class, the annoying boys. The fact was, Jenny had always been an intense child. She was all or nothing. She loved you or hated you; there was never any middle ground. He actually felt a little sorry for this new teacher — to be inflicted with Jenny's displeasure.

On the upside for the week, things were working out well with Amos Lapp. Chris had been patching jobs together whenever he could find work on the bulletin board at the hardware store, but he preferred working at one place for a while. Plus, Windmill Farm wasn't too far from his grandfather's house.

Amos paid Chris with cash at the end of each day. He said he didn't like being indebted, but Chris had a hunch that Amos wasn't quite sure if he should expect him again in the morning. He knew Amos was holding himself back from asking questions — he could just sense it. But he didn't ask anything, and for that, among other things, Chris was grateful. Amos Lapp had eyes so kind that they made you look twice just to be certain the kindness in them was real. It sure seemed to be.

It wasn't the meanness in people that surprised him. It was the good in them that he found so unexpected. Would he ever get over that?

Chris did a good day's labor for Amos. He hoped it would continue to work out. Not having to wait for cash until the end of the month meant that he could start buying supplies to fix up his grandfather's old house. Twice now, he and Jenny had driven into town to pick up drywall and tape. He was going to start by repairing the hole in the kitchen wall.

Chris climbed over the fence — the same spot where that cute girl had knocked him over yesterday and sent him flying into the ditch. He looked around for that red scooter, just in case she happened along. Not that he was interested. He wasn't. He had no notion to settle down — not for a very long, long time. He had too much on his plate, too many plans. But there was something about that girl that he couldn't quite get out of his mind. He got a kick out of how flustered she was. And then she was so exasperated with him! As if it was his fault that he was crossing the road like a normal person.

He wiped the back of his neck with his handkerchief. It was humid today. A wisp of a memory tugged at him as he walked down the hill. It had been a warm spring day, one of the first for the year. Chris was seven, and Jenny was an infant. She cried a lot as a baby, especially in the evening. Colic, he remembered a neighbor lady saying when she dropped off a meal to celebrate the new baby. The lady recommended goat's milk. "My son had it too," he remembered her saying as she stayed to rock Jenny to sleep.

It wasn't just colic. His mother had used drugs during Jenny's pregnancy. She and Jenny were both suffering from symptoms of withdrawal — edgy and hypersensitive. His mother had little patience for Jenny's ear-piercing cries.

Later that evening, his mother had become so agitated with Jenny's wails that she threw a frying pan against the wall and it made a gash in the drywall. And then she grabbed her purse and stomped out of the house. She didn't return for hours. Chris didn't know where his grandfather had gone to that evening — probably a gathering of old veterans at the local Grange Hall. He just remembered sitting by the front room window, holding Jenny, afraid to set her down because she might start hollering, watching for his mother to come home. When she did come home, she was high. Even at the age of seven, he knew the signs:

slurry talk, bloodshot eyes, clumsy movement.

He remembered how furious his grandfather had been when he saw the condition his mother was in and realized Chris had been left in charge of an infant. He had only allowed his daughter to move back home with two children if she promised to stop using drugs. They had a roof-raising argument that night. His grandfather said he would never fix the hole in the wall — he would leave it there to remind her of what she was turning into. He threatened to turn in his daughter to the authorities. "And don't think you're going to saddle me with them two kids!" his grandfather had hollered. "The cops are going to take 'em and plunk 'em into foster care!" At that point Chris ran to his room and pulled the pillow over his head so he couldn't hear any more.

Chris shuddered involuntarily. He hadn't thought about that night in years. It was strange how memories intruded into a person's mind, uninvited and unwanted.

That was going to be the first thing Chris fixed. That hole.

M.K. found Erma Yutzy out in the vegetable garden, picking the last of the summer beans. Feathery white hair stuck out in tufts around her head, except for that inch-wide strip of bare scalp along the crown of her head like so many other Amish old ladies — a result of years and years of hair pulled and pinned tightly into a bun. She was tiny and frail looking. A good stout wind could carry her off.

M.K. had never paid much attention to Erma Yutzy. She knew her as one of the many elderly ladies in her church, but she had never bothered to stop to talk to her or consider her, other than being careful not to trip her or bump into her at a gathering. She was afraid of old people. They reminded M.K. of a dried-up leaf that would snap in two and crumble if you accidentally bumped into them. Snap. Crumble. Collapse.

"I JUST WANTED TO STOP BY AND SAY HELLO," M.K. called out, loud and clear, as Erma shielded her eyes from the sun when she noticed someone in her garden. "FERN DROPPED ME OFF."

"I'm always delighted to have visitors," Erma said in her thin, wrinkly voice. "Nice to have a reason to stop working." Her face beamed. That was the only word for it. She positively beamed.

M.K. took the basket of beans from her and followed her into the house. Slowly, oh so slowly. It was difficult for M.K. to walk at such a snail-like pace. She never did anything slowly. But imagine — this woman was one hundred years old! M.K. was astounded. Erma had a pair of amazing eyes, brighter than your average blue eyes — maybe a little on the watery side — with a slight tint of something close to turquoise, the color M.K. imagined waters near Fiji to be, although she had never actually seen an ocean. Or maybe the hazy sky right before twilight in the desert of the Sahara, though she'd never seen a desert either.

Erma filled two glasses with lemonade. She added a little twist of mint and handed the glass to M.K.

"Thank you," M.K. said. "THANKYOU," she repeated, enunciating the words.

"You're welcome," Erma said as she settled into a chair. "Now, tell me why you feel the need to shout at me."

M.K. practically choked on her sip of lemonade. "Aren't you nearly deaf?"

"No. I thought maybe you were."

"Well, no. I just thought . . . I mean . . . you're one hundred years old. Uncle Hank roars at us and he's only half as old as you."

Erma smiled. "I've known Hank Lapp for years. He only has three settings on his voice-box. Loud, louder, and loudest." She started to giggle like a schoolgirl, her little shoulders shaking with delight.

Erma Yutzy was not what M.K. had expected. She leaned forward in her chair, intrigued. As the afternoon wore on, M.K. learned all kinds of interesting things about this woman.

When Fern said Erma had been a teacher, M.K. immediately assumed that she would be an old version of Alice Smucker. Erma Yutzy had three things in common with Alice Smucker: they were both maiden ladies and career teachers and they lived alone. Alice lived in a little cottage on her father's goat farm, not by choice. When her father remarried, Alice and her stepmother kept having disagreements about how to organize the kitchen. After Alice had reorganized the kitchen cabinets for the third time — to the way her belated mother had kept them — her stepmother gently suggested Alice might be happier in the little cottage, with a kitchen of her own.

Erma lived alone, by choice. She said she liked her peace and quiet. She had plenty of nearby relatives who kept an eye on her and her home.

But that was where the commonalities of Alice and Erma ended. Erma was winsome in every way and she was nearly one hundred with no plans of dying. Unlike Alice, who had her funeral planned — just in case — at the ripe old age of thirty.

The sound of horse hooves on the driveway caught their attention. Fern had arrived in her buggy. M.K. was shocked to discover that two hours had flown by. They were just scratching the surface! There was so much M.K. wanted to know about her — what was life like for her as a little girl? What changes had she seen in her lifetime?

Erma covered M.K.'s hand with hers. "Mary Kate, I was born into a world of horse-drawn carts on dirty paths, gas streetlights, when you could mail a letter for pennies and a box of Kellogg's Corn Flakes only cost eight cents. Now, I live in an age where there are eight-lane highways and men on the moon and strange little computers that fit in people's pockets."

"Most people call those cell phones."

Erma squeezed her hand. It didn't matter what they were called. She was trying to make a point. "Mary Kate, do you know what keeps me alive?"

M.K. leaned forward in her chair. "What?" She wanted to know.

"I want to see what happens next."

It was suppertime and Amos wasn't sure where Fern or M.K. had gone to. It looked like he was on his own for supper, though he smelled a pot of chili simmering on the stove top and noticed a pan of fresh-baked corn bread. He spooned chili into a bowl and eyed that corn bread again. As long as he was fending for himself, maybe a little bit of butter on that corn bread would be in order. Honey, too.

Just as he was lathering a chunk of corn bread with a thick layer of butter, the kitchen door blew open and in walked Hank carrying a cardboard box, Doozy at his heels.

"AMOS! WE'VE GOT TROUBLE!" Hank set the box on the kitchen floor. In it were four yellow puppies, squirming and wiggling and trying to get out.

"Where in the world did those come from?" Amos asked, swallowing a bite of buttered corn bread as he noticed Fern's buggy coming up the driveway.

"Edith Fisher sent them over with Jimmy. She included this note." Hank pulled his glasses out of his pocket and unfolded the crinkled paper. " 'I have given you plenty of notice to find homes for these puppies and yet you continue to ignore me. So I am ignoring you. Until you find homes for these puppies, you are not welcome for Sunday dinners.' " He stuffed the paper back into his pocket. "She is spurning me!" He shook his head solemnly. "Doozy had a moment of reckless abandon, and look at the dire consequences."

Doozy thumped his tail, pleased at his prowess, and Amos set down the bowl of chili. His appetite had just considerably diminished. "Well, I suppose that these things happen."

"What are we going to do with them?" Hank blurted out.

Amos, who was in the middle of putting the butter back into the refrigerator, stopped what he was doing. "We?" he asked. Out the kitchen sink window, he saw the buggy come to a stop by the barn and Fern and M.K. climb out to unhook Cayenne's traces from the buggy shafts. "I always thought of Doozy as your dog."

"He spends most of his time following M.K. around! Why, he's devoted to her."

"I'm not sure about that. He only follows M.K. around when you've gone off to visit Edith."

"He's not wanted at Edith's farm. She turns up her nose at him, you see. Particularly after this moment of indiscretion with her favorite poodle. Edith complains about Doozy an awful lot, mostly about his scent, which I just can't understand. After all, he is a dog. Dogs should smell like dogs." He crouched down to pat Doozy's head. "She refuses to see beyond a few little flaws."

"Think that she'll change her mind about the two of you?" Amos asked. "After all, you've been courting her for seven years now."

Hank sighed, looking wistfully at the ceiling. "I don't think there's much of a chance there. She says Doozy has to go. Said she can't deal with the both of us."

Amos nodded. Hank would be task enough for any woman. Adding Doozy into the equation would put anyone over the edge.

"Maybe you could compromise," Amos said. "Leave Doozy with us."

Hank shook his head. "No deal." A puppy was nearly escaping out of the box so he reached down and tenderly held it against his chest. "They sure are cute little buggers. It'd be a shame not to keep 'em."

Amos rinsed out his bowl of chili in the sink and put it back in the cupboard, dripping wet. He tried to imagine what it would be like to have five dogs in one house, especially in Hank's small apartment above his buggy shop. "Well, I don't know what to say."

The hinge on the kitchen door squeaked

as Fern came in. She looked at Hank, at Amos, at Doozy, at the box of squirming puppies, and shook her head in exasperation. "I know exactly what to say. Find homes for your dog's puppies, Hank Lapp."

Hank looked at her, wounded. "We were just discussing the possibility of keeping them."

"Absolutely not." She brushed past him and went into the kitchen to wash her hands at the sink. As she dried her hands on the rag, she noticed the missing piece of corn bread in the pan and eyed Amos, who was trying to skooch the remainder of the buttered corn bread behind his back on the counter. She saw. But before she could start scolding him for not waiting for supper, Hank snagged her attention.

"It is clear to me, Fern Lapp," Hank groused, "that you know nothing about the world of dogs."

"I know plenty about dogs. And even more about men." She took bowls out of the cupboard and frowned when she spotted the water drops in the top bowl. She pulled flatware from the utensil drawer and started to set the table, working around the box of puppies. They were curled into a pile in the corner of the box, sound asleep. "Both need very clear directions and expectations." She resumed setting the table. "The puppies go."

"Well, that answers that," Hank huffed. "I come here for sympathy, and all that I'm getting is heartless advice." He stopped. "Speaking of hearts, who's got a bigger heart than Sadie? Why, she's all heart. She might want one of Doozy's pups. Maybe even two! One for each of her little ones!" His face brightened, like the sun coming out after a rainstorm. He placed the puppy back in the box, picked it up, and opened the kitchen door. "M.K.!" he shouted.

M.K. was leading Cayenne into the barn and stopped short at the sound of Hank's loud voice.

"PUT THAT HORSE BACK IN ITS BUGGY SHAFTS! We've got ourselves an emergency errand!"

Fern came up behind Amos at the window. Together, they watched M.K. ooh and aah over the puppies in the box. "Poor Sadie," Fern said. "She'd better brace herself."

6

Jenny's shoulders ached from painting the kitchen wall after Chris had finished fixing the drywall. For the first time in her life she didn't feel like reading a book before bedtime. The problem with not reading, though, was that she couldn't ignore all kinds of creepy, frightening noises as she lay there in the dark.

This old house was awful, truly horrible. It creaked and groaned like it was in pain. She heard mysterious scratching sounds in the walls and the pattering of feet above her head. She closed her eyes and tried to imagine her happiest day, her tenth birthday, when Old Deborah had taken her to the prison and her mother was in a good mood.

Her mother could be sweet and charming at times, but you never knew what you were getting. You always braced yourself for the first minute, as you sized up the expression on Mom's face.

On this day, though, her mother was in a happy mood. She braided Jenny's hair, taming her long curls into two flat plaits down her back. She taught Jenny a dozen variations on cat-in-the-cradle. It was the happiest birthday Jenny ever had. To top it off, that day happened to be a Friday, a day that Jenny had always enjoyed, although Saturday was her absolute favorite. She had the usual feelings about Monday, a day that she had never heard anybody speak up for, for obvious reasons.

The wind picked up. Somewhere outside, a door banged. A branch tapped at the window. Something whirred past Jenny's face. Her eyes shot open to see a menacing dark shape flutter around her room. A bird? How had a bird gotten into her bedroom? She sat up in bed. It must have come in through the broken window. How many times had she complained to Chris about that broken window? Mosquitoes flew in every night, eager to torment her. It flew past again, swooping and dipping erratically. Wait. That was not a bird. It was a bat! She ran to Chris's room, screaming as she flew down the hallway.

"Who's there?" Chris sat bolt upright in bed. "What's happened?"

"Chris! Th-there's a bat flying around my room! It got in through the broken window pane!"

Chris signed and leaned back, closing his eyes. "It'll probably fly back out the window."

"But —"

"It's more scared of you than you are of it. Get some sleep. I've got a long day tomorrow."

Jenny crept back down the hall with the pillow over her head. She lifted the covers and checked every inch of her bed thoroughly before climbing in. As she lay there trying to sleep, she wasn't sure if it would be better to actually see the bat flying around again and know for sure where it was, or not to see it and wonder.

She hated this house. She hated Stoney Ridge. She hated school. She hated the girls at school who never asked her to eat lunch with them. Not one time. She especially hated the leader of the girls, Anna Mae Glick.

She wanted Old Deborah to be alive. She wanted everything to go back the way it used to be. She knew what to expect while she lived at Old Deborah's. The same friends at school. Meals waiting for her at home. People who cared about her. Nobody

120

cared about them in Stoney Ridge. Nobody.

She didn't want to cry. Tears wouldn't accomplish anything and would only make her pillow soggy. She bit on her lower lip to keep her eyes from filling with tears of self-pity. Once her tears started, they would never stop.

A floorboard creaked. The chimney moaned. Minutes ticked away. Everything went quiet. The bat must have flown out the window. It was okay, Jenny told herself, relieved. Everything was going to be okay.

No sooner were the words formed in her mind than the bat whooshed past her head, making squeaky bat noises, darting and diving and swooping and sailing as if it were putting on an acrobatic show for Jenny.

M.K. had a lot of time to think all that weekend, mostly because Sheriff Hoffman saw her at the post office and told her he would put a restraining order out on her if she got anywhere near that sheep farmer's pasture. He patted the gun as he said it too. So rude! She had merely asked him a few questions about how the case was progressing, and if he had discovered any unusual footprints. "Plenty of hoofprints!" he had told her, cackling in that rusty way of his as he said it. He refused to tell her anything more. He looked annoyed when she expressed the tiniest bit of dismay that it was turning into a cold case and suggested he consider putting more manpower into solving it — because that was when he brought up the restraining order. Outrageous!

At this rate, that poor sheep farmer was never going to have his murder solved. And what about the people of Stoney Ridge? They were all at grave risk with a murderer on the loose. Why wasn't anyone else as concerned about it as she was? It was just one of the many complaints she had about living in a small town. People in Stoney Ridge were more concerned about the price of eggs at the farmer's market than about random, senseless murders.

A plane left a long white trail across the sky, and she wondered where it was going. Maybe someplace like Buenos Aires. Or Tokyo. She wondered what it would be like to go somewhere like Moscow. Most of the people she knew were born and raised and died right in Stoney Ridge.

She was positive that the people who lived in big cities — Istanbul or London — *they* would be worried about random murders. Such a thought made her feel pleased that she had decided to pick up a second passport application at the post office today after losing the first one. She didn't have any specific travel plans, but it seemed like a good idea to have a passport. Just in case. A person never knew when she might need to leave the country in a hurry. Even Canada and Mexico required passports, she reminded herself.

What really irked M.K. was that she needed to go by the sheep farmer's field on her way home. It was her customary shortcut. But she wouldn't give Sheriff Hoffman the satisfaction. So instead, she took the long way home.

Saturday morning, Chris was ready to do battle with the exterior of the house as soon as he and Jenny returned from mowing Erma Yutzy's lawn. Starting at the front door, he swept his way up and down the porch, knocking down spiderwebs, dessicated insect carcasses, a long-abandoned birds' nest, and a forest of dead leaves. Jenny sloshed Pine-Sol all over the porch and attacked it with a mop. The water in the bucket grew grimy with the accumulated grunge. Four changes of water and two hours later, he decided the porch floor was done. He'd scrubbed the old boards so hard that he could see bare wood shining through the faded battleship-gray paint.

The windows were next. The panes were so caked with grime that he didn't even attempt to start with Windex. Instead, he hooked up a garden hose and splashed water all over the old wavy glass, sending a dirty river seeping down over his previously pristine floorboards. Shoot. He'd have to give the porch another rinsing later. But for now, he washed and polished and spritzed the tall windows that ran across the front of the house until they sparkled like crystal in the afternoon sunshine.

Chris had saved the front door for last. He scrubbed away layer after layer of dirt and dust. He spent the next few hours working feverishly. Jenny worked hard too. They scoured and scrubbed until their back and legs ached, and their hands were rubbed raw from all the bleach and disinfectant.

Chris looked over the list of things he needed at the hardware store. He couldn't do anything more until he got more cleaning supplies, so he decided to run into town. Samson needed some exercise — he hadn't taken him out for a few days. Jenny wanted to stay home and read a book in a bat-free room, so he hitched Samson to the buggy.

The hardware store was empty so Chris was able to get his supplies quickly. He loaded the buggy and hopped in, signaling

Samson to move forward. The stallion tossed his head and whinnied. He responded to Chris's slightest whistle.

On Stone Leaf Drive, he noticed two small figures in the road up ahead. As Samson gained on them, he saw it was a young Amish woman in a turquoise dress, with an old yellow dog trailing behind her. He recognized that young woman — it was the same one who careened into him the other day. He thought he'd seen her somewhere else, but he couldn't remember.

Chris reined the horse to a stop behind her. "Hey, you. Where's your red scooter?"

She spun around and looked at him. She didn't seem to recognize him, but then, how could she? He had been covered in mud.

Chris saw her puzzled gaze shift from him to Samson. She walked toward Samson and stroked his nose. "Why, this horse is beautiful. Just beautiful. He must be eighteen hands. And pitch-black." She stroked the neck of Samson. "Why, he's a stallion!" She looked at Chris with interest. "Are you going to breed him?"

"Someday. I want to have my own breeding business." He wasn't sure why he admitted that. It wasn't something he told many people.

She ran a hand along Samson's withers.

"Well, when that someday arrives, you'll be off to a fine start with him."

"Can I offer you a lift? It's getting awfully warm."

M.K. shook her head. "I'm almost where I need to be." She started walking down the road.

Chris clucked to Samson to get him moving, but he kept him from trotting to keep pace with the young woman and her dog. "I don't even know your name."

She didn't slow down a bit. "That's because we've never met."

"It might not have been a proper introduction, but we have definitely met."

She stopped abruptly and looked at him with a question on her face.

"I'm the one you knocked into the ditch the other day."

She squinted her face as if she was trying to place him. Just how many people did she crash into on that scooter? Clearly, too many to remember.

A frown pinched her face and she threw her arms in the air. "Join the long line of people who blame me for everything that goes wrong around here!" She started marching down the road.

Chris clucked to the horse. "I'm not blaming you. Well, maybe a little. You were heading down a hill, on a scooter, with your eyes shut. Probably going ten miles an hour!"

The young woman turned her face away, her jaw thrust out, and she picked up her pace.

Samson seemed to know to keep up with her. "Look, maybe we can start over. I'm Chris Yoder."

She balled her fists on her hips. "Which way are you headed, Chris Yoder?"

They were nearly at an intersection. Chris pointed straight ahead.

"Then I'm going this way. Come on, Doozy." She turned right at the intersection. As she swung to the right, something slipped out of her pocket. He tried to call out to her — a little awkward when you don't know a person's name: "Hey, you! You there!" — but she wasn't going to pay him any mind.

He jumped down to pick up the paper and unfolded it. A passport application. *What?* What was a Plain girl doing with a passport application? What kind of a girl was she?

He watched her march down the lane, head held high, until she and her dog disappeared around the bend. He couldn't wipe the grin off his face. He still didn't know her name . . . but he was going to find out.

■ ■ ■ ■

Jenny glanced at the clock on the kitchen counter. Was it already after two? Chris would be back soon. She had been completely absorbed in the book she was reading and simply had to find out if there was a happy ending. She loved happy endings. But now she needed to get this letter written and stick it in the mailbox before the postman came by. And before Chris returned from town. She took out one crumpled five-dollar bill from her pocket and tucked it into an envelope.

Dear Mom,

Chris and I are doing okay. I started school this week. There aren't any girls in my grade, just boys. I feel sorry for the teacher. She's not very bright and the big boys outsmart her. Mostly, she just sits at her desk and sifts through magazines. But at least it gives me a lot of free time to read my books. I miss you. Get better fast, okay? This is all the money I could get since my last letter.

Love you! Jenny

For one long, painful moment, Jenny remembered how her mother looked right before everything fell apart again this last time. She was so skinny that Jenny could see two scapula bones in her back that stuck out like chicken wings. She hardly ate any food. She hardly slept. And she kept getting bloody noses. Old Deborah had pulled Grace into the bathroom to stop the nosebleed.

You'd think her mother would care about what drugs were doing to her body. But all Grace Mitchell wanted, all she wanted, no matter what, was more meth.

That evening, Old Deborah talked and talked with her mom in the kitchen, long after Chris and Jenny had gone to bed. In the morning, when Jenny woke up, her mother was gone. Old Deborah told her that Grace had decided to enter the rehab center. Chris said he was pretty sure Old Deborah hadn't given Grace a choice.

Jenny had faith in her mom, though. This time would be different. Her mom would get better. She had cleaned up twice before. She could do it again. Absolutely. She licked the back of the envelope and ran out to the mailbox. Then she came back in to finish her story in the kitchen — the only guaranteed bat-free room in the house.

The kitchen clock ticked loud in the silence.

■ ■ ■ ■

M.K. hadn't intended to visit Erma today, but she did not want that flirtatious young man to continue to follow her, and she certainly didn't want to get in his buggy with him. Nosir! She had no idea who he was and had no desire to know, either — though anyone who had a horse like that couldn't be entirely bad. The horse was well cared for, sleek and strong, with intelligent eyes. Where had she seen that horse before? In town, maybe? No. She couldn't quite capture it — but she knew she'd seen him somewhere. She couldn't help but admire such a beautiful creature. But her admiration for its owner ended there. Her curiosity, though, was another story. She happened to notice that the young horse owner turned down the long drive that led to Colonel Mitchell's abandoned house. She hadn't even thought of that house in years and years. It was hidden from the road on a long flag lot, hidden from the road with a long dirt driveway for access.

But back to M.K.'s current situation. The road she turned down went right by Erma Yutzy's, and suddenly, there she was, walking up the driveway. The air was filled with the sweet scent of freshly cut grass — one of M.K.'s favorite smells. Erma was filling her bird feeders with oiled black sunflower seeds when she saw M.K. and her face lit up with delight.

"It won't be long until the skies will be filled with a thick black ribbon of birds as they head south for the winter. Don't you love to put your head back and watch them fly, Mary Kate? Don't you just wonder, 'Where is the end of that long ribbon?' " She sighed happily. "There's so much to wonder about in the natural world."

Imagine that, M.K. thought. Erma had seen one hundred autumns. One hundred years' worth of skies filled with migrating birds. The same skies, every year. And still, she found them fascinating.

The two women sat on the porch in the shade, with a slight breeze wafting around them, and drank iced tea, talking. The conversation began with news about Sadie's redheaded twins and drifted to school, as Erma asked M.K. what she thought about being a teacher.

M.K. groaned. "Awful. Just awful. Part of the problem is that I don't think these children are capable of learning." Maybe Danny Riehl would be the one exception.

"I have learned that most youngsters can

do what you ask them to do — even if they don't think so. They just need a little push sometimes to get them moving."

Apparently, Erma never had a scholar like Eugene Miller. He needed a push, all right, right out the window.

"So over the years I learned to give a little push in the right direction when I had to. That's what teachers do."

M.K. leaned forward in her chair. "That's the other part of the problem. I just don't know how to think or act like a teacher."

Erma tilted her head. "What do you think a teacher acts like?"

"Very, very serious. And solemn." Gid was serious. Alice was serious and solemn.

Teaching was serious business. M.K. had a difficult time acting serious and solemn on a full-time basis. It was exhausting.

"And why do you think that would be true?"

"The reason, I think, is because it is an overwhelming task to maintain order. Especially when Eugene Miller is in the room. I'm only five feet three and the older boys tower over me. They ignore me. They run roughshod over all of my attempts to keep the classroom from utter chaos."

"Mary Kate," Erma started. She was one of the few people who called M.K. by her full name and it made her feel rather grown up. "They will see you as a teacher on the day when you start seeing yourself as a teacher."

"But I do! I'm in that stuffy schoolhouse every day, from morning to night. I've been working myself to the bone. I've tried everything! I've tried to teach like Alice. I've tried to teach like Gid. Neither way works. I just can't do it. I can *not* teach."

"Oh, but I think you can," Erma said in that enigmatic way she had. "Mary Kate, there is a remarkable porosity in a one-room schoolhouse. A lesson given to one age group will find its way into others as well. You watch and see. Soon, you will have that entire schoolroom functioning like a well-oiled machine."

She asked about each of the students, and M.K. surprised herself at how much she knew about each one. Much, much more than she had thought she did. "There's a new girl who looks at me as if I'm a stray cat — pitiful and unwanted."

Erma stared at M.K. Then, her little shoulders began to shake, at first only slightly, and then more heavily, until her tiny wrinkled face broke open with a whoop of raspy laughter. She laughed and laughed until tears ran down her face. M.K. felt indignant. She wasn't trying to be funny! She was only trying to describe the way Jenny looked at her — as if she had no idea how M.K. ended up as a teacher. M.K. had the same thought.

An hour later, M.K. walked back to Windmill Farm feeling better about everything. Erma had that effect on her. She was an odd person in a lot of ways, full of contrasts. She was one hundred years old, but thought and acted like a much younger person. She lived alone but loved people.

As M.K. hopped a fence to shortcut through the Smuckers' goat pasture, there was something else about Erma that kept rolling around in her mind. When Erma was with you, she was really, really with you. She was totally focused on you. She fixed her eyes on you and looked at you as if you were saying the most important thing in the world. She would cock her head sympathetically, ask pertinent questions, and offer her opinions tactfully.

Unlike Fern, who never concerned herself with tactfulness.

As M.K. turned up the drive to Windmill Farm, she stopped to get the mail and braced herself to be met with a scolding from Fern. She knew she was running late.

But no! Fern didn't even seem to notice

she had gone missing all afternoon. Fern was turning the kitchen inside and out, looking for her coffee can of spare cash. She barely looked up when M.K. came inside.

M.K. tossed the mail on the kitchen table. "What are you looking for?"

"You didn't take my coffee can, did you?"

"No. Of course not."

M.K.'s father came inside and noticed the two women taking things out of cupboards.

"Amos, I can't find my coffee can," Fern said. "You didn't move it, did you?"

"No," Amos said, washing his hands at the sink. "Why would I?"

Fern eyed him. "Well, you were the last one who had it. You've been paying that new hired boy cash from it each night."

Amos grabbed a dishrag. "I always put it back where I found it."

"Wasn't gone yesterday." She opened up another cupboard. "Near on two hundred dollars, if a penny."

M.K. thought for a moment. "Dad, was the new hired hand in the kitchen with you when you paid him?"

Fern stilled a moment as she waited for Amos's answer.

Amos looked from M.K. to Fern. "Now, wait just a minute. You shouldn't be tossing accusations at anyone."

Fern frowned. "I have yet to meet this fellow. He's as skittish as a young colt."

Another mystery! M.K. was intrigued. "Who is this fellow, Dad?"

Amos frowned. "He's the hardest worker I've ever seen."

M.K. hopped up on the kitchen counter, then hopped off again when Fern scowled at her. "Dad, what else do you know about him?"

Amos tossed the dishrag on the counter. "I know that he didn't take money from Fern's coffee can. That's what I know." He noticed the mail on the table and skimmed through it. Then he took his mail to his desk in the living room.

M.K. turned to Fern. "Erma Yutzy said she was looking around for some cash that had gone missing."

"You were at Erma's today?" Fern looked pleased.

"I happened to be walking by her house."

"It's out of the way."

"Not today it wasn't." The more M.K. thought about it, the more she thought there might be a connection. According to the *Adventures of Sherlock Holmes,* a person needed motive and opportunity. She walked to the doorjamb of the living room. "Dad, do you happen to know if that hired hand is working anywhere else?"

"Yes," Amos said, leaning back in his desk chair. "Erma Yutzy's. She's been needing someone to mow her lawn once a week because her great-grandnephew fell out of a tree and broke his arm."

M.K. gave Fern a "See? I told you so!" look, but Fern didn't pay her any mind. She was looking through another cupboard for her coffee can. Clearly, this hired hand had plenty of opportunity. But what would be his motive? "Dad, tell me everything you know about this hired hand."

"I know two things. His name is Chris Yoder. And he's a hard worker." He put on his glasses to read a letter, a signal that he was done talking.

M.K. gave up trying to pry information from him and went back to the kitchen. She reached into the fruit bowl for an apple and took a bite, deep in thought. "I met a fellow named Chris Yoder on the road today. Strange man. Rather accusatory." She chewed and swallowed. "You know what I would do? I would keep a very close eye on that hired hand, that's what I would do. Sounds like this fellow might have a case of sticky fingers."

"You try to make things too simple," Fern said, her head in a cupboard. "You try to make life too simple."

But to M.K., it *was* all so simple. Chris Yoder had been on these very farms and money had gone missing. The two facts seemed to be inextricably linked.

7

M.K. couldn't sleep. Too much on her
mind. Too hot a night. Why did they have
school in September, anyway? It still felt
like summer. If she were on the school
board, she would only require pupils to attend school in January, when nothing much
else was going on. However, she was happy
to remember that she would not be teaching school in January, and not just because
she hadn't paid any attention to Orin Stoltzfus's instructions about that coal heater.

Three more days. Just three more days
and she could retire from teaching. Ah, bliss!

M.K. had the same feeling she got when
she came to the last chapter of a book: a
little sorry to see it end but already antici-
pating the start of a new story. Her time as
a teacher for Twin Creeks School was nearly
over. The ordeal had been grueling at times,
but she had done a good deed by substituting for Alice Smucker. No scholar had died

under her care, and two of Eugene's cohorts had started to stay for the entire day. She could leave with a sense of satisfaction. Her teaching career would be over. Done. Finished!

She wondered if she should give the class a formal farewell on Friday afternoon or simply disappear. In the end, she decided that she would make a formal announcement.

She got out of bed and crossed to the window. She sat on the sill and looked at the moon hanging low in the black velvet sky. Thin wispy clouds moved slowly in front of it. The sun would be rising in Athens, Greece, about now.

In her mind, she saw herself climbing up a steep path, walking past white stucco houses with blue shutters, and window boxes filled with red geraniums. She imagined stopping at one point to gaze at the Aegean Sea, far below the Greek village. What words would she use to describe the color of that sea? Turquoise? Azure? Cobalt?

In the quiet of the night, a horse whinnied and another answered back. She leaned her head against the window and set aside her imagined Grecian journey. She reviewed the sheep farmer's murder one more time. She was heading down the street, away from the farmer's pasture. Had she seen anything suspicious as she scooted past the pasture? Nothing came to mind. She didn't even remember seeing the farmer, but there were trees in the pasture. She did remember noticing some sheep along the fence, trying to eat grass outside the fence. She smiled — even animals thought grass was greener on the other side of the fence. Maybe it wasn't, maybe it was. But oh, wouldn't it be wonderful to find out?

When she had reached the far edge of the pasture, she heard the shot and practically fell off her scooter. An eerie stillness followed. One long minute. Then another. And then came a sound.

M.K.'s eyes went wide. Horse hooves! She had heard horse hooves! Somewhere, a horse galloped away. Why didn't she remember it? Was it such a familiar sound to her that she blocked it out? She squeezed her eyes shut — trying, trying, *trying* to remember. Black. Something black. A flash of black. Way down the road, a flash of black. A horse.

She gasped. Her eyes flew open.

It was that which put M.K. on high alert. A Pandora's box of accusations had cracked open in her mind.

She had seen Chris Yoder's black stallion

gallop away from the murder scene.

As Chris woke to the sound of rain on the roof, he stretched and yawned. His mind went through a checklist of tasks at Windmill Farm that he and Amos had discussed yesterday: hay cutting, apple picking, pear picking. Amos had said he would teach Chris how to prune the fruit trees, come winter. "Not a single cut is made without a reason," he told Chris.

Chris smiled. He could tell that Amos loved those orchards. He tended them like Old Deborah had tended her herb garden. Amos was a warm, loving man with a keen intellect. He was grateful to God for leading him to work for a man like Amos Lapp. Chris was learning quite a bit from him about how to manage a well-run farm, and he needed to get that experience if he were to have a farm of his own one day.

It was more than that, though. Chris was always drawn to wise, older men as father figures. He guarded his countenance carefully, but he valued those few men in his life who had taken an interest in him. He watched them carefully, studied them. They had taught him how to be a man.

He slipped his feet over the edge of his bed and walked to the window to see how hard the rain was coming down. He might try to get over to Windmill Farm today to talk to Amos about selling the apples and pears at the farmer's market in Stoney Ridge. A few days ago, he had wandered among the vendors. He recognized one person — that fellow who hung around Windmill Farm a lot. Jimmy Fisher, Amos called him. He was selling eggs at a booth to a long line of customers.

An empty booth sat next to Jimmy Fisher and that was when it occurred to Chris that Amos should consider selling apples and pears at the market. He knew Amos had an arrangement to sell most of the varieties to Carrie and Amos Miller so they could make Five Apple Cider, but this year, after a bumper crop, there would still be more apples to sell. More, even, than could be sold at Fern's roadside stand.

Chris sought out the market manager and learned that renting a booth would only cost 10 percent of the day's take. The market manager told him he could have the empty spot next to the Fishers'. That was an added bonus, the market manager said, because there was a local shortage of farm fresh eggs. Egg tended to draw customers to a produce stand. And those good-looking Fisher boys tended to draw customers, he added. Especially female customers.

Then Chris told him he wanted to sell Windmill Farm's apples and pears. The market manager's face fell. "Oh, we have more apples and pears than we can sell. If I let Amos Lapp's orchard fruit in here, it would drive down the prices for my other vendors." He scratched his neck, then his face brightened. "We're short on lettuces. There's big market demand. Ever thought of starting a market garden?"

Chris hadn't, but he did now. He didn't have the space he would need for a garden at his grandfather's house, but Amos had plenty of space. He wondered if he could talk Amos and Fern into letting him work a fallow section of the vegetable garden to sell produce at the market.

Farming was starting to interest him in a way he had never thought about — he had never felt more purposeful, more optimistic about the future. It *was* a good decision to come to Stoney Ridge. Everything, finally, was starting to come together. What he discovered about farming was that a man's worth was judged not by where he started, but where he ended up.

Mary Kate Lapp was no detective, but she was able to put two and two together and draw a conclusion in a matter of seconds — a new neighbor with a mysterious past had moved into Stoney Ridge just a month ago, money started to go missing in the sleepy little town, and a farmer had been shot dead in the middle of his sheep pasture. It was an alarming set of coincidences!

Early in the morning, an hour before school started, M.K. knocked on the sheriff's window.

He beckoned her inside and pointed to a chair facing his desk. "Can I get you some coffee?"

Coffee? Did he think she was here for a friendly chat? She shook her head. "I thought of something! Evidence! Significant evidence. The last piece in the puzzle."

The sheriff took a noticeable breath. "What's the puzzle?"

What puzzle? "The sheep farmer's murder! I've figured out who did it. I'm absolutely convinced. And I think he's also the coffee can thief!"

Clearly, the sheriff did not understand the full import of this discovery. He took a sip of coffee. Maybe he required a lot of caffeine to wake up. "What coffee can thief are you talking about?"

"The one who is stealing coffee cans in Amish kitchens! Everyone's talking about it. He's living at Colonel Mitchell's house. That would be considered squatting. Or maybe breaking and entering."

The sheriff stilled. "Colonel Mitchell's?"

She nodded. "That's what I've been trying to tell you! The murderer is right under our noses!"

"Slow down, M.K. Start at the beginning." He lowered his voice as he spoke, as if he was trying to talk someone out of jumping off the ledge of a tall building. Did he think she was crazy?

She glanced at the clock on the wall. She had to get to the school soon. Sometimes, it seemed as if she needed to do everything in this town.

"Looks like the rain isn't going to let up," Chris said. "Which means no hay cutting over at Windmill Farm." Chris gave Jenny that piece of news as they ate their breakfast of oatmeal and strawberry preserves. It was all she could muster together to eat quickly in the horrible kitchen, and besides, the stove wouldn't stay lit for more than two minutes. "We can get a lot done on the house today."

Jenny didn't respond. She didn't like the way Chris said "we" every time he decided something needed to be done. It meant that

Jenny's free reading time after school would disappear. And for what? This old place was a dump. She didn't know why Chris wanted to come here — she thought they could have moved in with some other family back in Old Deborah's church — maybe the Troyers. That's what she loved most about the Amish. It was like having this huge family, with aunts and uncles and a zillion cousins. But Chris was adamant that they needed to go back to Grandfather Mitchell's house and fix it up. He said it was their legacy. Whenever she objected, he only said to trust him.

Chris closed up the small Igloo he had bought for Jenny after she complained about carrying a brown bag, and set it on the tile countertop. "Okay, your lunch is packed," he said. "Don't be late for school." He pointed to the umbrella. "Don't forget that."

"You treat me like I can't remember anything."

"You forgot once."

"That was a long time ago, Chris. I was twelve." She grabbed the Igloo and stomped to the door.

"Jenny!" Chris called. When she spun around, he gently tossed the umbrella at her.

Maybe, she thought, as she opened the umbrella on the front porch, maybe after Chris fixed up the house, he would change his mind about having Mom come live with them. Then Mom could have a place to call home. They could start over, the three of them. Mom would stay off drugs after this last stint in the rehab center. Maybe they could finally be like everybody else, and Jenny wouldn't feel as if she was always on the outside looking in.

She passed by three Amish farms on her way to the schoolhouse. She would look up and see the family working around the yards, moms and daughters hanging laundry on the clothesline, fathers and sons walking to the barn. A deep, inside-out longing always swept through her. The hardest thing of all was when she caught a whiff of dinner cooking at someone's house. Those savory aromas made her eyes fill up with tears, sadness spilling over. She heard someone say once that you can't miss what you've never had. That was one of the dumbest things she had ever heard. She never had a normal family and she missed it every single day.

She saw a car heading toward her on the narrow road so she walked to the very edge and waited until it passed. She sucked in her breath when she saw it was a police car and didn't let the breath out until it passed her by. Police cars always reminded her of her mother.

It wasn't fair, no. None of it was fair.

It didn't bother Chris to have a rainy day today, even if it meant he missed a day's income. He could use a full day to work on the house. He walked around the downstairs rooms, coffee cup in hand, trying to decide where to start the day's work. He made a list of the things he had done and things still to do, which was much longer. Jenny would vehemently disagree, but it was in surprisingly good condition for an old, abandoned house. He wished he had a boatload of cash to do right by the house — new double-paned windows, new counter-tops in the kitchen to replace the cracked tiles. But all in all, his plan was coming along, right on schedule. Fresh paint was a wonderful resource too. He was doing the things he could afford to do and it was making a difference. It was the best he could do. In the silence that wasn't quite silence — the clock ticking softly, the rain dripping on the roof — his thoughts traveled to his grandfather. He thought the Colonel would be pleased with the repairs to the house.

Replace drywall in the kitchen. ✔

Sand and patch and paint the front
    door. ✔

Rip out dry rot in bathroom flooring. ✔

Replace flooring in bathroom.

Repaint interior and exterior.

Recaulk windows.

Sand wooden floors and stain. Varnish.

Chris went back downstairs to prepare the caulking gun to recaulk the windows. He had noticed some staining on the drywall under those windows that faced east — the direction most of the storms came from. When he examined where the water was coming from, he could see that the caulking was gone.

Chris started to caulk the windows facing east and, just to be safe, decided he would later seal all the windows. Outside, the storm was starting to ratchet up. The rain was coming down in sheets. He hoped Jenny had made it to the schoolhouse without getting soaked.

Someone knocked on the door, interrupting him. Had Jenny forgotten something? Chris opened the door to a police officer on his porch. He felt as though someone had punched him in the stomach. It was never good news when the police came to his house. The last time he had opened the door to a police officer, he found out that his mother had been arrested again.

"Are you Chris Yoder?"

Chris's heart thumped so violently he could hardly breathe. "I am."

"I'm Sheriff Hoffman. I'd like you to come down to the police station with me and answer a few questions."

"To the police station? Why? For what purpose?"

"I need to ask you a few questions."

"Am I being arrested?"

Sheriff Hoffman tilted his head. "Should you be? Have you broken the law, Mr. Yoder?"

"Of course not. But I have a right to know why you want to take me to the police station."

"I just want to talk to you." The sheriff looked past Chris into the house. "You're new around here, aren't you? Mind if I come in?"

Chris stepped away from the door and the sheriff walked in.

He took a few steps around and whistled. "Lots of work to do."

Chris held up the caulking gun. "That's what I'm trying to do."

"Mind telling me what you're doing here?"

"I'm fixing up my grandfather's house."

"Who was your grandfather?"

"Mitchell. Colonel Mitchell. I called him the Colonel. Everybody did."

The sheriff flipped a light switch but nothing came on. Chris had never called the electric company to turn the electricity on. No need.

The sheriff looked Chris up and down. "Mitchell isn't a Plain name."

"No."

"But you're Plain."

"I was raised Plain. I am Plain. I've been baptized."

The sheriff moved into the kitchen and pushed his booted heel against a worn-out spot in the flooring. "You thinking about ripping up that old linoleum?"

"Maybe."

"Might have hardwoods underneath. My mother's kitchen had indoor/outdoor carpet on top. After she passed, we ripped it up and voilà! Hardwoods." He snapped his fingers, as if it was easy.

Chris knew the sheriff was trying to make him relax. But he had a very bad feeling about this visit.

The sheriff hooked his hands on his hips. "Any chance you happened to be at the farm of Raymond Gould, a sheep farmer, on the afternoon of August 18?"

Chris took a deep breath. "Yes. I was."

M.K. started each morning with roll call. She wasn't really sure why it was necessary — but that was what Alice Smucker had done, and Gid too, so she thought it must be necessary. When she came to the eighth grade, she called out, "Jenny Yoder." Jenny raised her hand.

"Yoder? Jenny Yoder?" Something clicked. "Is Chris Yoder any relation to you?"

Jenny nodded. "He's my brother."

M.K. was a little stunned. She hadn't expected the sheep murderer and coffee can thief to be anybody's brother. She stood quietly, studying Jenny. Granted, Jenny didn't resemble her brother — she had dark auburn hair and he was fair-haired. Except for the color of her blue eyes, they looked nothing alike. He was tall and muscular, she was short and bird-thin. Still, how had she not put the two of them together? M.K. did have a lot on her mind — but she was usually so good at making those kinds of connections.

M.K. heard the rumble of thunder and hurried to shut the schoolhouse windows. Through the window, she noticed the sheriff's car drive slowly past the schoolhouse.

In the backseat was Chris Yoder.

As the car passed by, Chris looked over at the schoolhouse. For one brief second, their eyes met.

M.K. spun around to see if Jenny had seen her brother in the police car, but her head was bent over, tucked into the book she was supposed to be reading from. It was a strategy M.K. had used many times herself. A terrible feeling flooded through M.K. When she went to see the sheriff this morning, she hadn't really thought through that Chris Yoder might be arrested and hauled off to jail.

But if he was a thief and a murderer, jail was where he belonged.

Unless, pointed out a small voice in her head that sounded a good deal like Fern, unless . . . he's not guilty. Unless Mary Kate had no right to accuse another person of crimes. Unless he was another Plain person — one of her own. Unless she had no business meddling in police business.

M.K. felt the courage she had started the day with drip away like ice cream on a July afternoon. She interfered with something she should have left alone.

What if Chris Yoder were found guilty? But what if Chris Yoder *was* guilty?

What have I done? M.K. thought. *What*

154

As soon as Jimmy heard the news from his brother Paul, who heard it from a girl he was dating, who heard it from her friend who answered the phone part-time at the sheriff's office, he rushed over to tell M.K. He could hardly wait. This was going to be a delicious moment.

The Lapp family was just sitting down to supper as Jimmy rapped on the kitchen door.

Fern opened the door to him. "You have an unusual knack for appearing at meal-times," she said, as if she wasn't at all surprised — or excited, either — to see him.

Jimmy was in too generous a frame of mind to worry about that. Besides, Fern was already setting another place at the table for him.

Fern's cooking was legendary, so Jimmy was happy to be invited to stay. He took his time, waiting for just the right moment. The moment had to be perfect. M.K. had been cranky lately, with this school teaching and all, so Jimmy thought this would be just the thing to snap her out of her funk.

Finally, in between supper and dessert, Jimmy leaned back in his chair. "So, it turns out that the culprit has been found for the murdered sheep farmer."

"I know," M.K. said quietly.

"You knew? You knew?" Jimmy was astounded. How did she know things faster than he did? She was stuck in a schoolhouse all day! She looked at him strangely, pale and unhappy. "Are you all right? Are you sick?"

"I'm fine," she said, but she didn't sound at all fine.

Come to think of it, she hadn't talked during supper either. Uncle Hank did most of the talking.

"BOY, WE'RE ON THE EDGE OF OUR SEATS!" Uncle Hank roared. "Don't keep us waiting."

All eyes were upon Jimmy — his favorite moment. "As you know, the sheriff has been baffled over this murder."

"Tell us something we don't know," M.K. added mournfully.

Jimmy leaned forward in his chair. He lowered his voice to add suspense. "No one else was around, and no footprints led to or from the scene of the crime. But our trusty investigators sifted through the meager clues surrounding the farmer's death, and they have fingered the culprit." He pointed his finger in the air for a dramatic touch.

Uncle Hank sat straight up in his chair.

"WHO? WHO?"

"Turns out the farmer had fallen asleep amidst his sheep without securing his rifle."

"AND?" Uncle Hank yelled. Fern looked at him, annoyed.

Now Jimmy was in his dramatic element. "A moment of neglect, another one of leisure, a wooly hoof on the trigger, and a speeding slug sentenced the sleeping shepherd to his final slumber."

All faces were blank. It was Fern who put it together first. "One of his sheep stepped on the rifle?"

Jimmy grinned. "The coroner's report came back from the autopsy — something to do with the angle of the bullet. It was the only logical conclusion."

"When did they figure it out?" M.K. asked meekly.

"Today," Jimmy said. "I guess they found a witness who saw the whole thing and it all added up to what they had been thinking. You can all sleep easier tonight. The weapon has been confiscated from the flock. The perpetrator has confessed and the judge has handed down the sentence." Jimmy had been waiting to deliver this line all afternoon: "The guilty party has been sentenced to ewe-thanasia."

A moment of silence followed. Then,

Uncle Hank and Amos burst into laughter. Jimmy joined in. Tears flowed down their cheeks. Their guffaws were so loud and out of control that Fern and M.K. grew thoroughly disgusted. They gathered up plates and took them to the kitchen, leaving the men to howl like a pack of hyenas, Fern said. But Fern was not the laughing kind.

Jimmy wiped tears from his eyes. "One more thing, M.K. Now there's no reason keeping you from introducing me to Emily Esh!" He turned back to Amos and Uncle Hank and started laughing all over again.

M.K. felt a surge of jangly nerves as she sloshed the dishes with soapy water. The minute Jimmy walked through the door, she knew he had on his I-know-something-you-don't smile. Now she understood why.

She had been so sure, so absolutely, positively sure that Chris Yoder was the culprit. Maybe he had lied to the sheriff. But then, there was that autopsy finding. Forensic science was quite accurate. She knew that to be true because she read it in her *Unsolved Crimes* magazine.

Jimmy sidled into the kitchen. "So, I sure hope your dad and Fern don't have to leave town, thanks to you not setting a good example for the community. All eyes are upon the teacher, I hope you know."

"What are you jabbering about now?"

He grabbed a dish towel and pretended to help her dry the dishes. "Seeing as how you were escorted home by a very important means of transportation the other night." Carefully, he enunciated, "It involved a police car."

M.K. froze. The soapy dish she was washing was suspended in air.

Jimmy whistled two notes. "Did the sheriff cuff you before he took you home?"

She narrowed her eyes. "What do you know about anything?"

"You mean . . . your transportation in a police car?" he reminded. Again, he enunciated the words *police car* with utmost care. He took the dish out of her hands and rinsed it off, calmly drying it.

"I wasn't doing anything wrong," she spat out. "I was trying to help and —" Just then, Fern came into the kitchen with a few condiments to put in the refrigerator and M.K. knew enough to snap her mouth shut. This conversation with Jimmy Fisher would have to wait.

"Why, there it is!" Fern said. "I completely forgot I had put it there while I was cleaning out cupboards."

"What?" M.K. said.

Fern spun around. In her hand was the coffee can that held her spare cash.

M.K. dropped a wet, soapy dish on the floor and it shattered into pieces. *What have I done?* she thought. *What have I done?*

8

Chris tossed the forkful of hay into Samson's makeshift stall, in the garage-turned-barn. Then he clipped a lead rope to Samson's harness and led him outside to brush him down. He stroked the brush across Samson's withers, and the horse nickered, nudging Chris's shoulder with his nose. Normally Chris would laugh at the horse's antics, but not now. Not after a day like today.

Currycombing the horse was Chris's way to calm down and sort things out. Samson was annoyed that dinner was getting delayed, but tonight, it would have to wait. Chris still felt shaky inside after being hauled off to the police station like a common criminal. He was even more shocked by how the conversation with the sheriff had unfolded.

"So, Chris Yoder, tell me why you were at Raymond Gould's farm on the afternoon of

August 28th," the sheriff had said as he settled into the chair behind his desk.

"I had been doing odd jobs around Stoney Ridge. I found the jobs on the bulletin board at the hardware store in town. Raymond Gould needed someone to lift hay into his barn loft, so I went over to his farm that morning and he hired me for the rest of the day. Said he has — said he had — a bad back."

The sheriff scribbled down notes as Chris spoke. "Go on."

"I was up in the hayloft, using a pulley to haul bales of hay into the loft. I heard a gunshot go off and looked out the door at the end of the barn. Down in the pasture was the farmer, Raymond Gould, sprawled flat on his back, and a bunch of frightened sheep."

"No one else?"

"No one. I had a pretty good vantage point from the upper story of the barn."

"Then what?"

"I scrambled down from the hayloft and took off on my horse to call for an ambulance. I remembered that I had passed by a phone shanty near the schoolhouse."

"And then?"

"I went back to the farm, waited until I heard the police sirens, and left."

"You didn't bother to give Gould CPR?"

"I don't have any idea how to give some-one CPR." He turned the brim of his straw hat around and around. "Look, Sheriff, I've been around farm animals enough to know when a creature still has life in it. I have to say, Raymond Gould looked pretty dead from the barn." Chris pointed to his head. "The bullet, well, it —"

The sheriff waved that thought off. "Yeah, yeah." He jotted down a few more notes.

Chris was growing impatient. "Am I under arrest? I didn't do anything wrong."

The sheriff leaned back in his chair. "No. Your story checks out. We have two calls coming in, five minutes apart, from the schoolhouse phone. And the coroner's report corroborates your story. Turns out a sheep stepped on the rifle. The safety wasn't on."

"Then, can I go?" Chris started to rise in the chair.

"Not so fast. I've got a few more questions for you." The sheriff tossed down his pen and fixed his gaze on Chris. "If you weren't guilty, then why did you act guilty? Why did you leave the scene?"

Chris stifled a groan. He cleared his throat and tried to answer calmly. "I could see things were taken care of. I had nothing to add. I didn't see the actual shooting. I would have just gotten in the way."

The sheriff raised his eyebrows. "Or maybe you didn't want the authorities to know you were in town."

Maybe. "I haven't done anything wrong. Can I go?"

"Just a few more questions."

"Like what?"

"Like your real name."

"I've told you. Christopher Yoder."

"Your father's name was Yoder?"

"I don't know who my father was."

"Where'd you pick up the name Yoder?"

"My foster mother. She raised me."

"She adopted you?"

"No. Not officially."

"Then why don't you tell me what your legal name is?"

Chris sighed. "Mitchell. Christopher Mitchell."

"Tell me about your mother."

Chris snapped his head up. "What about her?"

"For starters, what is her name?"

"Grace. Grace Mitchell." Chris rubbed his temples. His mother's name always seemed ironic to him. It was as if his grandparents must have known she would require a lot of grace in life.

164

The sheriff scribbled it down. "Grace Mitchell." He looked up. "Where is she now?"

Chris wanted to tell the sheriff that his mother was none of his business. He hated sharing his personal life with anyone, much less this arrogant officer. But he feared the sheriff would continue to harass him unless he answered his questions. He cleared the lump from his throat again. "I haven't had any contact with her in quite some time." That was the truth.

The sheriff leaned forward in his chair. "Let me be straight with you, Chris . . . Yoder or Mitchell or whoever you are. And maybe, then, you will be straight with me. What I want to know is what happened in your grandfather's house, fourteen years ago."

Whoa. Why was the sheriff ripping the scab off this old wound? *Leave it alone!* Chris pleaded silently. That was such a long time ago. That was the last day he had ever seen his grandfather.

Jimmy Fisher left Windmill Farm after extracting a promise from M.K. to introduce him to Emily Esh. As soon as he disappeared around the bend in the road, M.K. set out for Erma Yutzy's house. This morning's storm clouds had been blown away by a change in the wind, and the evening sky was high and open. She found Erma, as usual, bent over in the garden, weeding.

"Hello, Erma," M.K. called out as she crossed over a row of spinach seedlings.

Erma lifted her head and blinked a few times. "Well, well. My new young friend is here." She leaned on her cane as she straightened up and shielded her eyes from the setting sun. "Can I get you a piece of apple snitz? I just took it out of the oven."

M.K. smiled and shook her head. No one came or went from a Plain home without being fed. "I just finished supper. I was passing by and thought I'd say hello."

But Erma couldn't be fooled. She took a few steps closer to her, pausing for a moment, sizing up M.K.'s mood. "Weeding is good for a heavy heart."

"Really?"

"When you weed, you get rid of the things that distract a plant from growing." Erma watched her for a long moment, then grinned. "It's a metaphor, Mary Kate."

Oh. *Oh!*

"And there are a lot of weeds." Erma pointed to a row of carrots and radishes. "I could sure use some help."

The two women worked their way down the row, carefully tugging weeds without uprooting carrot seedlings. About halfway down the row, M.K. quietly said, "Erma, how do you make something right when you've done something wrong?"

Slowly, Erma straightened up and leaned on her knees. "You ask for forgiveness and try to get things back on track, that's what you do."

"That's it?"

"That's it," Erma said. She pointed to the carrots. "Keep weeding."

Twenty minutes later, Erma's carrots and radishes were safe from the distractions of intruding weeds, and M.K. said goodbye.

As M.K. scooted down the street that led to Colonel Mitchell's house, she wondered what she might find — was Jenny left alone while her brother was thrown in jail today? Was Chris still in jail? M.K. felt terrible. When would she ever learn? This was just the kind of thing Fern was always getting after her for — she acted first and thought second. She had sent someone to jail today! And he wasn't even guilty. Oh, what would her father say if he found out? She hoped he never would.

She zoomed past Colonel Mitchell's driveway the first time, but found it on the second pass. The house was on a flag lot, sitting way back from the road, its long drive edged with overgrown bushes on both sides, hidden from the street. At the end of the long driveway, the house loomed, pale white in the gathering purple dusk. Fireflies flickered in the canopy of the trees, and whip-poor-wills chirped from the high grass. Fat, fuzzy bumblebees hovered in the warm evening air. Under normal conditions, she would stop to identify the variety of bumblebees. Maybe follow them to their hives. Not tonight, though. Tonight wasn't a normal night.

As she neared the house, she slowed, astounded. It was a stately old home, in utter neglect. Something wiggled around in her memory. She suddenly realized that the house backed up to the stand of pine trees on the far edge of Windmill Farm — not far from the honey cabin. If she didn't have the scooter, she could probably get home quicker by slipping through the fields. She set the scooter down, took a deep breath, and started for the porch but stopped when she saw Chris lead a horse out to a hitching post.

Well, at least he wasn't in jail! That was good news.

She smoothed her skirt and took another

deep breath before she approached Chris. "Hello."

He looked over the neck of the horse at her, didn't say anything, but calmly continued with his grooming, running the brush down the animal's flank. For a long minute M.K. just watched him. It struck her all of a sudden that he was a very handsome young man, clean-cut and wholesome looking.

She tried again. "We haven't been formally introduced. I'm Mary Kate Lapp. Apparently you have been working for my father, Amos Lapp."

"You look like a Lapp," Chris said.

He didn't seem at all angry. Maybe the sheriff hadn't told him who had turned him in. Maybe that piece of information could remain between her and the sheriff. In her detective books, the witness was always protected. Maybe that's what the sheriff had done. She stood up straighter. Everything was going to be all right! Maybe there was no harm done, other than a minor interruption in Chris Yoder's day. Maybe . . .

"Coming by to see if I got let out of the slammer?"

Oh. She knotted her hands, not knowing what she should say. No, that wasn't true. She knew what to say. She just wasn't accustomed to saying it. Finally, she pushed out the words that needed to be said. "I came over to apologize."

"For knocking me in the ditch? For treating me like I was a leper when I offered to give you a ride home? For turning me in to the sheriff on trumped-up charges?"

Okay. Maybe this wasn't going to be easy. It was obvious she had touched a raw nerve. "Yes. For all those things. I am . . . sorry."

"You should be."

"I am."

Chris walked around her and started brushing the horse's other side. He seemed to have forgotten she was here.

She turned to leave, when suddenly he said, "Any particular reason why you've got a grudge against me?"

She spun around. "No! I don't have a grudge. I just . . . I heard the gunshot that day and remembered your pitch-black horse galloping away and then Fern's coffee can had gone missing — and it all seemed to make sense. Like puzzle pieces that fit together. But I didn't think it all through. I got so excited that I didn't think it through. It's one of my worst faults, Fern says. Acting without thinking."

Chris looked at her, confused, squinting at her as if he couldn't understand her. She

170

knew she was babbling.

"Who's Fern?"

"She's my stepmother."

He nodded. But then he turned his attention back to the horse. "So what's this about the coffee can gone missing?"

"Oh that. Well, that, too, was a misunderstanding. Fern thought it was stolen —" she frowned — "come to think of it, she didn't really think that. She just couldn't remember where she had put it. Turns out she put it in the refrigerator while she was cleaning out cupboards. You see, she takes housecleaning very seriously. Always has. She takes it a little too seriously, I have often thought." She stopped, realizing she was babbling again. "So it's been found. The coffee can."

She turned to leave again, but then he said, "Since when do Plain people turn on each other?"

She spun around. "Well, you see, that was another thing I hadn't thought through."

He nodded, as if he agreed, and stroked the horse's long back with two soft brushes. One hand over the other, brushing, brushing, brushing, until that pitch-black horse shined like shoe polish.

She decided she'd had enough questions. It was time to ask Chris Yoder a few questions. "You have to admit it's a little unusual to have a young man arrive in this little town out of the blue."

"Something wrong with this town?"

"No, but it's pretty small. Everybody knows everybody's business. Except for your business. And you have a knack for staying out of sight. You haven't shown up at church or any singings. Fern says you won't have lunch with her or Dad. You don't go to church." She tilted her head. "You look Amish, you speak Penn Dutch, but you don't have an accent. It's like you learned it as a second language."

Chris took his time responding. He didn't look away. His gaze was as calm as morning, direct. He stopped brushing the horse and spoke carefully. "Is that what you think I'm doing here? Masquerading as an Amish man?"

Just like that, their fragile truce evaporated. She wasn't born yesterday. He was answering a question with a question. He was just like Sheriff Hoffman — information only traveled down a one-way street. Same thing. Well, she had done what she came to do. Again, she whirled around to leave.

"I've got something of yours. You dropped it on the road the other day. The day when

172

you treated me like I had a contagious disease."

She spun around. He pulled a piece of paper out of his pocket and handed it to her. She knew what it was the moment she saw it: the passport application. She glanced at him, wondering if he had looked at it. Of course he had. He was trying not to smile.

"Any particular reason why you might need to get out of the country quickly?"

She tucked the paper into her apron pocket, trying to look dignified. "One never knows what the future holds."

His face eased a little. "Especially when a person accuses innocent people of murder and burglary. I can definitely see how such a habit might require one to flee the country."

"I wouldn't call it a habit." She frowned.

"What would you call it?"

"A misunderstanding. And since we've cleared this little misunderstanding up —"

This time he did smile, but his smile did not warm the blue of his eyes. "Little misunderstanding? You accuse me of murdering a man? Of stealing from the home of the man who has given me work? You call that a little misunderstanding?"

Here, M.K. nearly faltered. She straightened her shoulders. "I felt it was my duty to

173

protect the citizens of Stoney Ridge." But she knew. She knew. She had made a terrible blunder. Her imagination had always been her biggest problem.

"From a trigger-happy sheep? And a coffee can hidden in the refrigerator?"

A familiar voice behind M.K. gave her a start. "*She's* the one who turned you in to the sheriff? She's the one who's been meddling in our business?" M.K. turned slowly to face the voice.

Jenny Yoder was staring at her with her sharp, birdlike look.

"How do you two know each other?" Chris asked.

"Because *she's* the substitute teacher I've been telling you about," Jenny said in a flat, cold voice. She looked at M.K. with unconcealed suspicion.

Chris looked at M.K., then at Jenny, then back at M.K. "This is the teacher you described as dumb as a box of rocks?" Then he looked back at M.K., shocked.

She was even more shocked! She had been called many things in her nineteen years — impulsive, overzealous, far too curious. But when, in her entire life, had anyone ever thought of her as dumb? Dumb? She was outraged.

M.K. had enough. She marched to her

scooter, picked it up, and zoomed down the drive.

The day had started out so nicely, but it was ending as a terrible day for M.K. One of the worst.

But she had discovered something tonight. Chris Yoder carried secrets. And M.K. wanted to find out what they were.

The ante was sky-high. Jimmy Fisher had found just the right horse to race — a two-year-old warm-blooded Thoroughbred, steel-gray, fresh off the racetrack in Kentucky. This deep-chested horse looked like it could run a gazelle to death. He had bought the filly for a song, though he had to weasel an advance from Domino Joe, the promoter of all races, to complete the transaction. This evening's race would wipe clean his growing debt and give him a little nest egg.

Domino Joe's day job was horse trading. He purchased two- or three-year-old Thoroughbreds straight from the track in Kentucky. The horses were retired for various reasons and, with some conditioning, became excellent buggy horses for the Amish. But before Domino Joe trained them for the buggy, he ran a little side business — pony racing on the racetrack.

The racetrack wasn't really a track but a level plowed section of Domino Joe's property, far from any paved roads that Sheriff Hoffman might be moseying past. It was common knowledge but nothing anyone talked about, and Jimmy had seen just about every male he knew, Amish or otherwise, at one time or another down at Domino Joe's track. Just quietly observing.

That's all Jimmy had done too. Just quietly watched. Until a few months ago, when Domino Joe asked Jimmy if he wanted to fill in for a scratched rider. Did he? Oh, yeah. Oh yeah! Jimmy had won that race, and the next one too. Soon, he was racing at least once a week. He won some, he lost some, but then the stakes kept going up and Jimmy couldn't stop himself. He loved competition of any kind. He owed Domino Joe several hundred dollars. Maybe a thousand, if he stopped to think about it, which he preferred not to.

But that debt led him to this particular race on a late evening in September, where the stakes were high. If he won tonight, his debt would be wiped out. He was just ten minutes away from winning. He could just picture Domino Joe's surprised face as he handed him the cash.

Jimmy's heart was beating at what he felt

was twice its normal rate, while the last few preparations for the race seemed to take forever. He thought Domino Joe needed to kill time while the rest of the crowd filtered in to place their bets with a quiet word and a firm handshake. Finally, Domino Joe got things under way.

"Everybody back, give 'em room," Domino Joe directed. "Line your horses up, men!"

Jimmy was racing against three other men on their mounts. As they all led their horses to the starting line, scratched in dirt, Jimmy felt the first taste of terrible doubt. It nearly did him in. These other horses looked as if they could step over him. This felt very different from the other races Domino Joe had arranged for him. Bigger. More serious. Jimmy slipped his feet into the stirrups and settled into the leather basin of the saddle. The reins were wrapped double around his hands.

"One," Domino Joe chanted.

There was not a sound from the entire crowd.

"Two."

Each horse's tensed ears were sharpened to a point now. Jimmy's were, too.

Boom!

The horses hurtled into action. Jimmy

managed a perfectly nice, orderly start, but soon, there was a wall of horses in his way, veering rumps that forced Jimmy's filly to fall back. Over the hoofbeats and horse snorts he could hear cheering and shouts of advice from the onlookers, but none of it truly registered. He was aware only that the riders of the other horses shouldered him out of the way, taking turns to rocket back and forth to keep Jimmy safely behind. He tried to collect his wits about him and focus on the turn ahead — that was where he hoped to gain his lead. By now they were thundering toward the last curve and Jimmy leaned as low as he could in the saddle, streamlining matters for the horse.

It worked. His horse seemed to sense that winning was imminent. Her ears pinned back as he stretched out and they edged ahead. They were nearing the lead! Her mane flew in the wind as Jimmy bent low over her neck. Hoof and tooth they flew, as one thought ran through Jimmy's mind: being on the back of a running horse — preferably a winning horse — was the most wonderful place in the world to be. Just one last bend in the track and he had this race won. In the bag.

But the horse didn't make the bend. Instead, she went straight and sailed over the fence. Jimmy lost his stirrups, then the reins, and tumbled off, landing in a farmer's hay shock. Shouts and hoots and whoops of laughter filled the air as men and boys ran down to get a better look at Jimmy's situation. Jimmy's horse raced on, solo, through the alfafa field.

When M.K. reached Windmill Farm, she was surprised to see Orin Stoltzfus's horse and buggy at the hitching post by the barn. Why would the head of the school board come visiting at such a late hour? Maybe he had news about Alice Smucker. Maybe her headache was gone and she was ready to come back to teach. That would mean that M.K. would be finished with teaching two days earlier than expected. Ah, bliss!

M.K. dropped the scooter and bolted up the porch stairs, two at a time, to the kitchen. She slowed before she opened the door — Fern continually pointed out that M.K. entered a room like a gust of wind. At the sight of Orin's face, she broke into a happy smile. "Orin, do you have some good news?"

Orin exchanged a glance with Amos, then Fern. Amos started to study the ceiling with great interest. Fern lowered her eyes and fixed them on her coffee cup.

Something wasn't right. M.K. felt a shiver begin at the top of her head and travel to her toes.

Orin scratched his neck. "Might as well tell you, M.K. Alice quit on us."

M.K. gasped. "But . . . isn't she getting better?"

"Actually, she said now that she's not teaching, she's feeling good. Real good. Sadie — your sister — has been trying to help heal her. Sadie told her that she thought it was the teaching that was giving her so many ailments."

M.K. understood *that*! Teaching could make anyone sick. On the heels of that thought came a terrible premonition — like a dog might feel right before an earthquake. Her eyes went wide. "You can't be thinking that I'm going to fill in for Alice for a full term. Friday is supposed to be my last day!"

Orin took a sip of coffee, as calmly as if M.K. were discussing tomorrow's weather. He avoided her eyes. "To tell the truth, Mary Kate, it's in the best interest of the pupils to have you remain. They're used to you. You're used to them." He chanced a glance at her. "And Fern tells me you're getting some mentoring from Erma Yutzy. Fern said that teaching has been a real good challenge for you."

Fern! So meddlesome.

M.K.'s heart knocked in her chest so fiercely she could scarcely breathe. This was terrible news! She looked to her father for support, but he didn't return her gaze.

She was doomed. She was only nineteen years old and already her life was over.

Later that night, as M.K. tried to sleep, a single, horrifying phrase kept rolling over and over in her mind: *Dumb as a box of rocks. Dumb as a box of rocks. Dumb as a box of rocks.*

There was no doubt in M.K.'s eyes. This was officially the worst day of her life.

9

Chris had just finished removing a broken windowpane in Jenny's bedroom and replacing it, adding a thin line of caulking around it to seal it in place. She was convinced a bat liked to come calling in her room each night to terrorize her. Chris was doubtful that the bat was so single-minded in purpose, but at least the new windowpane would keep the bat — or Jenny's imagination — at bay. He was changing the caulking cartridge when he saw a car pull into the driveway. A man got out of the car and stood in front of the house, looking up at it, before climbing up the steps.

Chris hurried downstairs and opened the door just as the man's hand was poised to knock. "Yes?"

The man looked surprised to find someone at home. Especially an Amish someone. "Well, well, you beat me to the punch." He thrust a business card at Chris. "I'm Rodney S. Graystone. Real estate salesman." He lifted one finger. "Numero uno."

Chris looked at the card.

Rodney flashed Chris a big plastic smile. "You probably recognize my face. I'm on every grocery cart at the Giant."

Chris didn't shop at the Giant supermarket. Too expensive. He and Jenny shopped at the nearby Bent N' Dent where they could buy bulk foods or damaged goods that were marked down.

"I've been interested in listing this house for years but have never been able to locate the owner." Rodney's eager eyes roved behind Chris, trying to peer into the house. "You are the owner, I presume? I, uh, didn't catch your name."

Before Chris could reply, Rodney S. Graystone spotted Jenny in the kitchen and waved boisterously to her in an overly familiar way. Chris stole a glance at the man's face and felt that his eyes were as flashy as the rest of him. His jacket was a brown plaid, and the elbows had been worn to a shine. Slippery, that's what came to Chris's mind.

Jenny disappeared from view, then peeked her head around the corner. "Adorable!" Rodney S. Graystone told Chris. "She's adorable. Same age as my niece. Is she

183

eight? Nine?"

"Thirteen!" Jenny snapped, poking her head around the doorjamb again.

"My next guess." The man turned back to Chris. "Looks like you've been doing a lot of work." He walked up and down the porch, peering in the windows. "I take it you're fixing it up to flip it. Say, I could probably give you some pointers on remodeling — what to do and what's a waste of time."

Rodney S. Graystone was itching to get into the house and have a tour. Chris started to close the door.

"I've got a buyer who's always been interested in this old d—, uh, diamond in the rough. I'm confident I could find you a buyer —" he snapped his fingers — "in the blink of an eye. Cash on the barrel."

"Not interested in selling." Chris closed the door in Rodney S. Graystone's surprised face.

"Keep my card handy, in case you reconsider. I'll stop by now and then, just to keep checking in. In case you change your mind," came a muffled reply.

On the way to the schoolhouse in the morning, Mary Kate noticed a squirrel perched on the limb of a maple tree. It chattered at the sight of a cardinal, darting around the squirrel with a bright splash of red. She watched for a while as the squirrel scolded the cardinal for coming too close to his tree. Then the bird flew off and the squirrel scampered away.

It wouldn't be so bad to be a bird, would it? Summers wouldn't be bad. Winters might get a little challenging. She liked the idea of being able to travel to far-flung places every spring and fall. No passport needed. Birds seemed so . . . carefree.

Unlike a nineteen-year-old Amish woman who had no say-so about her life. None whatsoever. Who was stuck teaching school for an *entire* term.

Fern! *This is all your doing,* M.K. thought for the hundred and thirteenth time.

Fern was always so certain that her opinion was the only one that mattered. Fern had always been so hard on M.K. And to make everything worse, last night her father had sided with Fern. Of all the times! All M.K's life, her dad had stuck right beside her, had been her ally, had been easy to talk into agreeing with her. But when it counted most, Amos turned around and took Fern's side — insisting that M.K. fill in Alice's void.

And why did her sister Sadie have to butt

her nose into it? Why did she have to point out that teaching was making Alice sick? Granted, Sadie was a healer and Alice was her husband's sister, but didn't blood sisters count more? She thought so.

M.K. wished her mother were still alive. Maggie Lapp had died when M.K. was only five and she only had wisps of memories of her. If M.K. squeezed her eyes tightly, she could conjure up a memory of her mother in the kitchen, with her black apron pinned around her waist. Under the apron, she was wearing a dark plum dress. She was humming. M.K. did remember that. Her mother was always humming.

Chocolate chip cookies. In this particular memory, that's what her mother was pulling out of the oven. They were M.K.'s favorites. Her mother would scoot them off the baking sheet with a spatula, slipping them onto a clean dish towel so they would cool. But she would always split one down the middle and hand half to M.K. "I think this cookie was hoping we would eat it first," her mother would whisper, as if they were keeping a secret from the other cookies.

Maggie Lapp would never have insisted that she finish out Alice Smucker's teaching term. She would have understood M.K.'s point of view, which was . . .

What was it? Well, that she didn't *want* to teach.

But maybe her mother would say that growing up meant you realized you didn't always get what you wanted. Growing up meant that you start to look for ways to give to others.

Wait. That sounded an awful lot like Fern.

How exasperating! M.K. was getting Fern's voice mixed up with her mother's voice.

As M.K. cut through the corner of a cornfield to reach the schoolhouse, her thoughts drifted to Jenny Yoder. *Imagine anyone calling me dumb!* Yet a little part of it felt true. About teaching . . . she did act dumb. She didn't teach. She just watched the clock.

A feeling of shame burned within her when she thought of how she handled a situation yesterday afternoon. She had caught Jenny Yoder with her nose buried in a book while the class was supposed to be doing arithmetic. M.K. took one look at the book's title, *To Kill a Mockingbird* by Harper Lee, and told Jenny to keep reading. No wonder Jenny thought she was as dumb as a box of rocks.

What is wrong with me that everything I touch turns out a chaotic mess?

She wished she could go home, fling herself across her bed, and put a pillow over her head.

Dry cornstalks started to rustle, like a small animal was following her. The brush crackled behind her and she whirled, ears straining. Suddenly, a boy's round face appeared out of the cornstalks.

M.K. let out her breath. "Danny Riehl! You gave me quite a start."

Danny looked down the dirt path at the school yard where the pupils were starting to gather. "I just thought you should know that the reason Eugene Miller leaves in the afternoon isn't because of your teaching. He slipped out a lot with Teacher Alice too."

"Why does he leave?" M.K. said.

"Because the upper grades read out loud after lunch." Danny poked his spectacles back up the bridge of his nose. "Eugene can't read very well. He doesn't want anyone to know." He squinted up at M.K. "You won't tell him I told you, will you?"

"I won't tell, Danny. Thank you."

Danny slipped back into the cornfield and disappeared. She heard more rustling, then she saw him burst through another section of the field and cross over the fence to meet his friends on the school yard. Danny could be a crackerjack detective, she thought.

Eugene Miller was drawing a picture in the dirt with a stick and stuck his foot out as Danny hurried past. Danny tripped, went flying into the dirt, picked himself up, brushed himself off, and joined his friends by the softball diamond.

So maybe Danny's detective skills needed a little bit of work.

She took a few steps, then stopped. *I am a bad teacher. I am!* M.K. realized. *And while I am not dumb, I have been acting dumb. I have been acting like a bad, dumb teacher.* There was no gainsaying what Jenny Yoder had said. It was just true. Just true.

But that was about to change.

The cramp of panic inside her chest eased a bit. She marched through the cornfield and into the schoolhouse, her sails full of wind, and dropped anchor.

Deep in the barn, Amos could hear Uncle Hank ranting and raving. He finished adding oats to Rosemary and Lavender's buckets — a small thank-you for a good day's work in the fields — and walked over to the buggy shop to see what was eating his uncle.

"I CAN'T FIND MY MONEY!" Hank roared when he saw Amos approach. "I kept it right there." He pointed to an open drawer in the workshop, filled with screw-

189

drivers and hammers and receipts. "That's always where it's been. Until now."

Now, that was an amusing thought. Hank Lapp was many things — inventive, big-hearted, a dedicated fisherman — but organized? That would be a quality Uncle Hank would never be accused of possessing. The buggy shop was a disaster. And his Dawdi Haas? Fern refused to step inside.

Come to think of it, Amos hadn't been inside Hank's apartment for over a year. For one, there was no free space to sit down. Everything was covered with newspapers and shoes and dirty laundry. And two, the heavy smell of cigar smoke made Amos hack and cough. And that brought back unpleasant memories of the year leading up to his heart transplant, when he would cough relentlessly, trying to get air.

Hank was pulling everything out of the drawers of his workshop. "Edith Fisher has been missing some cash lately too."

That was interesting. Not about the missing money — it seemed to Amos that Edith Fisher was always sputtering away about not having enough money — but it was interesting that Edith was talking to Hank again. Maybe the spurning over Doozy and the puppies wasn't as final as it first sounded.

That was another thing that puzzled Amos about women — they said things they didn't really mean. Just last night, M.K. said she wanted to move to Oslo, Norway. She thought it would be too cold for children to survive in Norway and that sounded like an ideal climate to her. Certainly, she didn't mean that. He knew she was upset about having to finish Alice's teaching term. He felt a tug of pity for her, but it vanished when he caught a warning glance from his wife. Fern knew best about this kind of thing.

Finally, Hank threw his hands in the air. "AMOS! I have come to the conclusion that there is a thief in Stoney Ridge. Maybe a crime ring. Targeting us older folks."

That, Amos thought, *or more likely, us older folks won't admit we're getting older. And forgetful.*

M.K. rang the school bell and called everyone in, five minutes before school began.

"You're too early, M.K.," Eugene Miller complained as he came inside and saw the clock.

She noticed a fresh bruise on his cheekbone. "Are you all right? How did you get that?" She reached out a hand to touch him, but he flinched and shrugged her off.

"I have some news to share," she said. "Everyone take your seats."

Eugene started to head back outdoors.

M.K. blocked the door. "I don't want any arguing. If I say something is to be done, then it is to be done. And here's another thing. From now on, you call me Teacher M.K. Is that quite clear?"

She gave Eugene a glance of reprimand. He straightened to his full height, towering over her as he glared at her. She glared back. She held his stare. She would not back down. There was too much at stake. Amazingly, he seemed to wither under her fierce glare. He smirked, turned, and plopped in his seat. The rest of the children remained still and silent, all but Barbara Jean. She nodded her small head enthusiastically.

"Teacher Alice is not going to be able to return to teach this year," M.K. said. "So I am going to be her replacement for the term."

Barbara Jean Shrock grinned.

Danny Riehl poked his glasses up the bridge of his nose.

Eugene Miller groaned.

Jenny Yoder clunked her head on her desk.

As Amos crossed the threshold of the farmhouse, he practically tripped over a cardboard box left by the kitchen door. It surprised him to see a box left out, unattended. Fern was a dedicated housekeeper — a bit on the fanatical side, he thought. He often teased her that he didn't dare release his fork during dinner for fear it would be washed and cleaned and put away before he swallowed the bite of food. To see a box left out was unusual, but there it sat, gathering dust, as Fern worked in the kitchen.

She was furiously whisking her new starter — the one she had made after M.K. had knocked over her great-great-great-grandmother's starter, which, Amos suspected, wasn't really as old as she liked to claim. But Fern did this every few days without fail — she called it refreshing her sponge. The tangy smell of yeast filled the air, so powerful that it made Amos sneeze. "A starter is a living organism," Fern often said in its defense, "that needs to be fed and tended. Like a family." He felt a wave of fondness as he watched her give the starter a good stir to bring in fresh oxygen. He sneezed and she glanced up, noticing him for the first time. "Look inside." The box, she meant.

He unfolded the top flaps of the box and crouched down to look. "Why, they're

M.K.'s detective books. Is she getting rid of them at last?"

"She came home from school, asked me for a few boxes, and packed them up," Fern said, still whisking.

Amos closed the box up and crossed the room to the kitchen. He folded his arms and leaned his hips against the kitchen counter. "What do you suppose has caused this? Teaching?"

"Maybe."

He grinned. "My little girl is finally growing up. You were right, Fern. This teaching job has been good for her."

Fern didn't seem as convinced. "Seems like something else happened lately, but I'm not sure what. Haven't you noticed how quiet she's been the last few days? Thoughtful and reflective. Very, very unusual."

Amos hadn't noticed. It always irked him that Fern was so observant about his own children, and yet he was grateful too. Irked and grateful. That just about summed up his feelings about his wife. And love. There was love.

They wouldn't even have Windmill Farm today, he was quite sure, if it weren't for Fern. The year his heart was failing, she had become his guiding force, his rudder. She had kept things going. She had kept his family together.

He took the whisk and bowl out of her hands, set them down on the counter, slipped his arms around her waist and kissed her. A kiss that meant serious business too. A down payment for later.

She put her hands against his chest, surprised. "What was that for, Amos Lapp?"

"That was for paying attention to the most important things."

Fern smiled, pushing him away playfully. She picked up the bowl as M.K. bounded down the stairs with another box.

"What are the most important things?" M.K. asked. "I want to know."

Amos looked at her. What were the most important things for his youngest daughter to learn? *Think before you act. Understand the big picture. Put the needs of others above your own wants. Start thinking long-term.*

He glanced at Fern. Or was the most important thing to find the right partner to help M.K. become the person he knew she could be?

Maybe it was all of those things. Serious stuff for a man with an empty stomach. Amos picked up the whisk. "Never miss a chance to refresh the starter!"

One week had passed and Chris hadn't seen

195

any sign of Sheriff Hoffman. He was just starting to relax, to not keep looking over his shoulder when he went into town or tense up when he heard a car drive by. And then one morning, after Jenny had left for school, he walked out of the barn after he finished feeding Samson, and there the sheriff was, leaning against his police car with one ankle crossed over the other.

"Morning, Chris," Sheriff Hoffman said. "Did you give some thought to our conversation?"

Chris put the empty bucket down. "I thought I was clear. I told you everything."

"I need ideas about anything else you can remember."

Chris took a metered breath. "I don't know anything."

"I know. I know you were only seven. I know you had already seen too much for a boy your age. But I'm guessing there might be something else. Something more you might remember if you really tried."

"And how do I do that?"

"Anything that might trigger a memory. Anything that comes to mind."

Two or three small bright-winged birds hopped about on the ground, pecking at the stale bread crumbs Jenny had sprinkled before she left for school.

The sheriff took a few steps closer to Chris. "Look, if you cooperate, I might be able to overlook the fact that you crossed a state line with your sister without the permission of Child Protective Services, and that you're squatting in your grandfather's house."

Chris snapped his head up. "This house will be legally mine as soon as I turn twenty-one. My grandfather wanted me to have it. He wanted me to take care of my sister. I have papers to prove that."

"But you're not twenty-one yet. I checked." The sheriff raised an eyebrow. "So maybe you want to try again to remember. Try real hard." He took his keys out of his pocket and went back to the car.

Chris took a few steps. "That day . . . the day we left . . . I might remember one or two things." There was, he understood, no going back.

The sheriff put his keys back in his pocket and took out his notepad. "I'm listening."

As soon as school let out for the day, M.K. went straight to visit Erma. She found her hanging laundry in the backyard. "Erma, why did you become a teacher?"

Erma continued to hang pillowcases on the line, gathering her thoughts. "I suppose it was because I had such a natural curiosity about people and things. I was always sticking my nose into other people's business. I've always thought of teaching as being a little bit of a detective."

Detective? Had M.K. heard Erma right? Did she say that teaching was like detective work? Her ears perked up.

"A good teacher has to hunt and dig to find the right way to reach each child — to give him a love of learning that will last his entire life."

M.K.'s heart started to pound. "Erma, help me become a good teacher."

Erma sat on the picnic bench and patted the place beside her. "What made Gideon Smucker such a good teacher for you?"

M.K. had to think that over. "He gave me extra math problems. He let me work ahead of my class. He brought me books he thought I would like."

"So he challenged you."

"Not just me. He made things interesting in the classroom. We didn't always know what to expect." She smiled. "Once, he had a handful of us meet at the schoolhouse at five in the morning, to watch the tail of a comet as it raced across the sky." She sighed. "He was a marvelous teacher — the kind that every child remembers fondly for the rest of her life. That's the kind of teacher I need to be, Erma. If I have to be stuck teaching, I want to be that kind of teacher."

Erma nodded. "Teaching has its advantages and disadvantages. But there are golden moments, when you connect with a child."

"But how do I do that?"

"Mary Kate, it begins when you try to see life through other people's eyes."

Erma went back to the business of hanging sheets on the clothesline, so M.K. joined her. She hung one blue-checked dish towel on the line, then another. She thought about each pupil, trying to imagine life through his or her eyes.

Anna Mae, she knew, mostly thought about marrying Danny Riehl. Barbara Jean wanted to be home, helping her mother with the new baby. She played dolls at every recess. What would it be like to see life through Danny Riehl's eyes? He could do math problems in his head and he was the runner-up in yesterday's eighth-grade spelling bee, even though he was only a sixth grader. The word that tripped him up was "Hallelujah." When Danny heard the letter he forgot, he slapped his forehead with the palm of his hand. "Ooh . . . silent *J*! I forgot silent *J*." She smiled at the memory of it.

She reached down for another towel and realized she had emptied the basket.

"Which pupil do you worry about the most?" Erma asked.

That was easy for M.K. to answer. "There's a boy, an eighth grader, who is smart as a whip, but I think he is having trouble reading. He tries to hide it, but he's going to be graduating soon. And then what? I feel as if I have just six months to help him."

"What's he like?"

"His name is Eugene Miller. He's a swarthy boy with a wiry build. He wins the sprint races on field day. He has an amazing talent for drawing."

"So he has some things he's good at."

"Yes. He loves drawing and he loves getting attention even more."

"In his own way, Eugene has found a way to get what he needs. I think he'll do all right for himself." Erma was observing a butterfly light on a white sheet, luffing in the wind. "I've found that it's often the people who don't call attention to themselves who have the most to offer."

Jenny. That's who M.K. thought of when Erma said that.

Amos grinned at the sight of watching

Uncle Hank try to harness the horse to the buggy with four puppies nipping at his pants legs. He kept hopping around as if he were barefoot on live coals.

A few days ago, Edith had re-reconsidered her spurning of Hank after he came calling with Doozy and four puppies in tow. Now, Edith meant serious business and Hank had been moping around the farm ever since. Yesterday, he tried to find homes for the puppies. No luck, not even from softhearted Sadie, though he tried again last night. She told him that twin babies and four puppies would unhinge her fragile balance. Hank returned home with a forlorn look on his face and four puppies in a cardboard box. Fern saw him coming up the porch steps and headed him off. She pointed toward his Dawdi Haas over the buggy shop.

Insulted, Hank spun around, muttering about women and their lack of understanding.

And then a happy surprise for Hank came late in the day. Edith Fisher had another change of heart. She still didn't want Doozy or his offspring hanging around her chicken farm, but she did pardon Hank. She sent her son Jimmy over to Windmill Farm with a note saying that Hank was invited for supper on Sunday. The spring was back in

Hank's step.

It was amazing what a little romance did for a person.

10

M.K. was surprised to see that Chris and Jenny Yoder were at church. They hadn't attended before today, so she figured someone — like Bishop Elmo or Deacon Abraham — had put a little gentle pressure on them.

It had been almost a week since that unfortunate misunderstanding with the sheriff. And nobody blabbed. That was the incredible thing. It was touching — to think Chris and Jenny would protect her from embarrassment. So kind! So unexpected.

By now, if they were going to say anything, they would have. Wouldn't they?

Ruthie's father was the first minister to preach this morning. M.K. had her own rating system for sermons: "boring," "boring boring," and "boring boring boring." Ruthie's father consistently earned three borings. One thing about his sermons: if you were unclear about the point he emphasized, another would be along in a moment.

Fern was forever telling her it wasn't the preacher's problem, it was the listener's. "Hald die Ohre uff." *Keep your ears open.*

Fern poked her with her elbow in a warning to sit up and pay attention.

Fern! So ever-present.

M.K. glanced across the room at Chris. He sat next to her father, who had greeted him warmly. Amos Lapp had a knack for tending to fatherless young men. Sometimes, M.K. thought it was a pity he hadn't had more sons. A houseful. Instead, he lived with a covey of women and he often seemed bewildered by them.

Chris's Sunday clothes made him look blonder and taller and grown up. And handsome. He lifted his eyes from the hymnal and looked directly at her, as if he knew exactly what she was thinking. He smiled, and it hit her in the solar plexus. She bowed her head, breaking away from his gaze.

Chris had to bite on his lower lip to stop smiling when he caught Mary Kate Lapp gazing at him in church. She blushed becomingly, he noticed. He still couldn't get over this was the teacher Jenny had been complaining about so bitterly. He was pleased to see Mary Kate had a full set of her own choppers. She didn't wear cloppety

204

shoes. She didn't jiggle when she walked. And she was awfully far from being old.

Mary Kate was sitting next to a young mother with two red-headed twin babies — a boy and a girl. The young mother had a dreamy smile on her face and a faraway look in her eyes, as if she were listening to a pleasant conversation that only she could hear. She didn't seem to notice that her little boy was teething and chewing on his shirt collar.

Speaking of teeth, Chris noticed that Jenny was sitting next to a little girl who was missing most of her front teeth. Jenny had talked about a cute little girl named Barbara Jean at school and he wondered if this might be her. He noticed that Barbara Jean kept sticking her tongue out, as if she was continually surprised to find the teeth had gone missing. He was glad Jenny had someone to sit next to, but he wished she had a friend her own age. The older girls had clumped together before church like clotted cream. Not one included Jenny in the cluster. He had worried it would be a mistake to come this morning. He knew the hearts of these people — they would fuss over the two of them as if they were chicks without a mother hen. They would ask questions about where they came from and want to stop by the house with casseroles and baked goods. As tempting as a good meal sounded — and it really did sound good — it wasn't enough to make him want to come to church and start joining into the community. Not quite yet. The whole notion of it worried him. If they could only lay low until January, when he turned twenty-one. But how could he have said no to the bishop? You just didn't do that.

But then, while the church was singing the *LobLeid,* Chris was filled with a wonderful sense of worship. It felt good, so good, to be back in church. He breathed in the familiar smells of starch and soap and shoe blacking. He had missed it more than he realized. The worship. Reminders that God was sovereign over all. It wasn't good to go too long without church.

The hymn ended and Amos Lapp, seated next to him, took back the hymnal and tucked it under the bench. Someday, in addition to the horse breeding business, Chris would like to have a farm of his own, just like Windmill Farm. Fields, orchards, livestock, bountiful vegetable garden. That was becoming his dream.

Amos had introduced Chris to some of the fellows who were close to his age. He wondered what their dream would be.

Jimmy Fisher, he noticed, had an eye for the ponies. By the barn this morning, he had already spotted Samson and asked Chris how fast he had been clocked. "I don't know," Chris said. "I've never raced him."

Jimmy Fisher looked at him as if a cat had spoken. "Never raced him? Never?" He ran a hand down Samson's foreleg. "I could do it for you."

"Why?" Chris asked.

"Don't you want to know how fast he could go?"

Chris shook his head. "No need."

Jimmy Fisher was amazed.

Right then, Chris knew what Jimmy Fisher's dream would be: Thrills.

Jimmy Fisher reached down to pat Doozy's neck. It was warm from the sun. This dog was devoted to Mary Kate and followed her everywhere, even to church. Or maybe he was just trying to get away from those little pups that were constantly pulling his tail and chewing on his ears.

Jimmy had known M.K. just as long as he had known his own brother, essentially his entire life. He treated her like a younger sibling too. He had put a billy goat in the cherry orchard when she was picking cherries. She had let the air out of the tires of his hidden ten-speed bicycle. He had tossed a racer snake into the girls' outhouse at school, knowing full well that she was inside. She had sprinkled water over his entire firecracker collection — just enough to make the gunpowder soft and ineffective. They raced their favorite buggy horses against each other. They were constantly competing, but it never meant a thing. They had a long history together — mostly as enemies, until one day when they put aside their feud and became friends. Good friends.

And now, suddenly, overnight, it had blossomed into love.

How to explain what happened? It was like a switch had flipped and in an instant the world had changed. His mind was racing.

M.K. had taken him along to a volleyball game and barbecue at the Eshes' home last night, so that he could meet Emily, his future missus. At least that's what he had assumed until he was actually introduced to Emily and tried to have a conversation with her. He was at his most charming, warm, and witty, thinking at first that she was just shy. Thirty minutes later, his charm had worn out. She had no sense of humor. None whatsoever. She took everything he said literally and tried to dissect it. "I don't think that could have really happened" or "That sounds like a gross exaggeration." It was like trying to talk to an IRS auditor.

Their lagging conversation was interrupted by gales of laughter. He turned his gaze to M.K., sitting by the fire pit, surrounded by four or five fellows and girls, telling a story about something funny that had happened at her school.

A burst of laughter shook Jimmy back to the present. It would be his turn at bat soon. They were having the after-church-after-lunch softball game and he had talked Chris Yoder into sticking around for it. He noticed how Chris stood at a distance, leaning against the fence, not joining in but not entirely separate either. Chris's gaze often drifted toward left field. That's where M.K. happened to be posted.

Jimmy gave a few practice swings before he stepped up to the plate. His thoughts slipped back to last night at the Eshes' as M.K. was wrapping up the story by the fire pit. The group was hanging on her every word. She was always good at storytelling — which she attributed to years of listening to Uncle Hank — but that was when it hit Jimmy like a two-by-four. He was dazzled by how she had suddenly become a different person. He was out looking for love and it was right in front of him. It had always been right in front of him.

He was in love with M.K. Lapp. He was a hooked fish. A goner.

He stepped up to bat, poised and ready for the pitch, but his mind was fully occupied. The question that faced him: how to convince M.K. that she loved him back? That was going to take some doing.

A week later, on Saturday, the sky was filled with dark clouds. The air felt damp and raw and smelled of coming rain. Chris Yoder was out in the west field of Windmill Farm, cutting the last of the hay. M.K. watched the work progress; it was painfully slow, even though Chris was always working when she looked in that direction — a tiny figure bent over the land.

She had just finished baking a few loaves of honey oat bread and decided to give one to him to take home. They weren't quite as light and airy as Fern's would be — her bread never was — but it would be good as toast. As she wrapped the loaf in a red-striped dish towel, she wondered what Chris thought of her. It was difficult to read him. He was polite, slightly amused, but just that and no more. The logical conclusion she reached was that he did not want to spend time in her company. And why should he? She had accused him of a heinous crime. Two crimes! One big, one small, but crimes nonetheless.

And yet he didn't tell anyone what she had done to him. Nor had Jenny. M.K. felt grateful to them both, but she wondered why. Maybe, Chris just wasn't interested in her.

M.K. wasn't used to having young men lose interest in her. And, the first few times they had met, Chris Yoder had shown a spark of interest in her — she could see it in his eyes. She could tell he thought she was attractive. That wasn't an altogether unusual experience for M.K. Boys had always been attracted to her. But that was just it — they were all boys.

M.K. wasn't the kind of girl who needed attention from boys, and she certainly wasn't the type who fell in and out of love like her friend Ruthie did. But she did like to be taken seriously. She liked that very much.

Chris Yoder did not take M.K. seriously. And Chris Yoder was the first boy M.K. met whom she considered to be a man.

She found herself thinking of Chris a great

deal. She tried to stop herself, but couldn't. He was a shy man, she decided, and that was another reason why he seemed reserved. Certainly that would pass, she thought, when they got to know one another better, but she wasn't quite sure how to achieve that. Chris didn't make it easy.

She crossed through the fields with the bread loaf tucked in one hand and a thermos of cool lemonade in the other. When he looked up and saw her, he stopped the horses and waited for her. The odd feeling that she had been experiencing lately came back. She felt her heart thumping. Ridiculous, she thought. Ridiculous.

She handed him the thermos. "Thought you could use something to drink."

He opened the lid and drank it down. "Thank you." He wiped sweat from his brow with a handkerchief.

She held up the bread. "I thought you and Jenny might be able to use a loaf of bread. Honey oat. The honey is from my own hives."

When he hesitated for a moment, she quickly added, "I made too many loaves. We can't eat it all. I'll put it in the barn by your coat."

"Jenny would put honey on everything if she could."

M.K. brightened with that news. Her confidence returned. Honey was an area of expertise for her, thanks to her sister's husband, Rome. He had taught her everything she knew about beekeeping. "I'll give you a bottle of my honey for her to try on this bread. My bees are brown bees — not very common, but they produce a delicious sweet honey."

His eyes crinkled with his smile as he handed the empty thermos to her. "She'd like that."

"Would you and Jenny like to come and have a meal at the house? Tonight?"

M.K. surprised herself. *Oh no.* This hadn't been planned. As he hesitated, she wished the words back. Why in the world had she said that? "My father's been wanting to have you." That was true, actually.

She was afraid to look at him too closely. His eyes, with that unsettling lucent quality, were on her. She looked down at the ground, at the rigging on the horses, at the shoes Chris was wearing, boots that had badly scuffed toes.

"Your father has been kind to me," he said softly.

"He thinks you're a hard worker." She glanced at the sky. "Looks like it's going to rain soon. I should let you get back to work.

If you decide you'd like to join us, we eat at six. Nothing fancy, but Fern's a terrific cook. If you're lucky, Uncle Hank might be in a storytelling mood." She started toward the barn.

"What's Fern got planned for tonight?"

M.K. whirled around. "Pot roast. Roasted potatoes. Green beans and bacon."

"Any dessert?"

"Pumpkin pie with homemade vanilla ice cream."

Their eyes met. This time, they held. Chris grinned. "We'll be there."

As M.K. walked through the field, she couldn't stop smiling. Ridiculous, she thought. Ridiculous. But she couldn't wipe the goofy grin off her face.

Chris flicked the reins on the horses' backs, to get them moving. He wasn't sure it was a good idea to accept Mary Kate's dinner invitation, but the mention of a good meal was a powerful temptation. Hardly a day went by that Amos Lapp hadn't extended the invitation to join him for lunch at the house, but Chris always declined. Other invitations had started coming in from other families too — he expected as much after he and Jenny attended church last Sunday. That's the way it was with the Amish —

they extended true kindness. It was one of the many things he loved about these people. He was starting to relax a little and think they should go ahead and accept a few dinner invitations. Help out at a few work frolics. Meet people. Get involved.

But then nagging doubts crowded in. Would they start pressing him with questions about his family? Would they want to help him fix up his house? He couldn't risk too much curiosity — look at what happened with Mary Kate Lapp. A few brief interactions, and she had him carted away by the sheriff. Unbelievable! But then again, there weren't too many Amish women who seemed like Mary Kate Lapp.

Still, there was something about her that intrigued him. True, she was easy on the eyes, though he was used to plenty of pretty girls in Ohio. Today, flour streaked Mary Kate's cheek, hiding some of her freckles. He thought about pointing it out to her, but she might feel embarrassed. She was trying to make amends — the loaf of bread, the honey for Jenny, the invitation to dinner. It was sort of sweet to see Mary Kate so ill at ease, so full of humble pie. He had a hunch it was a new feeling for her.

But here's what he hadn't expected about Mary Kate Lapp: she was funny. She had a way of looking at the world that was just off-kilter enough to surprise him into laughing. She wasn't trying to be funny, but everything about her was amusing.

And here's another thing he hadn't expected about Mary Kate: she was a good teacher after all. Mary Kate was starting to win over his reluctant-to-like-anyone sister. She had given Jenny a word puzzle to figure out and Jenny had spent hours deciphering it: "Beings highly deficient in cranial capacity hastily enter situations which celestial entities regard with great trepidation." A happy scream burst out of her when she figured it out. In common English it meant: "Fools rush in where angels fear to tread." Jenny had raced to school in the morning with the answer.

Encounters with Mary Kate Lapp felt as if someone threw a snowball down the back of his shirt on a blistering hot summer day. Unexpected, startling, shocking. But not unwelcomed.

Jenny was surprised when her brother blew into the house, galloped up the stairs to take a shower, and shouted down that they were expected for dinner at Windmill Farm.

That made no sense to Jenny. No sense at all. Chris was always telling her they needed to keep to themselves and not get too friendly with others. When she called out, "Why?" he opened the bathroom door, stuck his head out, and shouted back, "Pot roast and potatoes!"

Okay. That made sense. The thought of a home-cooked meal made Jenny's mouth water. Just today, she had looked longingly at Anna Mae Glick's lunch: slices of smoked ham between thick homemade bread. A slab of shoofly pie. She nearly threw away her own stupid lunch: stale crackers and rock-hard cheese, and a too-soft apple from the tree in the yard.

Pot roast and potatoes. She could practically taste them now. She was fully supportive of Chris giving in to temptation. In fact, she hurried to get ready!

But then they arrived at Windmill Farm and the family, including four wild puppies, came charging out to meet them. The puppies made a beeline for Jenny, jumping up and nearly knocking her down.

That's when Jenny became steaming mad. Until that moment, she hadn't made the connection that Windmill Farm meant she would be seeing her teacher. It was true that Teacher M.K. was showing a little glimmer of hope as a teacher, but that didn't mean Jenny wanted to be chummy with her. She was still outraged that Teacher M.K. turned her brother in to the sheriff. She was fiercely protective of Chris, and slow to forgive anyone who might cause him harm. She thought about feigning illness, but suddenly caught a whiff of pot roast in the air and decided she would stay. They would eat, and then they would leave. Old Deborah had taught her manners.

Fortunately, the food lived up to its aroma. As the platters were passed around the table, as she listened to the table conversation between Fern and Amos and M.K. and Uncle Hank — who did most of the talking by telling outrageously silly stories! — she felt a wave of missing Old Deborah. Of belonging at someone's table. How she envied these people. She wondered if Chris might be feeling it too. The last two months had been so filled with change that she hadn't allowed herself to think back on their old life. Not much, anyway.

"From your accents," Fern said, passing Jenny a bowl of green beans, "I'd say you didn't grow up in Pennsylvania. Not in Lancaster, anyway."

"Well, we sort of started here —" Jenny began. From the corner of her eye, she caught Chris's infinitesimal shake of his head.

"She's referring to the wave of nineteenth-century immigrants from Europe," Chris hastily filled in. He glanced around, taking in the blank looks on everyone's faces. He picked up the breadbasket and held it out to Amos. "William Penn and all that history."

Fern squinted her eyes at him as if he had completely lost his mind.

"NOW THAT," Uncle Hank interrupted, "reminds me of my great, great aunt Mathilda, who rowed over from the Old Country in a canoe." He helped himself to another serving of potatoes.

"A canoe, you say?" Amos said, calm as a cucumber. He reached out for the butter to spread on his bread roll, but Fern intercepted and moved the butter tray away from him. The man's dark eyebrows sprang up as he gave his wife a look of obvious merriment.

"A canoe and a pet parrot named Oscar," Uncle Hank said, winking at Jenny. "So she had someone to talk to. She liked to talk, that Aunt Mathilda. The problem came when the parrot started talking back to her." He jumped to his feet and shaded his eyes with his hand, as if looking for land. "Paddle faster, Mathilda! Faster! *Sqwuak! Sqwuak!*"

A laugh burst out of Jenny. She laughed

219

in absolute glee, and to her surprise the others joined in, creating a tangible joy that fell upon the room like soft goose feathers. Something bloomed inside of Jenny at that moment, a leaf unfurling in the spring. It felt so good to be a part of a family.

Fern rolled her eyes. "Hank has found a fresh audience for his old tales."

"Uncle Hank's tales are always worth hearing again," Teacher M.K. said. She leaned over to whisper to Jenny, "Unless you happen to be Fern, who says once is all she needs."

"I HEARD THAT," Uncle Hank bellowed. "You, Jenny Yoder, are welcome back every night!" Uncle Hank pinned M.K. with his good eye. "Now that M.K. has gone the ways of crotchety schoolmarms, I've been missing having someone appreciate my fine stories!"

Jenny looked at Teacher M.K. to see if she might be offended, but she was laughing. A warm feeling spread through Jenny. Amos and Fern told her to come back soon, to stop by anytime at all, and the way they said it, she knew they meant it. Fern had even told her to come over for a bread roll making lesson tomorrow afternoon after school, and Jenny thought she just might. She did love those sourdough bread rolls.

Then Jenny turned to Chris. She saw the
way Chris was gazing at Teacher M.K. and
she thought, *Oh, boy.*

11

When Fern Lapp told Jenny to join her after school and help her make bread rolls, Chris had a hunch that it would end up being more than a onetime occurrence. Jenny had been kind of lost and alone in Stoney Ridge, and he saw the look of longing on her face as they sat down to that pot roast and potato dinner. It wasn't about food — it was about having a place at someone's table. About belonging.

His instincts were right. Two weeks later, it was getting harder to keep Jenny home from Windmill Farm. Chris nearly gave up trying.

Now that Fern had an apprentice, she decided to try selling baked goods at her roadside stand that stood at the bottom of the driveway for Windmill Farm. She was even paying Jenny to work the stand after school let out. Townsfolk were starting to drive out to Windmill Farm to pick up a loaf of bread or cinnamon rolls, because it was cheaper than Sweet Tooth Bakery, fresher and tastier. The bakery owner, Nora Stroot, was livid.

Chris didn't think Nora Stroot should be too worried about it. When winter came, Chris was pretty sure that Fern would close up the stand and think of something else to keep Jenny busy. Because *that,* he knew, was the true motive behind Fern's bread making tutorials. For all her bluster, Fern Lapp was a marshmallow.

It did concern him, though, to see Jenny start looking and acting like Fern. Everything she talked about now was "Fern said this," or "Fern said that." Chris tried to have talks with her, about not getting too attached, and to not become a pest over there at Windmill Farm. In two weeks, she seemed far more attached to Fern than she had ever been to Old Deborah. But then, Old Deborah was . . . really, really . . . old.

"Pshaw," Jenny shot back. "Fern said it's not good to worry too much about what tomorrow holds." Then she would start scrubbing the kitchen sink as if it were a hotbed of germs. And Chris would sigh.

But he knew that every child deserved such moments — times of knowing that someone was looking out for you. He had his own: his grandfather lifting him up out of the backseat of the car after a long drive, carrying him into the house and up the stairs and putting him to bed. The scratchiness of his chin, the smell of his aftershave. Jenny deserved this time with Fern, time to make her own memories.

Jenny was wearing the heart-shaped Lancaster prayer cap now, and Fern showed her how to get her hair to stay pinned in a bun. Jenny was even starting to turn up out of thin air, the same way Fern had of doing. If you asked Chris, Jenny was turning into a cut-down version of Fern Lapp.

Jenny felt a little sorry for Eugene Miller. Today, he showed up at school with a big black eye. She had asked him about his black eye and he told her he was breaking wild colts for the rodeo in his spare time. She didn't think that was true. Maybe, but probably not. Anna Mae raised her hand, probably eager to tell the teacher that she was sure Eugene was lying about the rodeo, but Teacher M.K. never did call on her. She had just acted like it was nothing unusual for Anne Mae to keep her hand aimed for the sky. And in a way, it wasn't.

Jenny had expected Teacher M.K.'s new-and-improved teaching style would mean she would holler at them and hit her desk with the ruler, but now she would just look at the big boys, with her eyebrow up and her mouth a little pushed to one side. It wasn't a mean look — it was a smart look. So the big boys stopped and sat down. It wasn't any fun trying to get the teacher upset because it didn't look like she could be upset.

Teacher M.K. was different somehow. It started on that day when she put Eugene Miller in his place. Then she did something pretty smart, which was good for a teacher who had seemed pretty dumb.

She flip-flopped the day's work, so reading and arithmetic came in the morning. In the afternoon, she introduced a new period: art. Even Eugene didn't slip away for the afternoon when he saw what Teacher M.K. had planned. She brought out paper for everybody, and a wooden box with little metal tubes of paint. She showed everyone how to rule a margin for the picture so there would be a white space all around for a frame. She showed them how to wipe brushes carefully while they were painting. Pretty soon everyone just got quiet, they were so happy making pictures.

Barbara Jean Shrock painted a picture of her baby sister, but she forgot to add eyes and a nose and a mouth. Danny Riehl drew a picture of an airplane. He knew all the different names of airplanes and all about their engines and stuff like that. Anna Mae drew a picture of her and Danny on their wedding day. That made Danny's face go cherry red.

Jenny painted a picture of a rainbow with a pot of gold at the bottom of it. She had always thought it might be nice to find a pot of gold someday. Life would be much easier. Maybe then her mother would be happy.

But it was Eugene Miller's picture that was the best. He painted a falcon that looked so real it wouldn't have surprised Jenny if it had taken flight. He said it was a peregrine falcon and that there was a nesting pair at Windmill Farm that returned year after year. He said he had watched them across the street with his binoculars. Teacher M.K. nodded, and she looked really pleased. Eugene didn't seem nearly as annoying when he was talking about the falcons. Maybe there was hope for him.

Teacher M.K. had hung all the pictures on the wall. The room seemed much more cheerful after that. Everyone couldn't stop looking at them.

That was the day Teacher M.K. put Eugene Miller in his place. That was the day something happened. Something that gave Jenny more to think about than worries about her mom. By the end of that afternoon, the children looked different too. Like something good was going to happen.

On a gray afternoon in October, M.K. went into the Stoney Ridge public library. She sought out the head librarian and asked, "Do you have any books on reading problems?"

The librarian's face turned sad and pitiful. "Are you having a problem with reading, dearie?"

How insulting! "Not me," M.K. huffed. "A student of mine."

The librarian led her to a section of books at the far end of the library. The sunlight from the window was filled with dust particles. It looked like this section of books hadn't been visited very often. She pointed to the bottom row. "Those are the only books we have about reading difficulties."

M.K. pulled out a few books and went over to a table to sift through them. She wasn't exactly sure what she was looking for, but she knew Eugene Miller was a bright boy, imaginative and creative and artistic, but he couldn't read or write at his age level. Not even close. In fact, some of his papers looked like a second grader's. Untidy, mixed-up letters and numbers. He was easily frustrated, became bored, and that's when he would start some mischief in the classroom.

The more she read, the more she thought she was finding what was behind Eugene's reading struggle: something called *dyslexia*. She came across one paragraph that leapt out at her:

"Compared to the average person, a dyslexic generally has very strong visual skills, a vivid imagination, strong practical/manipulative skills —"

Oh . . . that definitely sounded like Eugene Miller.

"— innovation, and an above-average intelligence. Basically the right side of the brain is stronger than the left — and that's what a good artist needs. As a dyslexic you are likely to have a greater appreciation for color, tone, and texture. Your grasp of two-dimensional and three-dimensional form is more acute. You can visualize your art before reaching for the paint brush, and your imagination will allow you to go beyond the norm and create new and innovative expression."

M.K. thought about Eugene's peregrine

falcon drawing. It was shockingly beautiful — the minute detail, the haughty gaze in the tercil's eyes, the vicious-looking talons. It was as vivid and realistic as a photograph. That was it! It seemed as if Eugene had a photograph of it in his mind and was somehow able to transfer that image onto paper.

Eugene was always drawing something. A stick in the dirt, pencil sketches around the edges of his math assignment, caricatures on the chalkboard.

She closed the book with a sigh. If it might be true that Eugene had dyslexia, what could she really do for him? She was no expert. She had an eighth-grade education. Most of these words were entirely new to her, and she considered herself a first-rate philologist. Still, she checked a few books out and left the library.

As she walked down the front path of the library, she noticed Chris Yoder coming down the street in his horse and buggy. He saw her and lifted a hand to wave to her. She reached down to pick up her scooter, hoping Chris might offer her a ride home, but when she looked up, he had passed by.

She didn't mind too much about Chris. He was friendly enough, but either he was keeping his distance, or she was keeping hers. She didn't mind too much. Really, not at all, hardly.

Of all people! The very moment Chris was heading to the sheriff's office to have a talk with him, Mary Kate Lapp came strolling out of the library — directly across the street from the office. There was no way he was going to pull into the sheriff's office at that moment. No way at all. He hurried Samson down the street and pulled over at the Sweet Tooth Bakery Shop and waited until he saw Mary Kate zip away, heading in the direction of Windmill Farm. He couldn't hold back a grin from spreading over his face as he saw her zoom away. She was always darting around Stoney Ridge on that little red push-scooter.

He looped the reins around the hitching post and walked into the sheriff's office. Sheriff Hoffman was finishing up a phone call and motioned to the seat across from his desk. Chris sat down and took his black felt hat off, spinning the brim in his hands. Now that it was fall, he had switched from straw hat to felt, along with the other men in his church.

Sheriff Hoffman put the phone back on the receiver. "Chris Yoder. Got something for me?"

Chris shrugged. "I'd like you to tell me exactly what you're looking for."

The sheriff inhaled deeply, then blew the air out of his mouth. He leaned forward in his chair. "Look, Chris. This all happened when you were just a little kid. I've spoken to a child psychologist about this case. He's been clear that it's important to not put any leading thoughts in your head, to just see what you can remember. He said if I try to give you any clues, it might cause you to freeze up. All I can tell you is that every single thing you can remember is helpful to the case."

"So . . . it is a case. An actual criminal case. Something my mother was involved in."

"I don't know for sure. It's just a hunch." The sheriff scratched his neck. "Have you given any more thought to undergoing hypnosis?"

"Absolutely not. I will not. You can't make me. It's against my church, my beliefs —"

The sheriff held up a hand to stop him. "Yeah, yeah. I got it. That's what I figured. So, just keep trying to remember."

Chris rose. "It occurred to me that any information I give you might end up connecting my mother to a crime. Have you thought of that?"

231

Sheriff Hoffman lifted his eyes and looked directly at Chris. "My job is to find the truth. Somehow, I think that's what you want too. 'The truth shall set you free.' Isn't that in the Good Book?"

"The truth shall set you free." Chris had read those words all his life and never really thought about what they might mean. How would the truth of that day, fourteen years ago, affect him? And Jenny? What would it mean for his mother?

On the way back to the house, Chris pondered the conversation with the sheriff. Old Deborah made Chris read the Bible out loud to her by lantern light nearly every night after the supper meal. She claimed Scripture could be a powerful comfort and help if a person let the Lord's message speak to his heart. Old Deborah's faith was a big sweeping thing and his was faint and faraway.

When he reached his grandfather's house, he hopped out of the buggy and walked around to release Samson from his rigging. He tugged on the bridle, guiding him toward the barn as the new moon slid behind a cloud.

"The truth shall set you free."

But what if the truth meant Chris would lose everything?

■ ■ ■ ■

It was a sunny, breezy Saturday in mid-October. Working together, Fern and Jenny hung the day's laundry, shooing away those four little puppies that kept trying to snap at the luffing sheets. Fern kept surprising Jenny. She would have thought Fern would have no patience for something as silly as puppies. Instead, Fern stopped trying to hang laundry and gave her full attention to those crazy puppies. She tossed them sticks and tried to teach them tricks, until they finally wore out and curled up in a mound in the sun. Then she went back to hanging towels and sheets.

The comforting aromas of soap and sunshine scented the warm air as the damp sheets made a soft fluttering noise in the breeze. Fern said she liked doing laundry; the act of scrubbing something clean felt good to her. Ten minutes later, they went inside to bake cookies.

Jenny pulled a tray of cookies from the oven and set them out to cool. Fern stuck her thumb in the middle of one cookie. "Do this with each one," she said to Jenny. Then Fern carefully ladled a spoonful of raspberry jam into the indentation. "That's why they're called thumbprint cookies. They're my top seller. Folks love my raspberry jam."

Without thinking, Jenny said, "Old Deborah used to make these, but she liked to use blackberry jam."

Fern glanced up from spooning jam into another cookie. "Sadie got her start in healing from a woman in Ohio named Old Deborah. In Berlin."

Jenny's thumb froze, mid-squish. She didn't dare look at Fern.

"It was when Sadie was living with Julia and Rome for a few months, right after they got married. Julia is Amos's eldest daughter. She married Rome Troyer, the Bee Man."

Jenny swallowed. She didn't know what to say.

Fern put the spoon in the jam jar. "You know Rome and Julia, don't you?"

Slowly, Jenny nodded. "We lived with Old Deborah when our mother was . . . indisposed."

"Ah," Fern said in her knowing way. "I take it that Chris doesn't want anyone to know."

Jenny chanced a look at Fern. "Are you going to let him know I told you?"

Fern tilted her head. "But you didn't tell me. I guessed. And if Chris isn't ready to

234

tell us anything more, we'll just have to wait."

Jenny's eyes filled with tears. "Oh, thank you!" She flung her arms around Fern's middle and burst into tears.

Now it seemed to be Fern's turn to not know what to do. Slowly, she put her arms around Jenny and patted her. "Jenny, you know that you can always count on us to help you and Chris. Rome and Julia, too." She cupped Jenny's face in her hands, the same way Old Deborah used to. "You just need to let us know if you need help."

Fall's vibrancy was fading. Squash vines and tomatoes had withered to the ground; corn leaves were wispy brown paper flecked with fuzzy mildew, abandoned ears shriveled inside. But in the greenhouse at Windmill Farm, it looked and smelled as warm and humid as if spring had arrived.

When Chris had approached Amos about the market manager's suggestion that lettuce was needed at the farmer's market, Amos's face softened for a moment with pleasure. When he spoke, his voice was quiet and sure. "Good for you. The greenhouse hasn't been used since my eldest daughter married and moved away. Have at it."

He sent Chris directly to Fern, who

seemed equally pleased. "The market manager said folks will pay a premium for baby greens," Chris explained, though Fern didn't need any convincing. Together, Fern and Chris plotted out a plan to begin lettuce seeds in shallow wooden boxes in the greenhouse. Chris was discovering that Fern had the intuitive sense of a savvy merchant. She was already figuring out when the baby lettuce would be ready for the market, and how to bag them with a green polka-dotted ribbon. "We'll call ourselves the Salad Stall," she said, already at work on the sign.

Chris doted on those baby greens. Amos helped him with a few valuable tips: he added extra alfalfa meal into the soil to ensure a plentiful nitrogen supply. Lettuce, he said, needed a pH of 6.0 to 7.0. They selected a seed mix that included a variety of lettuces, since Chris would be hand snipping the leaves and not uprooting the plants. He showed Chris how to broadcast the seeds by hand and to tamp down the soil by gently massaging it with his palm. Keep the temperature of the greenhouse at 75 degrees, he told Chris.

None of this Chris knew. He felt as if he was getting a crash course in farming from Amos. He couldn't soak up enough knowledge from him. It embarrassed him how little he knew when he started this venture. Within a week, he had read every book he could find about lettuce. He learned that lettuce was a member of the sunflower family, and it was one of the oldest known vegetables — dating back to Persia, six centuries before Christ walked the earth. He knew now that the word "lettuce" comes from an Old French word, *laities,* meaning milk — probably referring to the milky white sap that came out of mature lettuce stems after the farmer snipped off the leaves.

Chris misted the seedlings three times a day and monitored them daily for any weeds. The greenhouse was the first place he went as he arrived at Windmill Farm in the morning and the last place he left at night. Thirty days after planting, Chris had harvested a small crop of baby lettuce to sell at the farmer's market on Saturday morning. He set up right next to the Fisher boys and their multicolored eggs. Jimmy helped nail Fern's elegant hand-painted "Salad Stall" sign up to the back of the stall. It was a bitterly cold day, with few customers trolling the aisles. Chris noticed there had been a change in the stands at the market. Many local produce stands were gone and crafts had filled their place: handmade wreaths, braids of garlic, shellacked gourds cut into birdhouses.

Maybe this was a mistake. It had seemed like such a good idea, but as the morning wore on and Chris had sold only three bags of lettuce, he felt like a fool. Only a novice would try to grow and sell lettuce in the late fall.

And then something miraculous occurred. First one customer bought a bag, then another, and soon he actually had a small line forming in front of his stand. At the end of the morning, he counted his earnings: forty-five dollars, minus ten percent for his stall fee. On the way back to Windmill Farm, he realized that he owed Amos money for the seed: forty dollars. That left Chris with a fifty-cent profit for a month's work spent sowing, watering, weeding, cutting, and bagging. Fifty cents.

He grinned. He felt like a real farmer.

Teacher M.K. had the scholars practice handwriting every day, right after lunch. She made sure everyone made sharp-nosed *e*'s and perfect *o*'s and straight *i*'s with the dot right smack on top, not floating off into space. Anna Mae liked to make little hearts to serve as the dots on her *i*'s and the teacher did away with those. Barbara Jean was still learning the alphabet. She made

Jenny laugh, because she was practicing so hard her tongue stuck out. Jenny wanted to make every letter just so. Perfect.

While they practiced their handwriting, Teacher M.K. read to everyone, walking up and down the aisles. It was a story called *The Jungle Book* by Rudyard Kipling about a young boy who was raised by wolves in the jungles of India. When Teacher M.K. read to the class, she acted out all the voices, and Jenny forgot right away it was just reading. It got real, like being inside the book. She felt as if she was in that deep, dark jungle with bushes thicker and denser than you could ever imagine, and when the teacher stopped, Jenny felt shocked, as if she had woken from a dream.

Even Eugene Miller liked hearing about the boy raised by wolves. He had stuck around all week.

One afternoon, Teacher M.K. handed the upper grades books she had made with paper stapled down the center. "This is for you to write a story," she told everyone. "Don't worry about the spelling, just write. Anything you want to."

She told the students they could even make things up. The stories didn't have to be true.

Anna Mae and Danny and the other upper grade students were excited about writing a book. But not Eugene. He crossed his arms against his chest and looked mad.

12

Eugene didn't come to school one morning. M.K. felt discouraged. Things had been going so well. She had been trying all kinds of ways to help Eugene: she stopped having him read aloud in class, saving him that painful ordeal. Instead, she had a private time with him when he read aloud.

She had been surprised to discover that he could hardly read at all. He had to read slowly, so very slowly, and the big words gave him fits. She provided reading books for him far below his grade level, to help build his confidence. For the spelling bees on Fridays, she gave him the list of words to practice on Thursday. He needed so much practice. In mathematics, her goal was to teach him to estimate, and to finish a problem by asking himself, "Does this answer make logical sense?" She gave him a box of index cards for key words and formulas. She was doing everything she could to help him.

After school let out for the day, M.K. wiped down the chalkboard. She heard the door open and turned around to see Eugene standing there. He was so tall he was scraping the top of the door, and growing still.

He scowled at her. "I'm quitting school. I already turned fifteen. I don't need it."

M.K. turned back to the chalkboard and calmly finished wiping the last section. She knew this was a critical moment. "You can quit school, Eugene. But you're going to have to keep learning all your life." She put the rag in a drawer. "You can't spend your life quitting things just because they get hard."

He narrowed his eyes. "It wasn't hard with Teacher Alice. I was getting along just fine until you showed up. It's because of your teaching. You couldn't teach a dog to bark. You couldn't teach a fish to swim. Or a bird to sing."

M.K. snapped her head up. She marched up to him and pointed a finger at his chest, which took notable courage because he towered over her. "I am trying to help you. You're a smart boy, Eugene, but your mind works a little differently than other students. That doesn't mean you can't get faster with reading and writing and arithmetic. You can. It's just going to take you a lot longer and you're going to have to practice a lot more to keep up."

He backed up a few steps. "Maybe I don't care."

M.K. stiffened. "Maybe you don't. I can't make you care. I can only offer you a chance." She fixed her eyes on him. "But I think you do care. I think you care very much."

Eugene held her gaze, narrowed his eyes, and called her an unrepeatable name, then whirled around and slammed the door behind him.

Out of habit, Jenny stopped by the mailbox on her way home from school and opened it. She wasn't sure what might be inside, but it was a bright spot of the day. Usually, all that the rusty old mailbox contained was junk mail. Today, there was a thin, gray envelope, addressed to her. Jenny stared at the letter for a long minute. Her heart leapt into her mouth and she felt a little strange, kind of dizzy and a little bit sick to her stomach. Looking over her shoulder, she hurried up to the house, dropped her lunch box, sat on the porch steps, and tore open the letter.

Hey there, Jennygirl! I was so happy to get a letter from you. Doing good here, though I sure am missing our monthly visits. Sorry to hear about Old Deborah. She was a nice old lady but she's been old for as long as I can remember. Write to me soon now honey and tell me about school. And what is Chris doing these days? Has he still gone whole hog over to them kooky Amish? I couldn't imagine why you're in Stoney Ridge until I figured out that my daddy's old house must still be empty. That's where you are, isn't it? Don't you worry. I won't tell. Makes me feel real happy to know where my babies are, safe and sound. Don't never forget that I love you. And don't never forget that I will always be your mama.

XOXOXOXOXOXOXOXOXOXOXOX-
OXOXOXOXOXOXOXOXOXO

P.S. Listen, honey, if you can send me some money, it would really help a lot. Cash is king here in the pokey — I need it for cigarettes and stamps and that sort of stuff.

How had her mother figured out where they were living? She had taken such care not to mention anything in her letters and not to supply a return address. She glanced at the envelope. *Stupid me!* The Stoney Ridge postmark would have given it away.

Chris would be furious.

Should she write her mother back?

She looked up at the sky and was surprised to see how thick the gray clouds had become. It would rain soon. She slipped the letter back into the envelope and put it into her apron pocket. Later. She would worry about writing back to her mother later. For now, it was time to start dinner.

You could hear a rumble in the late afternoon sky. Cayenne, the favorite of all the horses, was in her stall. M.K. reached over and touched her nose, and she nickered at her. She could see the horse's breath in the cold air. There was silence, the only sound was Cayenne's steady breathing. Her father had told M.K. once that the barn was the most peaceful place he knew. No voices, only the sound of the animals, their breath and bodies so warm.

M.K. had never felt so thoroughly exhausted in all her life. Physically and mentally. Teaching must be the hardest job in the entire world. And she was never done! Even on the weekends, she found herself thinking up a new way to help Jenny Yoder not shut down when faced with an arithmetic problem or wondering how to keep a mind like Danny Riehl's challenged. Or how to just keep Eugene Miller attending school.

It was too much. It was all too much.

She let her mind drift off to her plan of escape: she would finish the school term, take her passport, and travel to a land without children.

Raindrops started to splatter the metal roof of the barn. A crack of thunder split the sky. The storm would soon pass by. She stroked Cayenne's nose. She should get up to the house before the downpour started.

The barn door slid open and she turned to find Chris Yoder coming in, leading the draft horses, Rosemary and Lavender, by their bridles. He didn't notice M.K. as he led the horses to their stalls and attended to their needs: filling buckets with water and mangers with hay. She saw him rub one of the mares' forehead. The horse nudged closer to him, and though M.K. couldn't hear what he said, his lips moved as though he were singing to the animal. He bent and ran a hand over each of the mare's legs.

Such gentleness.

As he dipped the bridles into water to clean off the bits, he caught sight of M.K.

and startled. "I didn't see you there." He looked around the barn. "I thought I might wait out the rain before heading home, but what's the use of weather if you're not out in it anyway? I'll leave —"

"No, wait. Don't go on my account. It should pass soon." Just as she finished that sentence, a loud BOOM blasted overhead and made her jump. She shivered. "When I was little, Uncle Hank would say that thunder meant the angels were moving furniture in heaven."

"Then that would have been the armoire," Chris said. He hooked the bridles on the wall pegs and picked up a broom. He started sweeping down the center aisle of the barn.

It had become so dark in the barn that M.K. lit a lantern and hung it on the wall. She watched Chris for a while. "You don't have to work all the time."

"Yes, I do." He swept the loose straw into a stall. "You work pretty hard yourself. I've seen the glow of lampshine in the school-house early in the morning on my way to work."

Someone had noticed? For some reason, the thought pleased her. "I know why I'm working so hard. I'm trying to prove than I can teach school."

247

He grinned. "You're making a little progress, from what I hear."

That pleased her too, and she felt her cheeks get warm. "So what about you? What are you trying to prove?"

His grin faded.

She had gone too far. When would she ever learn? Just as Chris started to relax, she scared him back into his shell, like a turtle. "I'm sorry. It's none of my business. My curiosity is one of my worst faults."

The rain was really coming down now. It sounded like a work crew was hammering nails on the roof. Chris put the broom away and leaned his hips against a hay bale, facing

M.K. He crossed his arms against his chest and one booted ankle over the other. "I'm trying to prove that I am my own man."

"Was there ever any doubt of that? You seem like a person who knows who he is and where he's going."

He went very still, and for a long minute he frowned at her. She worried that she had said the wrong thing again. "I'm sorry. What do I know?" A cat wove between her feet. She bent over and scooped up Buzz, the long-haired cat who spent most of his day snoozing. Nuzzling the cat's warm fur, she said, "It's just that sometimes I . . . I don't know who I am or what I'm meant to be doing. Fern says I have a terrible restlessness inside of me. She's right. I want to travel and see the world and swim in the Mediterranean Sea — but I love my family and I love my church and I love my bees — and I don't want to disappoint my father or Fern or my sisters. Or Uncle Hank." She ran her hand down Buzz's furry back and he responded with a low purr. "Though, Uncle Hank, of all people, would understand." She set Buzz on the ground and looked at Chris. "But I just can't figure out which way to go sometimes." She was babbling. She had to wrap this monologue up. "Do you ever feel that way? Do you understand what I mean?" *Please, please understand.*

Chris's face grew tight. He shook his head. "No. I don't."

Oh. This wasn't going very well, and the rain wasn't letting up at all. If anything, the thunder and lightning were coming steadily. Even the horses seemed uncomfortable, shuffling their feet restlessly. It was a very dramatic stage for M.K. to bare her soul — to practically a stranger — and she had just made an utter fool of herself.

Chris rose to his feet and crossed the

space between them and put his hands on her shoulders. M.K. had never seen eyes so blue, the purest cobalt, like windows to the soul. For a split second, the way he was looking at her, the nearness, she was certain he was going to kiss her. She had never let a boy kiss her before, had never *wanted* to be kissed before. When she had observed Sadie and Gid kissing — which she had done on plenty of occasions — she thought kissing seemed ridiculous, involving odd noises and a lot of awkward nose bumping.

Ruthie had kissed a couple of boys — but only the ones she had fallen in love with. She had described kissing that made her stomach flip-flop and her palms sweat and her head start to spin. M.K. told her she might be confusing kissing with coming down with the flu.

But standing so close to Chris right now, kissing took on a different light. Chris Yoder wasn't a boy. He was a young man. He looked away, then looked back, and gave her shoulders a gentle shake. Something flickered behind his eyes. "I don't feel sorry for you. Not at all. You don't realize what you have here. You have something that most people would give their eyeteeth for in a heartbeat. A family, a place of belonging.

A purpose — you're needed in that school-house."

He was practically nose-to-nose to her. Her heart was thumping so loudly she was sure he could hear it. He brushed his fingers over her cheek. She had never felt anything like it: a touch more quiet than a breath.

"You might be the prettiest girl in Stoney Ridge, but if you don't have the smarts to appreciate that — all that — then you don't deserve the life you've been given." He reached behind her and plucked her dad's black slicker, hanging on a wall peg. As he slipped it over his head, he said, "Jenny will be pacing the front room like a circus lion if I don't get back soon. She hates storms. Tell your dad I'll bring this back in the morning." He slid the barn door open, just enough to slip through, then he disappeared.

Through the opening, M.K. watched Chris run down the driveway in the pelting rain. How dare he! How dare he speak to her like she was a child. Why, he was using the very same tone she had used to scold Eugene Miller barely an hour ago. Chris Yoder had a regular way of dousing any momentary warmth she might have felt for him.

Insults. That's all she was getting today. Eugene told her she couldn't teach a dog to bark and Chris told her she didn't have much smarts. Boys! So rude.

Then a small smile crept up on her face. Chris had said she was pretty. The prettiest girl in Stoney Ridge.

No one had ever called her pretty. They had called her nosy and sneaky and overly imaginative. Not pretty.

Jimmy Fisher had just delivered another one of his mother's notes to Hank Lapp. He didn't know what was in this note, but he didn't really need to know. Hank read it and started sputtering away about how insensitive and heartless some females could be. Jimmy's mother, he meant. It wasn't hard to figure that she must have spurned Hank again.

Those dogs of Hank's really irked Jimmy's mother. Granted, Edith Fisher was a woman who was easily irked, but these dogs set her teeth on edge. Hank would promise not to bring them to the Fishers', and that would last a time or two, until he arrived at the door surrounded by yellow fur and black noses. Doozy always smelled like he needed a bath, which he did. Add four little Doozies to the mix. It was too much for any woman to bear! Edith had declared. And Hank was spurned again.

Jimmy listened to Hank's rants and raves

for a while, until Hank got distracted by a tool he had just spotted underneath a buggy part. "DADGUMIT! I've been looking for that screwdriver for days."

With Hank's head under a buggy, it was a perfect time for Jimmy to slip out undetected. He headed over to the house to find M.K. Wooing her wasn't working out quite the way he had hoped — mainly, because she didn't seem to realize he was wooing her. A few days ago, he brought a bouquet of flowers and she asked if he was heading to a graveyard. He stopped by the schoolhouse and invited her for a hamburger at the new diner, and she said she had just eaten. Jimmy was flummoxed. Never, ever, ever had a girl turned down an opportunity to spend time with him.

Tonight, he had crafted a new plan. He was going to look for an opportune moment — hidden from Fern and Amos's sight — and kiss M.K. One kiss from Jimmy Fisher, and she would be his. He was an expert kisser. Ruthie had said those very words, right before he broke up with her. He always felt a little bad about that timing. Unfortunate.

Fern turned Jimmy away at the door. She said that M.K. was out. Nothing more. Just out. As he walked down the driveway, he wondered if it was just his imagination, or if Fern seemed more prickly toward him than usual. As prickly as a cactus.

He heard a woman's voice and turned to locate the source. Coming down the orchard path was M.K. in her beekeeper's getup, with her big netted hat tucked under her arm. By her side was Chris Yoder. Jimmy raised his hand, getting ready to yell out to them, when he saw M.K. turn toward Chris, her face animated, talking to him intently. Her hands waved in the air, the way they did when she got excited. Chris was loping beside her, hands in his pockets, but he was listening carefully to her. Jimmy could hear M.K.'s voice float all the way down the hill. Then he heard Chris's laughter join with M.K.'s.

What story could M.K. be telling? What could have possibly made Chris Yoder laugh? Whatever it was, why hadn't M.K. told Jimmy that story? Jimmy felt strangely unsettled.

M.K. snapped open a fresh sheet and watched it settle gently over her bed. She smoothed the wrinkles and tucked in the corners. She had always loved the feel of cool clean linen beneath her hands, had always loved to crawl between crisp sheets at night.

Why couldn't these simple pleasures be enough for her? They were more than enough for Ruthie and Sadie and Julia. What was wrong with her? Yesterday, she was helping Fern tackle the basket filled with clothes needing ironing. The sweet smell of steaming cotton filled the room. Treading carefully, M.K. asked Fern if she ever wanted to see parts of the world.

"No." Fern kept ironing. "We should want nothing more than the life God has given us. The problem with you, M.K., is you lack contentment."

Contentment. She didn't have it. Not much of it, anyway. In truth, it sounded boring. Cats and dogs were content, and they slept all day.

Fern acted as if gaining contentment was as easy as taking a vitamin pill and M.K. knew it wasn't.

So M.K. took her scooter out to pay a visit to Erma and ask what she thought about contentment. "Personally, I think everyone should be able to seek their own contentment," M.K. said, as she helped Erma gather ripe grapes from her vineyard.

"The only problem with that thinking," Erma said in her calm way, "is that if one can't find contentment at home, one is unlikely to find it anywhere else."

Oh. *Oh.* Could that be true? Did the fact that M.K. had been discontented living in Stoney Ridge mean she was doomed to a life of discontent?

Then, typical of Erma, she turned the whole thing around. "Mary Kate, I have discovered that I am happiest of all when I have learned to be content at home."

Jenny hated arithmetic. She always just wrote any old numbers down before, so she wouldn't have to think about it. Even if writing stories became fun when Teacher M.K. gave them their handmade books, there was no way she could make arithmetic fun. The teacher had an oven timer on her desk and Jenny kept one eye fixed on it. As soon as it went off, math would be over for the day and they could be excused for recess.

Jenny ran behind the far maple tree and sat on the ground, leaning against the tree. This was where she spent every recess and every lunch. She definitely did not want to spend her precious free time with Anna Mae and her group of giggling girls. Besides, they had never asked her to join them.

Jenny pulled out a paper and pencil from her pocket.

Dear Mom, I miss you a LOT.

She chewed on her lip, thinking. What else could she say to her mother? Chris would be upset with her for tipping their mother off to where they were living. He thought their mother would never be able to stay out of jail for long. The counselor at the rehab center explained that using drugs short-circuited your brain so you weren't the same person anymore. Jenny refused to believe that her mother couldn't change. She believed in her, even if no one else did. When she had asked Old Deborah what she thought about that, a sad look covered her sweet wrinkled face. "I believe God can work miracles, Jenny. But our faith is in God, not in people."

I know you probably don't feel very good, but remember: you can do it! You got clean before and felt really good, remember? Keep getting better and better.

Chris is working really hard to fix up Grandfather's house. He has done so much! It is still awful because no one was in it for a long time, except for a creepy bat. The house looks a lot better than it used to. Chris has big plans for the house because he wants to be a horse breeder. He really likes it in Stoney Ridge. Maybe when you are better, you can come live with us. The Colonel left the house to Chris and to me. Old Deborah said so.

Love, Jenny

P.S. I am trying to save as much money as I can to send to you. Please quit smoking! It's not good for you.

A softball bounced on the ground next to her. As Jenny leaned over to pick it up, Eugene Miller ran up to her. She braced herself. You never knew what was going to pop out of Eugene's mouth, and it usually wasn't very nice, though he hadn't actually been unkind to her. Not yet, anyway. She tossed the ball to him, expecting him to catch it and return to the game.

"Nice throwing arm," he said. "Why don't you come play? We need a good shortstop."

She looked up sharply at him, thinking he was making a crack about her height. She had heard all kinds of smart-aleck comments about her small stature: Thumbelina, Oompa Loompa, Shortcake, Peewee, Itsby Bitsy. If Eugene thought "shortstop" was a new nickname to Jenny, he was sorely mistaken.

But he actually seemed sincere. When she hesitated, puzzled that he was being nice, he put his hand out to help her up. "Come on."

Under Eugene's shaggy bangs were bright blue, smiling eyes. Even though his complexion was marred by acne, he had an attractive smile that made dimples in his cheeks. She was surprised to realize how cute he was, up close like this. She shook her head to erase the absurd idea.

She looked at his hand, waiting for her. She folded the letter to her mother and put it in her pocket. The letter could wait. She took Eugene's hand and jumped to her feet.

It had taken Jimmy Fisher more time than he had expected to figure out where Chris Yoder was living. It was strange that no one seemed to know. He was sure someone at Windmill Farm would know, but Amos was away at a farm equipment auction and Hank didn't have any idea where Chris lived. Even Fern didn't know — and she knew just about everything. He finally tracked down M.K. and she knew. He should have known. M.K. knew all sorts of facts about people in Stoney Ridge that no one else knew.

That afternoon, Jimmy rolled into the long narrow driveway of Colonel Mitchell's old house and found Chris replacing rotted boards in the covered wraparound porch floor. Jimmy couldn't find a hitching post to tie the reins of his horse and buggy and finally decided on a tree branch. He waved to Chris, who had stopped sawing a board when he saw Jimmy drive in. "Looks like you could use a hand."

Chris looked surprised. He hesitated, then said, "I wouldn't refuse it." He handed the saw to Jimmy across the sawhorse.

Jimmy waved away the saw. Instead, he picked up a hammer. "You keep cutting boards and I'll nail them in place. There's an excellent chance I would lose a finger or two by cutting. I'm not known for paying too much attention to details. Too risky." He held up his hands and bent a few fingers down, as if he was already missing a few. "It's killing my career as a classical pianist."

He got a laugh out of Chris at that. That meant a lot to Jimmy, to get a laugh out of a serious guy like Chris Yoder. He had the impression that Chris didn't laugh much. Jimmy would change that, if they were going to be friends.

The two worked side by side for the next

hour or so, not speaking unless it pertained to the porch. When all of the rotted boards had been replaced, a small girl brought out a pitcher of water and two glasses. Jimmy had seen her at church and at Windmill Farm once or twice. He had figured out she was Chris's sister, Jenny, but he had a hard time believing she was in eighth grade. She reminded him of an elf. She stared at him as she handed him a glass, as if she had never seen anyone who looked like him before. It was a stare he was accustomed to by women of all ages. He knew he was handsome, had known it all his life. He wasn't being proud. It was just a fact. He gave Jenny his most charming smile and she practically gasped. Her little feet barely made a noise on the steps as she hurried away. She wrenched the door open. It banged shut behind her.

Chris and Jimmy sat on the new porch floor and gulped the water down.

"Did you just happen to be passing by?" Chris asked. "How did you figure out where I live?"

"M.K. Lapp told me."

Chris took a sip of water. "Know her well?"

"I do. Very well. I'm planning to make her my missus."

Chris started coughing, as if he had taken in a sip of water down the wrong pipe. Jimmy whacked his back with enthusiasm. He was always trying to be helpful.

"I owe you a favor," Chris said. "You saved me more than a half day's work."

"Glad to help," Jimmy said. He turned around to look at the old house. "Looks like you've got a lot of work to do. I could try and come over now and then to help."

"I could use the help, but I can't pay you cash. If there's some other way I can return a favor, let me know. I don't like to be beholden."

Jimmy took another swig of water, his mind working. He wiped his mouth with his sleeve. He looked at Samson, grazing in the paddock. He grinned. "Well, now, if that's the case, we might just be able to figure something out."

13

Chris jerked awake from a heavy, dreamless sleep and sat straight up, blinking, trying to gather information as fast as possible. Where was he? Was there any trouble? What had his mother done now?

The soft light of dawn splashed on the slanted walls of his bedroom.

No, he didn't have to worry about his mother. She wasn't here. She was in Marysville, Ohio, in a rehabilitation treatment center. And he was in Stoney Ridge, Pennsylvania.

With a sigh of relief, he fell back on the soft bed and scrunched the pillow under his head like a nest. It was still super-early. Too early to get up.

He didn't want to think about his mother. He didn't want any news about her.

But he did.

When it came right down to it, it just wasn't that easy to give up completely on the family you were born into. As much as he wanted to, he couldn't rid himself entirely of the hope that one day his mother would be well.

Chris wished he'd been born into a regular family, one where everyone was just a normal person. But right from the start something was wrong, because there was no father, and his mother was not equipped for motherhood. She was young, immature, selfish, and loved to party. Chris ended up living with his grandfather, who never did know what to do with his rebellious daughter, even less with a baby. Then his mother moved back home again and life took on a reasonable calm, until his mother and grandfather started fighting all the time and his mother started using drugs for the first time. The thing about methamphetamine was that it was highly addictive. One time, two times, and she was hooked.

The counselor at the rehab center said that meth changed your brain chemistry, so you weren't the same person. There was always hope, Old Deborah would say. Always, always hope.

Hope. He turned that word over in his mind, the way a gold miner might examine a rock for specks of promising glitter. No sooner would he feel the comfort of the word and fear would swoop in from the sidelines to snatch it away. He lifted his head and peered out the window to see what kind of day it was, but his mind was still on Old Deborah.

Old Deborah talked so strangely, so intimately about God, as if the Almighty spoke to her the way he spoke to people in the Bible.

Chris believed in God, of course. He had attended church ever since he started to live with Old Deborah after they moved to Ohio — when he was eight and his mother had been put in jail the first time, for using credit cards from a lady who had asked them to housesit while she visited her sick daughter. His mother was in and out of jail or rehab after that, mostly in. She believed the world owed her something, and she had no problem helping herself to it. Her chief income strategy was to live off the generosity of others, and she always seemed to find kindly people who were willing to give her another chance. Chris didn't believe his mother had the capacity to change. Old Deborah would tell him that nothing was outside of God's capacity to redeem. But it wasn't God whom Chris doubted — it was his mother.

The morning was chilly. Winter was coming. Chris got up, dressed, and went to the living room. He made a fire in the fireplace and it finally began to heat the downstairs. He stayed by the fire for a moment, warming his hands. Samson would be expecting breakfast soon. As he put his boots on, he looked around the room. The walls were repaired and painted. The broken windows were replaced. The stair railing was fastened. The broken latticework around the porch foundation had been fixed. He had ripped out the rotting kitchen flooring and laid new linoleum — he was able to buy linoleum tiles for a bargain because the hardware store had ordered the tiles for a lady and she didn't like the tan color. He didn't really like the color, either, but he liked the price.

He still had a long list of things to do, but the house was getting into shape. He thought his grandfather would be pleased. Memories flashed at random intervals, faster than he could take them in — the way his grandfather ducked his tall frame when passing through a doorway, his uncanny accuracy at reading the night sky and knowing tomorrow's weather, and how his old dog would respond to his slightest whistle. He remembered the way his grandfather would scold him for slamming doors, how mad that used to make him. Chris could never figure out why that was a big deal.

Flashes of his previous life surprised him like this. He sure wouldn't mind hearing his grandfather scold him about those slammed doors now. No, he sure wouldn't.

The sun was hanging low in the sky, casting a mellow autumn glow across the garden. Amos checked the ripening pumpkins. Soon, they would be ready to pick so Fern could can them. He whistled for Doozy and strolled out to the orchards, with the dog trotting behind him.

As he reached the orchard, he feasted his senses, turning his face into the warm breeze. He sampled a still-tart, late-to-ripen variety of apple off the tree and examined the pears, swelling toward perfection. M.K.'s brown bees had worked their magic again.

Ah, Mary Kate.

Amos had stopped in at the schoolhouse this morning to drop off M.K.'s forgotten lunch, and thought he might stay for a few moments, quietly observing in the back. He ended up spending two hours, mesmerized.

Amos glimpsed a side of his youngest daughter he had never seen before. Her quick brown eyes took everything in — she could listen to one scholar's recitation while simultaneously managing the entire wild pack of big boys. It seemed to him that she was a born teacher — patient, creative, dedicated. If a pupil had trouble grasping a concept, he saw her search for a new approach. He observed her trying a different explanation until the light of understanding finally lit a pupil's eyes. He never saw her lose her temper or grow impatient, no matter how thick-skulled or stubborn the pupils could be at times. And Eugene Miller, he noticed, could be both.

Usually, he cut M.K.'s descriptions about people in half. Some truth, heavily embroidered with exaggeration. Not so for Eugene Miller. Watching that boy's sulky behavior, he decided that she was telling the complete and total truth.

"You can do this," she would urge him. "It's not as hard as it seems, take your time." The satisfaction on her face when Eugene finally caught on told Amos that for M.K., the joy of teaching was its own reward. Who could have imagined it? Fern had been right all along — M.K. would rise to the challenge of teaching.

Children. You think you have a sense of who they are, the person they've become . . . and then they surprise you by becoming another person entirely.

He squinted against the sun. His eyes swept over the orchards. These orchards, planted by his grandfather years ago, added to by his own father, had kept Windmill Farm solvent during some lean years when Amos had heart trouble. He stood there for a while, amid the long, even rows of trees, branches weighed down with heavy fruit. A farmer always looked forward, sacrificing long hours in anticipation of a good harvest. A reflection of God's character.

The trees were lovely reminders to him of God's steady reassurance — that goodness and gentleness will someday prevail. He ran his fingertips over a branch and almost marveled, as if he could imagine his grandfather planting the tree as a mere twig. He lifted his head, breathed deeply of the pear-scented air, felt his heart tighten with gratitude.

Herr, he thought, *denki.* Lord God, thank you.

A Saturday came, silent and sun-dazzled. M.K. turned off the burner under the pot of beans. She sprinkled some brown sugar into the pot, then a little ketchup. She stirred in some more of each, then added salt and pepper. She tasted it. *Not bad.* She got the apple cider vinegar out of the cupboard and stirred in a little of that and tasted it again. *Better.*

M.K. moved the pot to the oven, where it could bake peacefully.

She opened the kitchen door and stepped out into her yard.

There, coming up the driveway, was Jenny Yoder. M.K. crossed the yard to reach her.

Jenny was soaked with water. "I'm looking for my brother. Do you know where he is?"

"My uncle Hank talked him into going into town to pick up some buggy parts at the hardware store," M.K. said. "He shouldn't be too long, if you want to wait. What happened to you?"

Jenny looked uncertain. "I was trying to fill a water bucket for the horse and when I turned this, it broke off in my hands." She held up a water spigot. "I can't get the water to stop. It's shooting everywhere, like a geyser!"

Amos was on the far side of the barn, hooking Cayenne's bridle to the buggy shafts.

"Let's ask my dad what to do," M.K. said. She took the water spigot from Jenny and explained the situation to Amos.

He looked at the rusty edges of it. "M.K., get my wrench from my workbench. And see if you can find another spigot in the top

270

right drawer." He looked at Jenny. "Hop in. We'll get that water shut off in the blink of an eye."

"I'll come too," Fern said, appearing out of the barn like magic, startling Amos. He practically jumped.

"Everybody knows Fern has a knack for turning up out of the blue," M.K. whispered to Jenny. "You'd think Dad would be used to it."

The way Jenny looked at her then, almost giggling, filled M.K. with some relief. It was the first time Jenny hadn't peered at her with that suspicious, birdlike glare. Maybe she was finally thawing out.

Chris decided that he wouldn't seek the sheriff out on his trip to town today, but if he happened to see him, he would tell him about the memory — or was it a dream? — that seemed to pop into his head last night.

Maybe. But maybe not.

Of course, just as he pulled into the edge of town, he saw the sheriff's car at the silverstream diner, The Railway Station. Chris thought it was a strange choice for a diner name because Stoney Ridge didn't have a train running through it, but he had heard the burgers were good. If he ever had an extra ten dollars to spend, he should take

271

Jenny out for a burger and shake. If he had an extra twenty dollars, he might consider asking Mary Kate Lapp out for a meal.

Maybe. But maybe not.

After all, she was spoken for by Jimmy Fisher. A pang twisted Chris's gut, and he knew it wasn't hunger. Thinking of M.K. with someone else didn't set well.

Chris had taken pains to avoid Mary Kate after finding out that particular piece of news. This morning, he was even a little rude to her. She brought him coffee in the barn and he refused it, brushing past her as if he was on his way to put out a fire. He wasn't the kind who would ever take another fellow's girl, especially a friend's. And Jimmy Fisher had been a friend to him. He had come over again last Saturday afternoon to help Chris tackle the overgrown yard.

Chris knew Jimmy had an angle — he was itching to borrow Samson for a horse race. That wasn't going to happen, not ever, despite Jimmy's strong hints. Still, Chris couldn't help smiling at the challenge. Jimmy Fisher was the type who made a competition out of everything. How fast you could hammer nails. How quickly you could rip boards off the porch. Everything was an opportunity for a race. Even stupid things, like thinking you could race a hot-blooded stallion at the tracks. Everybody knew you didn't take a stallion to the tracks. Too distracting. Stallions instinctively tried to create a harem. Everybody knew that.

Besides, the thought of gambling repulsed Chris. It reminded him of his mother — always wanting something for nothing.

Jimmy Fisher had an answer for gambling, when Chris asked him why a Plain person was at the tracks. Jimmy said that horse racing was in the best interest of the animal. "These horses are trained day after day to forget the instincts they're born with." Jimmy insisted that racing helped a horse work out its desire to be free, to roam wild, so that it could return to the fieldwork as a happier beast, knowing it had reached its full potential.

There was no point in responding to such a bogus explanation. Jimmy had an answer for everything, Chris had quickly discovered. Still, he found himself enjoying Jimmy's company. Jimmy was hard not to like.

Chris pulled the horse over to the side of the road, trying to decide if he would go in to talk to the sheriff or not. Maybe. Maybe not. Should he? Or shouldn't he?

He'd come so far these last few months, and the slightest misstep could wipe all that out.

"Got something else for me, Yoder?"

Chris practically jumped at the sound of the sheriff's voice right at his buggy window. "Last night," he said, "I woke up from a dead sleep. I had a vision so real that I couldn't remember if I dreamed it or it was real." He took a deep breath. "There was a woman who had come over to help us sometimes. She took pity on our family and used to bring food. She would give me her son's hand-me-down clothes. Stuff like that."

"Go on," Sheriff Hoffman said, leaning his arms against the open buggy window.

"One afternoon, my mother sent me upstairs to check on the baby. Jenny was crying, and I remember hearing my mother's voice get louder and louder. I crept down the stairs, and I saw the neighbor lady holding my mother's arm as if she was trying to stop her."

"Stop her from what?"

This was what was hard to say. "From doing drugs. My mother is — was — is a drug addict. Methamphetamine. Back then, she would buy a lot of Sudafed and make her own meth."

The sheriff didn't miss a beat. He was probably used to this kind of thing, but it

274

still shamed Chris. "Go on. What happened next?"

"My mother became angrier and angrier at the neighbor. She saw me on the stairs and yelled at me to get upstairs." Chris paused to collect himself for a long moment. "The neighbor lady was trying to calm my mother down, but my mother was shouting at her to leave and mind her own business. Then, suddenly, there was silence. A strange silence. The next thing I knew, my mother raced upstairs, grabbed a suitcase, and started to throw things into it. She picked up the baby, told me to get in the car, and we left Stoney Ridge."

"Did you see the other woman leave the house?"

Chris shook his head. "No. We went out the back door of the kitchen to get to the car."

Sheriff Hoffman rubbed his chin. "What do you remember of this woman? Do you remember her name?"

Chris squinted his eyes, thinking hard. "No, I can't remember her name. Only that she was Amish." Out of the blue, a name popped out at him. "Mattie. No — Maggie." A cold chill ran through Chris. He had a feeling that he had just made things much, much worse by telling the truth. He should not have said anything at all. But he had to know. "Why? Did something happen to that woman? Did something happen that day?"

Sheriff Hoffman gave an infinitesimal nod of his head. "I was just a rookie that spring. I was told to make an arrest for accidental manslaughter. I did what I was told. I made the arrest. But something never added up to me. Something always bothered me about it."

"But . . . who did you arrest?"

Sheriff Hoffman's penetrating stare was unnerving. "Your grandfather. Colonel Mitchell."

Was it possible? How could this be? Amos followed Jenny Yoder's instructions to drive to her house. He felt a shiver up his spine when she pointed to a narrow drive that led to Colonel Mitchell's house. He hadn't been to this house in fourteen years, and he had never wanted to cross the threshold again. Not ever.

Fern and Jenny were debating bread dough and starters and yeast and he couldn't even make any sense of their conversation. All that he could do was to pray one prayer, over and over and over: Herr, hilf mich. *God, help me.* When Amos reached the house, he saw the water spewing out from the side yard pipe. He hopped out of the buggy and went straight to the pipe. He needed time to think and was grateful for something to do.

When he noticed Fern climb out of the buggy, he called out, "This won't take but a moment. You stay put."

She snapped her head up at the sharp tone in his voice and gave him a strange look. "Jenny is going to show me the house. It won't take long." She turned her attention to Jenny and helped her out of the buggy.

Fern didn't understand. But how could she, when he had never told her how Maggie had died? He had only told her it was an accident. That God had been merciful and Maggie hadn't suffered. He hadn't told her that she had been trying to help the English neighbor that bordered their farm, because there was no father, and the mother wasn't quite right. The woman had a little boy, a few years older than M.K., and a baby girl who cried a lot. And she lived with her father, Colonel Mitchell. A tough guy, he liked to call himself. A former Marine. And a former football player, in the days when helmets were flimsy, he would say.

His mind racing, Amos looked around until he found the main water pipe to the house and turned it off. Then he went to the broken spigot, wrenched off what remained of it, screwed on the new spigot, turned back on the main water. Checked to see if there was any leak, gathered his tools.

Why was Chris Yoder living here? *Why, why, why?*

And then it hit him — so hard he had to sit down. A melee of emotions — dread, anger, guilt — struck him all at once. He realized why he thought Chris looked vaguely familiar. Chris was the Colonel's grandson. Chris was that little boy Maggie was always worried about. Too serious, Maggie had said. Much too serious for a little boy. Always worried about his mother and his baby sister. It was as if he hadn't been allowed a childhood.

And Jenny — she was only a baby. A baby with colic, like his own son, Menno. Maggie had found goat's milk helped Menno's indigestion as a baby, so she wanted to take goat's milk over to the Colonel's house. He vividly remembered the day — it was the first warm day of spring after an exceptionally cold winter. The crocuses were blooming, and Maggie had been so excited to see her first robin that very morning. "Spring is finally here," she told Amos as she explained where she was headed. Julia and Sadie were in school. Menno and M.K. were in the barn with him, playing with some new kittens.

"Let them stay and play," he had told Maggie. "I'll watch them."

She had kissed him on the cheek and promised she wouldn't be long.

But she never returned.

Looking back, Amos viewed his life as if divided into two halves: before Maggie died, and after. He believed that God's hand was on Maggie's passing. He believed that her life was complete. He believed that God had a purpose. God had a plan. He believed that with his whole heart. He banked his eternal life on that belief. But the reality of living without Maggie was a harsh one. He likened it to how someone must have felt if he lost his sense of taste: a person might continue to eat, to provide sustenance and nourishment to his body, but life had lost all flavor. Grief-stricken was just the word: grief had literally reached out and struck him, and left a permanent mark.

"Amos, are you all right?"

Fern and Jenny appeared beside him, shocking him into the present. He picked up the wrench and the broken spigot. "Yes. Yes. I'm fine. I'm ready to go."

Fern looked at Jenny and dusted her hands together the way she always did when she was making up her mind. "I think we should organize a work frolic to help Chris with some repairs."

Jenny's face scrunched up. "I don't think Chris wants any help."

"Nonsense. It's our way," Fern said, being annoyingly practical. "Come back to the house and we can make plans." She started back to the buggy.

Jenny looked to Amos to intervene. "I don't think Chris is going to like that."

Amos had no idea how to respond. He still felt as if he was trying to process through a mountain of buried memories. "We can count on Fern to know what to do," he managed at last.

Back in the buggy, Amos flicked the reins over the horses' backs. Slowly the buggy started off again. His heart and mind, though, remained at Colonel Mitchell's house.

14

Early Monday morning, Teacher M.K. stood by the schoolhouse door, waiting for the scholars, smiling and talking with everyone in her mile-a-minute way. As hard as Jenny tried not to, she found herself growing increasingly intrigued by Teacher M.K.'s unique teaching style. And Teacher M.K. wouldn't let Jenny fade into the background like she usually did. She simply wouldn't allow it. She would call on Jenny in class even when she didn't raise her hand. She would read parts of her story out loud as if she thought they were any good. And they weren't. Jenny was sure they weren't. Anna Mae Glick told her so.

With Teacher M.K., the world got bigger and then it got smaller. Jenny was amazed. She was starting to notice things she had never noticed before.

First, Teacher M.K. taught them about the stars in the sky, and how the ancient mariners could find their way across the oceans by charting the stars. She brought in seashells and pieces of coral that she had found at a garage sale. She pointed out how a conch seashell looked like the inside of a person's ear, and that coral looked like veins and arteries.

Next, she brought in an old microscope she had bought for $5 at that same garage sale. She had the class look at things that were too small to see. She said there were much stronger microscopes that could see things even smaller than they could see with the garage sale microscope. A drop from the water pump became a regular sideshow of squirming cells. Jenny hadn't taken a sip of water from that pump since.

Today, Teacher M.K. had brought in fern leaves and put one on every single desk. "Tell me what you see," she said.

The room went very still as the scholars counted the leaves. Even the rowdy boys who usually whispered and snickered throughout the lesson sat as still as mannequins.

"The lines on the leaf are like blood vessels," Danny Riehl said. He adjusted his spectacles for a better look. Danny had this way of looking at things very carefully, even little things. He was always taking things apart and putting them back together. Anything he was curious about. Jenny was a little sorry that Danny was younger than she was, and even more sorry that Anna Mae had dibbs on him. Jenny thought he showed great promise. "And would that be the nervure?"

"He's always making up them big words," Eugene Miller sputtered. "He talks like he's playing Scrabble and is looking for points."

"*Nervure* is a word for the rib of a leaf," Teacher M.K. said. "It's just a more precise way of explaining something."

Danny looked at Teacher M.K. and smiled that smile of his, like when she told him about black holes in the sky and stuff like that. In a strange way, Jenny thought they understood each other.

Teacher M.K. said that there were all kinds of illustrations in nature that pointed to the Creator of the universe. God's handprint was on all of his work, just like when we sign our drawings. Just like that.

Gazing at the fern leaf, Jenny blurted out, "Count the little leaves! They come out just right! Look. On each row there's just one more leaf less, until it gets to the top."

Teacher M.K. looked pleased. "You, Jenny Yoder, just figured out today's arithmetic problem."

Imagine that, Jenny thought. *Me. Arithmetic.*

Mary Kate had been teaching for nearly ten weeks now. She had good days and she had bad days, but she wasn't thinking quite as often about running off to Borneo. Last week, she had a terrible, awful day and promptly sent off her passport application in the mail. Eugene Miller had gone too far, yet again, and put a snake in her pencil drawer. She hated snakes! Always had. She blamed Jimmy Fisher and a certain black racer snake.

Getting her picture taken for the passport made her feel as exposed as if she had run through Main Street in her underwear. She waited at the post office until she was sure no one was around whom she might recognize. Then she quickly had her picture taken by the postal clerk. As soon as it was ready, she signed the application, stuck the money order in the envelope with the application, and handed it to the clerk without allowing herself a second thought. It was a weak moment, one she wasn't proud of, but knowing it was a done deal gave her a feeling of satisfaction.

In the meantime, she had taken Erma Yutzy's advice to heart. She tried to find ways to connect to each pupil, to look for that golden moment. Teaching had become strangely satisfying, though winning the affection of the pupils was proving to be harder than she had expected. Not with the little ones, like Barbara Jean, or the bright ones, like Danny Riehl. But some of the older boys and girls were harder to convince, like there was Jenny Yoder. Jenny remained cool and distant. A bright spot occurred today when Jenny started to notice the patterns in the leaf and connected it to math patterns. That was good. Very good.

But later in the day, she had asked Jenny and Anna Mae Glick if they might like to stay after school and help her set up the art project for the next day. She had hoped that if Anna Mae could get to know Jenny, she might start including her with the other girls. But Anna Mae wrinkled her nose and scrunched up her face so tightly that M.K. thought she might suddenly be in pain. "Danny likes me to walk home with him from school." She swiftly made her escape without a word of farewell.

M.K. knew that wasn't true. Danny usually burst out of the schoolhouse as soon as she rang the dismissal bell and disappeared into the cornfield before Anna Mae had time to gather her things.

Jenny watched Anna Mae flounce out of the schoolhouse. And then she said, almost in a whisper, "She acts like I'm invisible."

"You're not, you know," M.K. pressed.

Jenny hesitated, her intense eyes searching M.K.'s face. "Not what?"

"Invisible."

Jenny looked at M.K., then looked away, but not before M.K. saw the way her eyes narrowed and two lines formed between her thin little eyebrows. "Fern is expecting me." She turned and hurried out the door.

M.K. could have kicked herself. Why did she always seem to say the wrong thing or do the wrong thing when she was around those Yoders? Just when they started to open up, she had to say something that scared them off. A turtle in its shell.

Wouldn't it be nice, Jenny thought as she walked to school, if you could shorten the bad days and save up the time to make a good day even longer? This morning, for example, she would like to swap out for two Christmas mornings.

She knew the entire day was headed in the wrong direction when she overcooked the scrambled eggs for breakfast. Fern had warned her to cook eggs slowly, but Chris was in a hurry, so Jenny turned up the flame on the stove. She burnt her finger on the hot pan handle and couldn't find a bandage. Then the eggs ended up looking like rubber cement. They tasted worse. Chris didn't complain, but Jenny was disappointed. Yesterday, Fern had given Jenny those brown eggs, still warm from Windmill Farm's henhouse, and Jenny had wasted them. Eggs were precious.

Chris hurried off to work and Jenny got ready for school. She heard a knock at the door and ran to get it, thinking it was Chris. But no! Rodney Gladstone, that overeager real estate agent who was always dropping by, stood at the door with that greasy smile on his face. He held out a handful of mail to Jenny. Her mail. On top was a thin gray envelope with her mother's familiar handwriting on it.

"I bumped into the mailman just a few minutes ago," Rodney said, still smiling. "Thought I'd save you a trip."

Jenny grabbed the mail from him and closed the door, but Rodney stuck the toe of his shoe in the threshold, leaving two inches of space to talk through. "I happened to be at the county clerk's office. Happened to discover that the legal owner of this house is a woman named Grace Mitchell. No one seems to know where she might be."

Jenny squeezed the door harder on his foot.

"I happened to notice the letter you just received is from a Grace Mitchell." Rodney's voice rose a few notes from pain inflicted on his foot. "The return address says Marysville, Ohio."

Jenny leaned against the door and pushed as hard as she could, and Rodney finally yelped. He pulled his foot out of the threshold and Jenny closed the door tight.

"Any chance that Grace Mitchell is the daughter of Colonel Mitchell?" Rodney called through the closed door. "Any chance Grace Mitchell is your mother?"

Jenny locked the door behind him. She tore open her mother's letter:

Hi sugar! How ya doing? Listen, Jennygirl, I could sure use some extra cash right now. Would you believe they make us buy our own toothpaste here? I'll bet Chris has some moola tucked away. Check under his mattress — that's where he keeps it. SHHHHhhhhh! Just our secret, you and me. Thanks, babygirl! Never forget your mama loves you! XOXOXOXOXOXOXOXOXOXOXO

Jenny folded the letter and put it in her

pocket as she heard Rodney Gladstone's car start up and drive down the driveway.

She had a very bad feeling about today. She often had bad feelings about days, especially Mondays, but this was different. This was worse.

M.K. had been certain Chris might drop by the schoolhouse or accept Fern's standing invitation to come to dinner. She thought she might bump into him somewhere. But she hadn't seen him in nearly two weeks. Their friendship had been progressing, and then, boom, it just ended. M.K. wasn't good at handling rejection. It had never happened to her.

It was a beautiful fall afternoon — slightly crisp, with the tangy smell of burning leaves in the air. Fern had planned to can garden-grown pumpkins all day, so M.K. was in no hurry to head home. No sir! Canning food in a steamy kitchen might be her least favorite activity. She took the long way and stopped at the cemetery where her mother and her brother, Menno, were buried. The tops of the trees swayed gently in the breeze. She walked up to her mother's grave and dropped down to clear away the dandelions and brush a bit of moss off the gravestone. Her mother had been gone for most of

M.K.'s life, and she couldn't quite recall her like she wanted to. Sometimes, she thought she only remembered remembering her.

She closed her eyes, trying to think what life had been like before her mother died. The images were so mixed up they never made much sense. She remembered a time when her mother had lifted her into the air and laughed as they whirled breathlessly around the room. Her mother smelled like cookies. And she remembered her father coming into the room and wrapping his arms around the two of them. A sandwich hug, he called it, and his littlest girl was the filling.

That was it. That was about all she clearly remembered of her mother.

"Are you all right?"

M.K. lifted her face, and there stood Chris Yoder, his brow furrowed in concern.

"Are you all right?" he repeated.

She stumbled to her feet. "Where did you come from?"

"I was passing by and saw your red scooter by the fence, then I saw you drop like a stone — I thought maybe you'd . . . fainted or a crow was dive-bombing at you . . . something like that."

"I'm fine," she said, feeling oddly nervous,

oddly pleased. Chris had been worried about her! She pointed to her mother's grave. "I was just pulling weeds."

Chris walked up to her and read the tombstone out loud. "Margaret Zook Lapp, beloved wife and mother." When he read the date, his eyebrows lifted. "You must have been young when she died."

She nodded. "Only five."

He half smiled. His smile was soft. He inclined his head as if he was weighing how much to say. "You must miss her."

Would she ever stop missing her mother? "I think about her every day. But you know what that's like. Don't you miss your folks?"

"Yeah, sure." But Chris looked away when he spoke, and M.K. could tell that he was lying. Too late, she recalled how Jenny had evaded the question about her parents, or where she was from, just like Chris was doing.

But then he smiled at her and his eyes crinkled at the corners. A funny sensation flitted through her. She felt that peculiar moment of connection weave between them, as if they shared something. Then the moment passed. He was gazing deeply into her eyes with his bright spring-water blue ones and he began to have a mesmerizing effect on her, the same way he had in the barn on that rainy day. She couldn't have moved away from him any more than the poles of two magnets could be pulled apart. "Are you coming from town?"

Chris nodded. "Your Uncle Hank needed a part for a buggy he's working on."

"You're working as much for Uncle Hank's buggy shop as you are for Dad's orchards."

"I don't mind. I need the work." Cayenne tossed her head and whinnied. Chris turned to look at her standing on the road, tied to a fence. "Your uncle is expecting me. I'd better get the part to him." He turned to leave, then stopped. "Do you need a ride home?" A slight smirk covered his face. "Unless, I suppose, your boyfriend is coming to get you?" He started to walk toward the buggy.

What? "Wait!" she called. "Who's my boyfriend?" She hurried to catch up with him.

Chris didn't answer. He helped M.K. into the buggy, tossed her scooter on the backseat, and climbed up beside her. He gave a quick "tch-tch" to the horse and a light touch on the reins and they were on their way home. He whooshed past a slow-moving car as if in a hurry to deliver M.K. as quickly as possible.

M.K. tried once again. "Why do you think I have a boyfriend? Because I don't. I don't know who told you otherwise, but I do not have a boyfriend."

"I see." He was trying not to grin, but she thought the news pleased him. She hoped so.

"Are you going to tell me who is spreading rumors about me?"

Chris remained quiet for a moment, then gave her a sideways glance.

Right, M.K. thought. The information flowed only one way.

Fern had left Jenny in the kitchen at Windmill Farm, waiting for the oven buzzer to go off and remind her that the last few pies were done, while she took one pie over to a sick neighbor. Jenny and Fern had made six pies this afternoon — three apple, three pumpkin — and the kitchen was filled with spicy cinnamon. Fern had showed her how to roll out dough and how to keep a bottom crust from getting soggy in the middle.

Jenny found a piece of paper and an envelope and sat at the kitchen table to write her mother a letter.

Dear Mom,
    I met a nice lady who is teaching me

how to bake. First she taught me to bake sourdough bread rolls. The first batch could have chipped a tooth, but by batch four, they were tasting pretty good. Now she's teaching me to make pies. Here's a secret: adding a teaspoon of vinegar into the crust helps to make it flaky. Did you know that?

Of course she didn't. Her mother had never baked a piecrust in her life.

Jenny didn't know what else to write. She didn't want to sound too happy, and she didn't want to seem as if Fern was replacing her role as a mother. Her mom could be touchy about that kind of thing. She had never wanted to hear about what Jenny had learned from Old Deborah either, and she always made fun of their Amish clothing. She used to whisper to Jenny, "As soon as I get out of here, I am giving you a makeover. The works!"

The first time that she could remember her mom getting released from jail, they moved from Old Deborah's into a halfway house. Her mom gave Jenny a short haircut and took her to a thrift shop for some new old clothes and plunked Chris and Jenny in a public school. Her mother stayed clean for a few months, but it didn't last long.

She had found some work cleaning houses for rich ladies and might have helped herself to their credit cards.

That time, her mother was sent to jail for a longer time. Something about having priors — whatever that meant. Chris and Jenny settled back comfortably at Old Deborah's. They had made friends and quickly picked up the Pennsylvania Dutch language from Old Deborah and their friends. Three years later, when their mother was released, she yanked them away from Old Deborah and set up housekeeping in a grungy apartment with cockroaches. Chris and Jenny started yet another public school, but they hated it. They felt as if they were walking a tightrope between two worlds: Amish and English. Kids made fun of them for the way they talked or mocked them because they didn't know television shows or video games. Just as they had finally made a friend or two and life was beginning to be tolerable, their mother started using drugs again. She bought some meth from an undercover police officer.

Back Chris and Jenny went to Old Deborah's.

The third time Grace Mitchell was released from jail, Old Deborah convinced her to let the children stay at the farm and keep going to the Amish school. She offered to let Grace live with them too. Jenny's mom complained the entire time that her children had been brainwashed, but Chris noted that she didn't mind eating Old Deborah's food or sleeping in a clean bed. She stayed off drugs longer that time — six whole months, but it didn't last.

Jenny wanted her mom to get out of the rehab center, but she didn't want another makeover. It took years to grow her hair out again. She liked being Amish and she doubted her mother would let her remain in the church. Chris said not to worry too much about that because he didn't expect their mother to ever stay clean.

Jenny looked around the big kitchen at Windmill Farm. She loved being here. Everything was calm and predictable. Three meals were planned for, each day. Like right now she could open the cupboard and there would be cereal, and on the counter were some apples and pears, and there was milk in the fridge. It was the nicest family Jenny had ever known, and they were all so kind to her and Chris.

There were moments, like now, when she felt an overwhelming sadness. Why couldn't she have been born a Lapp? Why couldn't she have had a mother like Fern and a father like Amos? Not fair. It just wasn't fair.

The oven timer went off and Jenny peeked inside. She thought the pies needed just a little more time, so she set the buzzer for another five minutes. She noticed Fern's coffee can by the buzzer, the one where Fern kept cash. She peeked out the window to make sure no one was coming and opened the can. So much money! There must be hundreds of dollars in that can. What would it be like to have so much money that you could keep extra stored in a coffee can? For she and Chris, it seemed money was barely in their pockets, and it was gone. *Whoosh.*

Then she saw Fern's buggy turn into the driveway. She put the lid on the coffee can and tucked it behind the timer. She hurried to the table and picked up the pencil. It was always so hard to know exactly what to say to her mom. Finally she added:

Here is a little more money. Sorry it can't be more, but I have to be careful. Love you! Jenny

P.S. I've grown so tall you won't believe it!

She smoothed out two five-dollar bills and

put them in an envelope addressed to her mom. Everybody had someone to depend on — but Jenny's mom only had Jenny. Even Chris didn't want anything to do with their mother. Taking care of her was up to Jenny.

It was one of those days that made you feel happy to be alive. On a chilly Saturday morning in mid-November,

M.K. decided it was high time to winterize the beehives. The weather this fall had been unseasonably warm. Maybe not warm, but not freezing. Still, she knew winter would arrive, fast and furious. She had spent the morning in the honey cabin, bottling the last of the season's honey. Now she covered herself with netting and prepared the smoker. As she stapled fresh tar-paper on the outside of the hives, her mind wandered to the first time she had worked with her brother-in-law, Rome, to prepare the hives. It took months before he would let her come close to the hives — he said she had to learn how to be patient before she could be a beekeeper.

Had she learned to be patient?

In some areas. Wasn't she patient with Eugene Miller's fits-and-starts path to becoming a better reader? It was a slow, slow process, but just when she thought he would never make any progress, there was a break-through. Just this week, he had joined in recitations with the rest of his class. She hadn't asked him to, but she had given him the reading assignment a few days ahead so he could prepare if he wanted to. She had been doing that for weeks now and he had always refused. But this time, he read out loud in a clear, steady voice. Nearly flaw-less. Her heart swelled with pride for him. As Eugene's confidence grew, he was far less annoying to the other children. She couldn't wait to fill Erma Yutzy in on the changes in Eugene. She only hoped that he would have the skills he needed by late May, when he would graduate. Should graduate.

Such a thought amazed her. She was actu-ally thinking about the end of the term. Wouldn't Rome be pleased? She was defi-nitely becoming a woman of patience.

She stapled the last roll of tarpaper and stood back to examine her work. It had to be perfect. The cold weather would slow the bees' activity, but they could survive by keeping the hive at a comfortable tempera-ture. These bees came from a strain of brown bees that Rome's mother had be-queathed to him, and he had bequeathed a hive to M.K.

A jolt shot through her — no one knew how to care for her bees like she did. When she thought about traveling to see a Maori village in New Zealand, she hadn't taken into consideration what would happen to her bees. How in the world could she ever leave her bees?

Jimmy Fisher finally located Hank Lapp in the weeds behind the barn. He had his hands held out in front of him, holding onto dowsing rods, gazing at the ground with intent concentration.

"Looking for water?" Jimmy asked.

Hank startled and dropped the rods. "I was," he groused.

"How do you know when you get close?"

"When I find it, the rods will move by themselves and cross in my hands."

"Let me save you some trouble," Jimmy said. He went over to the spigot and lifted the hose. "I'm pretty sure the water comes out of the faucets."

Hank scowled at him. "For your information, dowsing is a very lucrative skill."

"How so?"

"Let's say you're going to invest in a piece of land. Don't you want to know what's under the surface?"

"I'd probably hire a well company."

"But who's going to tell the well company where to dig, eh?" Hank picked up the dowsing rods, holding them lightly in his hands. In spite of the fact that the faucet and the pipes were just a few yards away, over by the barn, the rods did not jump in his hands or twitch or cross. Hank frowned.

"I just came to tell you that Bishop Elmo is over at the buggy shop. Mad as hops that his buggy isn't repaired yet." Hank threw down the dowsing rods and pinned Jimmy with a look with his one good eye. "BOY, DON'T YOU HAVE SOMEPLACE YOU NEED TO BE?"

"I do, actually. I came over to look for M.K., but Fern said she's off visiting her scholars' homes." Jimmy mulled that over. "Why would she bother to waste a perfectly good Saturday afternoon on that?"

Hank wasn't listening. His good eye was peeled on an approaching figure. Bishop Elmo had spotted him from across the yard and was heading his way.

15

In the schoolhouse, the countdown to Christmas had begun. A secret gift exchange was planned, and parents were coming for a special program. A light dusting of snow one afternoon caused the scholars' pent-up enthusiasm to explode, like a shaken can of soda. The schoolhouse nearly vibrated with excitement.

M.K. handed out poems for some of the children who volunteered to recite. Anna Mae Glick chose the longest piece to recite. She was sure she had her part down pat. M.K. wasn't as sure.

Each day, the children rehearsed Christmas carols. Day after day, the strains of a miniature heavenly host singing "Joy to the World" wafted out of the schoolhouse. M.K. scanned the ranks — the sun glinted off Danny Riehl's spectacles. Barbara Jean's grown-up front teeth were about halfway in now. She didn't whistle and spit so much when she talked, but her little tongue kept sticking out. She'd grown accustomed to Jenny Yoder's earnest, birdlike look. A well of fondness rose within M.K. for these children. Imagine that! Fondness.

And here was another unexpected surprise in the schoolhouse this Christmas season: Eugene Miller. The boy had a beautiful tenor voice. M.K. started using him as a pitch pipe — to set everyone on the right note. He would roll his eyes whenever she asked him for a G or an E flat, but then he would sit up straight and open his mouth and the exact note would float out of his mouth, right on key. He tried hard not to look pleased, but M.K. could tell he was secretly delighted. The changes she had noticed in him lately were astonishing. There were good days and bad days, but Eugene Miller was becoming a different person.

She had known Eugene all his life, but for the first time she was catching glimpses of how vulnerable he really was. For all his outward swagger, he was a hurt little boy inside, hiding his pain behind pranks and laughter.

How had she not realized? Eugene Miller was starved for attention.

■ ■ ■ ■

It was late in the day, and the day was late in the season. Winter was coming. The shadows were growing dusky. M.K. had just finished grading papers at the schoolhouse and had one more thing to do: she wanted to tape the scholars' new artwork up on the window as a surprise to them in the morning. She had pushed a desk up against the window and stood on top of it when she heard the door open and spun around to find Chris Yoder standing at the threshold.

He looked at her. "What are you doing up there?"

"Hanging pictures." Startled by his sudden appearance, she felt her face grow warm, so she reached over to smooth a piece of tape out against the window. "What are you doing here?"

"Jenny forgot a book she wanted to finish reading tonight. Which desk is hers?"

She pointed to the far desk in the back row.

Chris crossed the room, opened the desktop, and plucked a book out. "You shouldn't be teetering on a rickety desktop when you're alone in the schoolhouse. You could fall and hit your head and no one would know until morning."

She started to climb down because she had reached as far as she could on that desktop. "That's true. That's actually how my mother died."

Chris helped her down. "Then you should definitely know better." He was so tall he didn't need to stand on top of a desk. She handed him the pictures and he taped each one up, more precisely and evenly than she had been doing. He came to a picture of a snowy owl and stopped. "This should be hanging in a museum."

"I know. It was drawn by Eugene Miller. He's been my most difficult student and my most rewarding one. Both."

Chris looked at her. "Sounds like Samson as a foal. Stubborn and feisty. Every day was a challenge. But he's the one I've learned the most from." He taped Eugene's picture up on the wall. "I love that horse."

The way he said it touched M.K. She didn't know many men who would admit they loved an animal. They talked about the scholars' artwork as he continued to tape the pictures to the window. It struck her that she and Chris were actually having a conversation, getting to know each other, without any need for her to have to apologize for something stupid she had done to him. First time.

She made the mistake of looking up into his eyes, which were as blue as the sky on a clear autumn afternoon. She felt breathless, as if she were treading water and trying not to drown. *Think, think, think. Get my mind on something besides his beautiful blue eyes.* "Tell me about your family, Chris. Where did you grow up?"

A shadow passed over Chris's face. "Raised on a farm outside a town you probably never heard of."

Oh. That was it. It was as if someone had turned the lights off. She had frightened him off again. When would she ever get it right?

Silently, they worked through the last few pictures, then he handed her the tape dispenser. "Did you ever send away for a passport?"

She hesitated. He remembered that?

He read her mind. "The application you dropped that day I passed you on the road. That was *before* you turned me in to the sheriff."

Sheesh! What a memory. Would he ever let that go? "I did," she finally admitted. "It will take awhile before it arrives, though."

"Why did you want one? Are you planning a trip to Canada?"

He was gazing into her eyes, and suddenly, she lost her train of thought altogether. It took her a moment to remember the question. "Uh . . . yes. Canada. Maybe Mexico." She sighed. "Shanghai, Borneo, Istanbul, Paris. Those are just some of the places I want to go to someday. I want to see the whole world."

Chris gave a two-note whistle, one up, one down. "Why?"

Why? "Because . . ." Why? Why? "Because it's exciting. And interesting. And fascinating to see other places. Other people and other cultures." There. That was why.

No. That wasn't why. She had a restive search going on inside of her. She wanted to discover someplace that made her say, "This is it! This is what I've been looking for."

The sound was so faint she couldn't be sure, but she suddenly realized that she was saying these thoughts out loud. She wondered if she might be losing her mind. It was entirely possible. She blamed teaching. Too overwhelming. She hoped it was getting too dark in the schoolhouse for Chris to notice her flushed cheeks.

He smiled. A genuine one. He wasn't laughing at her. "My grandmother would have answered that in a hurry."

"What would she have said?"

He picked the book up from Jenny's desk. "She would have said there's nothing out there that isn't right under your nose." He started toward the door.

"What would you be, if you weren't born Amish?" she blurted, suddenly wanting him to stay.

"I'd be doing exactly what I'm doing right now."

"And what is that?"

"Fixing up a house. Planning to start a horse breeding farm on Samson's fine lineage. Hoping for a farm of my own one day." He stopped and glanced at her. "And if I weren't born Amish, I'd become Amish."

One thing about Chris Yoder — he was not one to linger. He started toward the door again, so she grabbed her sweater and keys to follow him out.

"So if things were different, if you weren't born Amish, and you could be anything in the world, what would you be?"

"I suppose . . ." Should she tell him? This was her deepest secret, after all. "I suppose I would be . . . a detective."

He groaned. "That should put fear in the hearts of all criminals."

"I would love to solve mysteries and help catch criminals. Though," she glanced at him, "I suppose there are some who think my reputation as a detective might not have gotten off to a very good start."

He guffawed. "Might not have?"

She gave him a playful punch on his arm and he ducked away, but it caused her to miss a step on the porch and she lost her balance. He reached out to steady her and somehow ended up with his hands around her waist. She put her hands up against his chest — her face was so close to his that she could even smell the pine soap he showered with — and before she thought twice, she closed her eyes and lifted her chin, expecting him to kiss her.

Nothing. Nothing happened.

When she blinked her eyes open, he was looking at her strangely, as if she might be a little sun touched. He released his hands from her waist as if she were a hot potato. He moved backward one step and held up Jenny's book.

"I got what I came for. So . . . uh . . . so long." He swiveled on his heels and walked away.

Oh. *Oh.* She felt a massive disappointment. Massive.

Jimmy Fisher had two serious things weighing on his mind, and that was unusual for him. First, he needed to find a way to convince Chris Yoder to loan Samson to him for a quick lap or two around Domino Joe's racetrack. Second, he needed to convince M.K. Lapp that she loved him.

First things first. He had done everything — dropped hints, offered to barter — everything but ask Chris outright for the use of Samson. He didn't know Yoder all that well, and he was one of those guys who kept his cards close to his vest. That was an expression Jimmy had picked up on the racetracks and liked to use. In the right company, of course. Never around his mother. But there was something about Chris's manner that made Jimmy hesitate to ask to borrow Samson. That, and he could probably beat Jimmy to a jelly if he took a notion to.

Today, he stopped by Chris's house with the intention of directing the conversation to the temporary loan of Samson. Somehow, he ended up helping Chris patch shingles on the roof before winter arrived. Chris was up on the roof, bareheaded and without a coat, though there was a bitter wind. He was muscled like a bull, tight as a tree. One after another, in a couple of mighty blows, Chris drove the nails into the shingles. Jimmy tried to keep up and finally just became Chris's assistant — handing him nails and shingles as he needed them.

Jimmy kept getting close to the topic of Samson, but Chris was preoccupied with how many more shingles he needed and didn't pay him any mind. That was the way it went with Chris. If he didn't want to answer your question, he'd just pretend you hadn't said anything.

Finally, Jimmy just came out with it. "Chris, I just need Samson one time. Just one little race. Half a day, and he'll be back in the barn. Or . . . garage. Whatever you call it."

Chris was on the other side of the roof peak, peering down at the front of the house.

"One time, Chris. That's all I'm asking for. I'm an expert horseman. You can have complete confidence in me." Still, Chris ignored him. Or maybe he couldn't hear him?

Jimmy climbed to the peak to see what Chris was staring at. M.K. Lapp had driven up in the buggy with Cayenne. Jenny climbed out of the buggy and M.K. leaned out the window to hand a pie basket to her. M.K. looked up at the roof and gave a small wave with her hand. "We brought some extra apple pies!" she shouted up to Chris

311

and Jimmy after she climbed out of the buggy. "Come down and try a slice while it's still warm!"

M.K.'s timing couldn't have been worse. Jimmy needed to nail down borrowing Samson with Chris. Now. No distractions, even for Fern's apple pie and the girl who was destined to be his future missus. Time was running out. "So, what do you say?"

"Sure, whatever," Chris said absently, watching M.K. cross to the house, and the way she gathered her skirts. "I sure do like apple pie. I sure do."

That was a yes, Jimmy concluded.

M.K. rode better than a mile in silence. Her chin was set and she gripped the reins. For the last two weeks, she had taken Erma's advice and made a point to visit each of her pupils at their home. It was amazing what layers of understanding she had uncovered, even though she had known these families all her life.

Barbara Jean's mother seemed to be in very low spirits since this new baby had been born. She seemed frail and unhappy and overwhelmed. No wonder Barbara Jean constantly worried about her mother. M.K. was going to ask her sister Sadie to go fix her up with one of those teas or remedies she concocted. Sadie was good at helping new moms get over the blues.

Here was another thing that surprised M.K.: she had known that Anna Mae was an only child, but she never thought much about it. As she sat in the kitchen of the Glicks' home, she noticed that everything revolved around Anna Mae. M.K. was the youngest in the Lapp family, and nothing had ever revolved around her. Nothing. Not ever.

The Glicks had invited M.K. to stay for dinner, which she did, and ate a meal that was customized to suit Anna Mae's peculiar tastes. Everything was beige because Anna Mae didn't like to eat things with too much color or texture: meatloaf without onions, white bread, mashed potatoes. No vegetables or fruit because she didn't like them. Even the chocolate cookies didn't have walnuts, because Anna Mae thought walnuts tasted yucky.

On the way home from the Glicks', M.K. had two thoughts. One: what in the world would Fern have done with a child like Anna Mae? And two: Danny Riehl had better watch out — because Anne Mae Glick was a girl who got what she wanted. And she wanted Danny Riehl.

The last pupil to visit was Eugene Miller.

She had held it off as long as possible. Dread swept her as she turned Cayenne into the long lane that led to the Millers'. She smelled the farm before it ever came into view: pigs. The smell watered her eyes. She had a fondness for most animals, but she took exception to pigs.

The house was in worse shape than the barn. M.K. turned Cayenne to the hitching post by the never-shoveled-out barn and climbed down out of the buggy. She made her way gingerly to the house — everyone knew you wanted to be careful where you stepped around the Miller farm. The only time it was mildly cleaned up was when it was the Millers' turn to host Sunday church, once a year. Deacon Abraham would ask for a work frolic for the Millers, two Sundays before they were due to host church, and there was always a quiet shuffling in the seats as people were loathe to volunteer. Finally, Amos would raise his hand and others would follow suit.

M.K. knocked on the door but no one answered. She turned around and shielded her eyes from the sun, and then she saw Eugene crossing over from the barn, a pitchfork in his hand.

"Why are you here?" he hissed as he approached her.

"I've been visiting everyone's home, Eugene. I just wanted —"

The door opened then and a large, grim-looking man appeared. Eugene's father. His dark mean eyes shifted from Eugene to M.K. and back to Eugene. "What do you want?"

"Good afternoon." M.K. tried to make her voice sound casual.

"Daddy, she's my teacher," Eugene said.

Could she have heard him right? Did M.K. hear the word "daddy" coming out of the usually sneering lips of Eugene Miller?

He pointed to Eugene. "Is he giving you any trouble?"

M.K. glanced at Eugene, who had lost all color in his face. He seemed to shrink the closer he got to his father. "No. No trouble at all." She turned back to Eugene's father and said, rather primly, as she smoothed the wrinkles of her dress, "I just wanted to stop by and say hello. To let you know that Eugene has been a real . . . pleasure . . . to have in the classroom."

Eugene's father looked suspicious. "He's not the sharpest tool in the shed."

M.K. looked at Eugene and felt a wave of pity for him. "I think he's one of the smartest eighth graders I've ever taught."

Eugene's father lifted a bushy eyebrow.

"Ain't you new at teaching?"

She pulled out a manila folder. "I thought you might want this." She handed him the drawing of the snowy owl. "Eugene drew this. Isn't it wonderful?" She wasn't quite sure her voice carried a seasoned teacher-authority as she wanted it to, but she did the best she could under the circumstances.

Eugene's father squinted his eyes at the drawing. He grunted, gave Eugene the once-over, then, to M.K.'s horror, he wadded it up into a ball and tossed it on the ground. "That's how you'll give the boy a big head." He turned to go back into the house, stopping at the threshold to point at Eugene. "Get back out to the field with your brothers. Farms don't run themselves." He shut the door behind him, muttering something about "Just useless."

M.K. bent down to pick up the drawing and smooth it out.

Eugene clenched his jaw.

"I'm so sorry," she said. She saw a glassy sheen in his eyes.

He spat out an unrepeatable word before running out to the field.

Chris woke up one morning to a silent world. No birdsong, no wind rattling the windows. Groggily he lay there, wondering why he felt as if his ears were stuffed with cotton. The strange grayish light that filtered through the window slowly registered on him. The world outside was covered with a blanket of snow.

During breakfast, Jenny complained bitterly about the snow. "That schoolhouse is going to be freezing."

"There's a heater in there," Chris said. "A big thing. It should warm that room up quick."

"Teacher M.K. doesn't use it," Jenny said sourly. "She says it's good for our brains to be slightly chilled." She shivered. "My fingers are so cold in that room that I can't even hold a pencil."

Chris thought about that for a while as he ate his watery oatmeal. Jenny had been complaining about the chill in the schoolroom for a few weeks now, ever since the weather had turned brisk. Why wouldn't Mary Kate use the heater? Then it dawned on him. Of course! He bolted from his chair and grabbed his coat and hat from the wall peg. "I've got to go. I've already fed Samson. Turn him into the paddock before you leave for school."

As he hurried down the street to the schoolhouse, he found himself grinning. He loved the first real snowfall of the year, damp and clinging, like winter was trying to decide if it was ready to come yet. He picked up his pace when he saw a small black-bonneted figure down the road. He broke into a jog.

"You know, Jenny has been complaining about the temperature in the schoolhouse lately," he said when he caught up with Mary Kate. "But I told her just to wear an extra sweater or two. That her teacher must be feeling the need to save coal."

M.K.'s cheeks were red from the cold air and her brown eyes were snapping. "Absolutely. It's important for the children to learn to be frugal."

"Then she started wearing mittens all day, and scarves and ear muffs. Then she asked to borrow my coat. I told her that her teacher must have a pretty good reason to keep the schoolhouse well chilled."

"Well, the theory is that cold helps to keep them awake. Especially the big boys."

"Or maybe . . . the teacher doesn't know how to get the heater started."

Mary Kate stopped short, opened her mouth to say something. Snapped it shut. She looked up at him with those dark-fringed eyes. "Maybe I forgot to pay attention when Orin Stoltzfus was giving me his lengthy tutorial on the fussy heater." She cringed. "Oh Chris, I have tried to get it started every morning for two weeks now! I just can't make it work." She frowned. "The truth is, I think this heater has it in for me."

He laughed, and then she laughed. "Why didn't you just say something to someone?"

"I did ask Jimmy Fisher for help and he promised to stop by, but that hasn't happened yet."

"Why didn't you just ask your dad? Or your uncle Hank?"

She frowned. "Fern is forever telling me to solve my problems by myself. I nearly asked Uncle Hank, but he has a tendency to make problems worse. Yesterday I thought I had it figured out at last. Then it blew up and sputtered coal dust at me. Ruined my apron. And today, I wake up to find snow!"

They were at the schoolhouse now. Mary Kate unlocked the door and Chris went right to work. It was a temperamental old coal heater, he had to admit. But it wasn't too different a model from Old Deborah's old heater. Soon, he had a small fire started in the base of the heater, added coal, and it wasn't long before the chill in the air tapered off. Just in time too. He heard the sounds of children arriving.

Mary Kate was staring out the window, stunned. Chris came up behind her to gaze at the schoolhouse scene. Whoops and squeals, snowballs firing through the air, exploding on the back of one child or another, laughter as bright as sleigh bells. Excellent snowball fighting weather. He grinned, wondering how Mary Kate would adjust to the classroom climate today. The first snow substantially altered the environment. Boys would be chomping at the bit to stampede their way outside for recess. Remembering his own school years, it wasn't long before there was as much snow being flung through the air as was resting on the ground. An all-out free-for-all.

"Well," he said, "I could help you with the heater, but that, out there, is all yours." He grinned and turned to go.

He was practically to the door when she called out, "How did you know that I didn't have any idea how to work the heater?"

He shrugged. "Wasn't hard to figure out." He rolled that over in his mind as he walked down the lane to turn onto Windmill Farm's drive. It occurred to him that he was starting to understand the illogical logic of Mary Kate Lapp. The first few times he met her, he tried to follow her line of thinking and was often left pawing the air. Why was she starting to make sense to him?

Lately, thoughts of Mary Kate Lapp rose

up time and again. He tried to kick her image aside the way he might scoot a cat out from underfoot, but back it came, silently slinking in. All he could think of were those eyes. Those deep, brown, lovely eyes.

Whenever his thoughts drifted toward Mary Kate, a sense of well-being sneaked up on Chris, which he normally only experienced after a hard day's work, when he was too tired to think straight.

Such a feeling worried him. And pleased him too. Both.

16

That first snowfall was just a tease of winter's coming, but Chris stopped by the schoolhouse every single morning to help M.K. start the heater. She thought she had a pretty good handle on it after watching him work that first morning, but she decided not to share that particular revelation with him. She liked having him there. Each morning, they would talk a little. He loved hearing stories about the scholars. A few times, he even laughed out loud.

Little by little, M.K. was discovering more about Chris Yoder. He fascinated her. Ever since that first predawn conference when he helped her start the coal heater, several days ago now, it seemed natural to be together. They met early on the way to the schoolhouse, talking as they walked, their breath puffs of fog. It intrigued her that as Chris went about the business of firing up the heater, his experiences seeped from him,

322

episode by episode, as if they wanted out. But if she asked anything, he clammed up. Door shut. Conversation over.

So she *was* learning to be patient. Wouldn't Rome be proud of her? Wouldn't he be amazed? Mary Kate Lapp, starting to be patient. Learning to wait for a person to choose to share his past, in his time, rather than going after that information with reckless abandon, like she usually did. She was very pleased with herself. And those early morning moments with Chris were becoming her favorite of the day.

Late on Friday afternoon, she was wiping down the chalkboard. She heard her name. She turned and there he was. Chris, alone, standing by the door in front of the cloakroom. He had a smile that hitched up on one side. That smile of his, especially when it reached his eyes and made them crinkle in that way, it made her stomach do a flip-flop.

"Jenny left her lunch Igloo." He lifted it up. "Didn't want to leave it here over the weekend."

M.K. tossed the chalk rag on her desk and walked to him. "I was just finishing for the day." She grabbed her coat and bonnet off the wall peg in case he was in a hurry to leave, as he often was. But he wasn't. He held the door for her and stayed on the school porch, waiting for her to lock up. Something was on his mind. By now, she knew not to press him.

"I wondered if . . . maybe . . . next time there's a decent snowfall, maybe you'd like to go on a sled ride with Samson. I'd need to borrow your dad's sled, though." His cheeks flamed and he looked down at his feet, kicking a loose board with his boot top.

"Yes!" It burst out of her.

Chris's head snapped up. "Really? I mean, uh, good." His eyes crinkled into a smile.

Oh, there was that smile again. She thought for sure her knees were going to go right out from under her. A quiet spun out between them.

The most wonderful surprise happened next. *Don't breathe,* she thought. *Don't move.* Chris bent down to lightly graze her lips with his. Just a featherlight kiss. Her first.

Amos Lapp had gone to the schoolhouse phone shanty to see if there were any messages, and to place a call to his eldest daughter, Julia, who lived in Berlin, Ohio. Communication required patience — he would leave a message for her, and when she had time to check messages, she would return the call by leaving a message back for him. They were planning to head out to Ohio for Christmas to visit Julia and Rome and their four boys.

While they were there, they would take some time to visit little Joe-Jo, the child of his now-in-heaven son, Menno. Joe-Jo lived with his mother, Annie, in a Swartzentruber colony not too far from Berlin. Imagine that, Amos thought, pleased. Counting Sadie's two little ones, he had six grandsons and one granddaughter. Could a man ask for any greater gift? And he had a sneaking suspicion that it wouldn't be long before M.K. and Jimmy Fisher married. Seemed like that boy was at Windmill Farm on a daily basis. Perhaps Amos would have a dozen grandchildren before long. An even dozen!

Fern had a long list of things she had started for the trip and more than a few questions for Julia. He grinned — he never knew anyone who liked to make plans like his list-making wife. Except for Julia. She was like Fern in that way, wanting everything to be orderly.

He left Fern's questions for Julia on the message machine and closed the shanty door. It was getting dark — that gloaming hour of the day. As he turned the corner and came around the front of the schoolhouse, he stopped abruptly. There, on the school porch, was an Amish couple, kissing. He turned like a top and hurried back to the shanty to think things over.

He was uncertain of what he was supposed to do — he needed to pass in front of the schoolhouse to get home. He wished Fern were with him. What would she do? She would probably think it was appalling — to think of a young couple kissing out in public like that, though he had to admit he had done plenty of public kissing when he was a teenager.

But that was different. That was long before he had daughters. He had a different perspective on affection after he became a father of teenaged daughters. He knew what was on the mind of a boy. It occurred to him that he would be doing that girl's father a favor if he interrupted the couple right now. Better if he was the one to interrupt them than the bishop or ministers. Or imagine if Edith Fisher happened along! He was going to have to tap the boy on his shoulder and send him on his way.

Wait a moment. He suddenly realized something. The girl on that porch wasn't just any girl. He recognized that turquoise blue dress. Mary Kate had one just like it. She had worn it this very day. That girl *was*

Mary Kate! A sick feeling came over Amos. That wasn't Jimmy Fisher she was kissing. This boy was too tall to be Jimmy Fisher. If he wasn't mistaken, that boy's thatch of blond hair belonged to . . . Chris Yoder.

Shocked and distressed, Amos had to sit down on the little stool. When had this romance begun? How could this have happened? This was terrible, terrible news. Of all the boys in Stoney Ridge, how could his little girl be involved with Chris Yoder? Should he fire Chris on the spot? Definitely. He definitely was going to fire him.

He took a deep breath, opened the shanty door, gathered every indignant bone in his body, and marched to the front of the schoolhouse to confront them.

But there was no one there.

HI JENNY GIRL!

Your momma is sure proud of you for getting so much money to me. You must be working really hard. What are you doing to get so much dough? Baking a lot of pies, huh? Ha!

I've got some AWESOME news! But, ssshhhh! baby, you got to keep this secret from Chris. I want to surprise him. They're letting me out of this crummy joint early cuz I'm clean! Clean as a whistle.

I want you to be here when I get out. You could take the bus, meet me, and we could surprise Chris together back in Stoney Ridge! It'll be the three of us, together again, for Christmas. This time it'll be different, Jenny. I promise. I'll stay clean. You know your momma is the only one you can depend on. Promise me you'll come, okay? Tuesday, December 23rd, 11:30 a.m. SHARP. DON'T LET ME DOWN! And remember: this is top secret! I'm counting on you!

For a long time, Jenny sat right there without moving, feeling a weird hollowness in her chest, like all her air had been sucked out. When she took a breath, it didn't go away. She didn't want to go to Marysville all by herself. She didn't think Chris would be at all happy to have his mother arrive in Stoney Ridge as a Christmas surprise. But how sad for her mother — to not have anyone waiting for her when she got out of rehab. To not have anywhere to go for Christmas.

Jenny's hands were shaking as she read through the note a second time. And then she began to make a plan.

■ ■ ■ ■

M.K. heard someone call her name and looked up to locate the voice.

"Mary Kate!" Chris Yoder stood at a distance and waved to her. "I'm not coming any closer to those bees."

Her heart lifted like a balloon. She was repairing a loose piece of tarpaper that the wind in yesterday's storm had ripped off. The bees needed her, but this could wait. For Chris, they could wait. She put the staple gun down and set the smoker aimed at the beehives before she walked over to him. She hadn't seen Chris since that kiss at the schoolhouse last Friday and she felt giddy with anticipation. It was never far from her mind, that kiss. That sweet, tender, wonderful kiss.

She had woken in the night and relived it, over and over again. His lips had touched hers, as softly as a butterfly landing, and rested there for a moment before he moved closer and his mouth seemed to melt into hers. His arms slid around her waist and she felt the stubble of his chin as his face brushed against hers. The sensation was the most amazing, terrifying, wonderful, frightening one she had ever felt. All of it — the feel of his strong arms around her, his sturdy body next to hers, the way he breathed, the way he smelled. As his warm lips brushed against hers, she decided that a kiss was the most wonderful sensation in the world. It started where his tender lips joined hers and traveled slowly through her like a wave of warm water. That kiss was a moment in her memory that went on forever and ended too soon. M.K. finally understood why her friend Ruthie liked to kiss so much. Now M.K. got it.

She thought a lightning bolt had struck her, and she thought it was love.

She was glad she had the netting over her face as she walked toward Chris. M.K. was beaming. Beaming!

But something was wrong. Chris looked upset. "Do you know of any reason why your dad would fire me?"

"Fire you? What did he say?"

Chris looked past her to the hives. "He said there wasn't any more work to do at Windmill Farm for the winter." He looked back at her. "It wasn't long ago that he talked about all kinds of things he wanted me to do for him this winter. He even talked about expanding the Salad Stall with some winter crops — kale and cabbage. Did something happen? Could he be worried about paying me?"

"Not that I know of." Her father didn't share any financial problems with her. That never stopped M.K. from eavesdropping, but she hadn't overheard her dad and Fern talking about money lately. In fact, if anything, her father seemed awfully quiet lately. Quieter than usual.

Chris frowned. "You didn't say anything about . . . what happened between us at the schoolhouse, did you?"

"Of course not!" Did he think she was crazy?

He turned to leave, then turned back. He gave her a long, lingering look, like he was memorizing her face. "Look, about that. I apologize. It should never have happened. It won't happen again."

Why won't it happen again? M.K. thought, watching him stride down the hill. *Why not?*

Maybe getting fired was a blessing in disguise. Chris had been letting his guard down. He should stick to the plan — fix up the house, start looking for the right mares to breed with Samson. That's what brought him here — that was his grandfather's gift to him. A fresh beginning.

He would be twenty-one in six weeks. Then, he would feel safe. He would have

331

kept his unspoken promise to his grand-father. He would have provided for his and Jenny's future.

It was the Lapp family that was starting to get to him — each one of them. Fern and Jenny were thick as thieves. Jenny was act-ing more and more like Fern. Baking bread, fussing over a clean kitchen, ironing his shirts with so much starch that they could stand up by themselves. It was preposter-ous.

And Amos? Over the months of working for Amos Lapp, Chris had developed a great admiration for the man. Amos had always been fair with him. He possessed a natural business sense that Chris respected. More than a few times, Chris had thought that Amos was the kind of father he wished he'd had. Caring, calm, kind, wise. There had been a subtle change in the way Amos treated Chris. He used to work beside Chris. For the last few weeks, he would start Chris on a task and leave him to complete it. Or he would send him off to work for Hank in the buggy shop. Chris thought Amos might not be feeling well, that maybe his heart was acting up. He didn't know much about Amos's heart problem, but he did see all those pills he took at meals.

At least, that was what Chris had assumed

about Amos's cool treatment — up until thirty minutes ago, when he had been abruptly and inexplicably dismissed. For no apparent reason.

Chris felt like he'd had the wind kicked out of him. He racked his brain and couldn't think of anything he might have done wrong. He had no idea what had gotten into Amos. The only thing he could come up with was that kiss. Maybe Mary Kate had told him. But she looked stunned when he mentioned it, and she wore her thoughts on her face. If she were lying, he would have known.

Then there was Mary Kate. He had to get *that* girl off his mind. Kissing her like he did the other night — it shocked him. Where did that kiss come from? One minute they were talking, the next . . . he had leaned over to kiss her. He had always prided himself on his self-control with girls. He noticed women on occasion. What fellow didn't? But with discipline, he always guided his focus away. Something not as easily done with Mary Kate Lapp.

He wasn't like some of his friends from Ohio, who talked about girls constantly and, given the opportunity, could barely keep their hands off them. What was happening to him?

But he knew. He knew. He really was totally and hopelessly smitten with this girl. This had to stop. This wouldn't last. He had to keep remembering that. *This. Will. Not. Last.*

Maybe all this was a good reminder. Chris's only true family was with Jenny. That was the one person — the only person — he needed to take care of.

Chris passed by Hank's buggy shop to walk down the driveway. As soon as he realized Bishop Elmo was involved in a deep conversation with Hank over the state of his buggy, he veered away from the shop.

Normally a lighthearted, softspoken man, Elmo sounded exasperated. "You haven't made a lick of progress on fixing this buggy, Hank Lapp!"

Hank was shocked. "I've been utterly swamped!"

"Swamped, eh?" Elmo's hands were on his hips.

Chris tried to make himself invisible, but those yellow puppies spotted him and charged happily toward him, barking and yipping. Elmo turned to see what the commotion was all about.

Too late.

"Chris Yoder! Come over here."

Chris crossed over to the bishop, puppies

tangled at his feet.

"Hank said you've been giving him a lot of help around here. Seems like Stoney Ridge could use another buggy shop. Hank is going to volunteer to teach you everything he knows about buggy repair."

"I am?" Hank asked.

"And when he's done sharing all of that vast knowledge, you are going to open up a buggy shop."

"I am?" Chris asked. He felt a shiver of dread run down his spine.

"You are." Bishop Elmo popped his black felt hat back on his bald head. He pointed to his buggy, up on blocks. "Starting with that one. I need that before Christmas. My wife's entire family is coming to visit." Then he marched across the driveway to his waiting horse and buggy. "Before Christmas!" he called out, as he slapped the reins on the horse and it lunged forward. "You have one week!"

Chris looked at Hank, shocked. "What in the world just happened?"

Hank was at an unusual loss for words. Hands hooked on his hips, he crinkled his wide forehead in confusion as he watched the bishop drive away. "There is one thing I have learned in my life. Don't waste your time arguing with a bishop." He

335

tossed a wrench to Chris. "So, boy, let's get to work."

After supper, Amos went out to his favorite spot on a hill, overlooking the orchards, to watch the sun set. It was a habit he had when he needed reminding that God was sovereign, that he held the world in his hands. Amos stood watching, arms crossed against his chest, as the sun dipped below the horizon. How many times had he stood in this same spot when the sorrows of life overwhelmed him?

As his gaze shifted from the sun to the first sign of the North Star, he realized Fern had followed him and stood beside him. "That might have been the quietest meal we've ever had. Hank is bothered with Elmo for making Chris his apprentice. Mary Kate is bothered with you for letting Chris go. I'm bothered with all of you. Mind telling me why you told Chris you didn't need his help anymore?"

Amos glanced at her. His dilemma bounced back and forth across his brain like a volleyball in a match. *Tell her. Don't tell her. Tell her. Don't tell her.*

"Something's eating at you," she said. "It has been for a while now. Weeks."

He kept his eyes on the star.

"Is your heart giving you any trouble? Did the doctor tell you something at your last checkup that you didn't tell me —"

"No," he interrupted. "My heart's not the problem. Not in the way that you mean."

A long silence spun out between them. Finally, Fern sighed. "I can't read your mind, Amos."

He turned and gave her a sad smile. "Sometimes, I think you can."

17

Jenny jerked awake from a dreamless sleep and sat straight up, blinking, trying to gather information as fast as possible. Where was she? Was she late for school?

No. She was on a bus to Columbus, Ohio. Once there, she would catch another bus to get to Marysville, and then a city bus to meet her mother. She had sneaked out of the house before dawn and left a note for Chris:

> Needed at the schoolhouse early. After school too. Don't worry if I'm late. Lots to do.

It was tricky getting a bus ticket, since the woman behind the counter said she needed an adult to buy it for her. So Jenny lied. She *lied.* Her first lie ever — no, wait. It was her second one. She had lied to Chris in the note she left him. She wasn't proud of it.

She told the ticket lady that she looked small but she was actually over eighteen. She said she had a genetic disease that kept her from growing like a normal person. She said it was a common ailment among the Amish and the ticket lady's eyes softened. Then she sold Jenny a ticket for forty-one dollars and told her to be extra careful.

As Jenny settled into the seat by the window, she felt like crying and didn't know why. The bus was quiet and a toddler in the back row with his mother fussed a little. It seemed like the loneliest place in the world. She wanted to be home, making soupy Cream of Wheat for her brother. She wanted to bake bread with Fern after school. She looked forward to being with Fern all day long, every day. Her stomach twisted in hunger as she thought of the smell of baking bread. Was there any better smell in the entire world?

Why did she do this? What was she thinking? Jenny felt that tangle of anxiety and sorrow and relief that always came up when she thought about her mother.

Get off the bus and go home, said a voice in her head. *Home.* Windmill Farm came to mind as she mulled over the word. That was how she felt when she was baking in the kitchen with Fern. She was thirteen years old and she felt she had found what she'd always wanted, even without knowing that she wanted it. She was home.

That was Jenny's state of mind as the bus rumbled along the freeway, passing on a rusty bridge over a winding river as it headed through West Virginia, then another bridge as it sped into Ohio. Every mile, pulling her farther and farther from Stoney Ridge. Tears choked her. She pressed her fist really hard against the bottom of her jaw to keep from crying.

But then she thought about her mom, who was counting on her to be there when she was released today. Her mom had been clean for a while now, so she would be in good shape. She wouldn't be a bundle of raw nerves. Maybe, at least for Christmas Day, her mother wouldn't say mean things to Chris. Jenny didn't know how her brother stood it — but Chris never fought back. He just quietly absorbed the awful things their mother said to him. That his birth had ruined her life. That Chris was stupid, just like his father, even though Grace often admitted she had hardly known the man. That Chris was a hypocrite — joining the Amish church was just his way to get back at her.

She didn't say such horrible things to

Jenny. Only to Chris. She even talked about Jenny's absentee father in a nice way. "He works for the government, top secret stuff, so he can't let anyone know about us. But someday, he'll be back for us," she would tell Jenny. Or, if Jenny complained about her height, she would say, "Your dad isn't very tall, either. Good things come in small packages."

It didn't make any sense to Jenny. She had never known her father. Chris had never known his. Both men had gone missing long before their babies were born. She liked to hear those stories about her CIA father, but she knew they probably weren't true. Maybe, but probably not. She hated to hear how her mother talked about Chris's father. Her mother had a nickname for him: W.B. Why Bother.

Chris never defended himself, never said a word back to their mother. Somehow, his steadfast calm made her even more angry.

Sometimes, Jenny wished Chris would go ahead and argue back, tell their mom to stop. She had admitted as much to Old Deborah once. Old Deborah had cupped her liver-spotted hands around Jenny's small face. "Years ago, your brother read something from the Bible that spoke to him and settled deep. Something Jesus had said.

From Matthew 10:16." Then she closed her eyes, as if she were reading the words in her head. " 'Behold, I send you forth as sheep in the midst of wolves: be ye therefore wise as serpents, and harmless as doves.' " Old Deborah explained that Chris was wise enough to know that words were like tools. "Your mother uses her tools to tear down. Chris uses his tools to repair and fix up."

Her brother amazed her. Every single day, he amazed her. So kind, so faithful, so determined to live a better life, to be a better person, to build new memories.

Despite everything, despite how confused she felt, it was her mother whom Jenny couldn't stop thinking about. Her mother needed her. She should be there when her mother was released from rehab.

When the bus pulled into Marysville, Jenny hurried to the bathroom and washed her face. She was hungry but didn't want to miss the city bus that would travel to her mom's rehab center. She had brought all of the money she had earned by working for Fern — nearly one hundred dollars. She had visited her mom at this rehab center before, so she went to the right bus, paid the fare, climbed aboard, and sat down. Without Old Deborah beside her, the city felt especially lonely.

Why was she doing this? What was she thinking? Why didn't she tell Chris about this plan? He would know what to do. If Jenny had only talked to him about it, they could have figured out what to do together. Why did her mother want this to be such a big surprise? Suddenly, the bus came to a stop a block away from the rehab center and she jumped up. This was it. She was here. She had come this far. She might as well see it through. Jenny felt sick to her stomach. She knew this was the stupidest idea she ever had, but her mom needed her. She had to remember that.

At the rehab center, she sat for a long time in the dimly lit waiting room. Finally, the receptionist at the desk called her name. A door buzzed, then opened, and suddenly the room filled up with her mom.

"JENNY!" her mother yelled.

For a fleeting second, the sound reminded Jenny of the booming way Uncle Hank would enter a room and everyone would cringe.

But when Jenny saw how much healthier her mom appeared, her whole being came to rest and she was glad she had come. She jumped up to cross the room and hug her. "Mom!"

Her mother smelled like cigarettes and shampoo. Her arms were strong, and she had gained weight. Even her hair looked shiny.

"You've grown half a foot since I saw you last!" her mother said, pulling back to look at her.

"One-and-a-half inches," Jenny said, laughing. "Can you believe it?"

Grace stepped back to look Jenny up and down, holding on to her hands. "You look so beautiful! Even in that kooky get-up."

Jenny ignored that. "So do you, Mom." It was true. Her mom's face didn't have open sores anymore, and her shiny hair was pulled back into a tidy ponytail.

Grace looked at the clock on the wall. "Let's get out of here! Let's go to Mc-Donald's and get us a Big Mac. I've had a craving for one for months and months."

They walked down the street to Mc-Donald's. Jenny took her wallet out of her backpack and saw her mother's eyebrows lift in surprise when she pulled a twenty from it to pay the cashier. They went outside and sat on a bench in the sunshine. It was chilly, but the sun felt good.

Her mom wolfed down the Big Mac and then ate half of Jenny's. As she sipped on her giant soda, Jenny felt so happy to see her mom's healthy appetite. When her mom was doing drugs, she didn't care about eating. After her mom polished off the french fries, she took a cigarette out and lit it, blowing smoke away from Jenny. She smoked restlessly, her eyes constantly glancing at her wristwatch.

When she finished one cigarette, she lit a new one from the butt, then tossed the butt on the ground and stamped it out with her shoe. When she saw Jenny's frown, she said, "I'm cutting back. There's just not much else to do but smoke in there. Gotta do something with my hands." Her mother looked uneasy. "We need to catch that bus pretty soon."

"It's only 12:30. The bus to Columbus leaves at 1:00. We have just enough time. If everything goes according to plan, we'll be home by dinnertime. Chris will be worried if I'm not back before he gets home from work."

"Chris was born worrying." Grace flicked the ashes off her cigarette. "He thinks he does a better job raising you than I do. He thinks he's better than me." She took a long drag on her cigarette, blowing smoke away from Jenny but looking at her hard. "But he's not."

Jenny tensed, like she always did when her

mother criticized Chris. Things had been going so well since her mom had left the center, a full twenty minutes without any digs about Chris. She desperately wanted this Christmas to be different. Her mom had promised. "He's been working really hard on the house, Mom. He works a full day job, then he comes home and fixes the house up till almost midnight. Starts all over again the next day. The house is looking great too. The yard is all cleaned up now and he patched the roof so it stopped leaking and he fixed broken windows so bats can't fly in."

Grace looked pleased. Very, very pleased. "Bet Rodney the Realtor is licking his chops."

Jenny's head snapped up. "How do you know about him?"

Grace kept her eyes fixed on a grease spot on the picnic bench. "You must have mentioned him in a letter."

Jenny couldn't remember mentioning Rodney Gladstone in any letter to her mother. Had she? Her mind skimmed through the different letters she wrote to her mother —

"We should get going if we want to catch that bus." Grace looked at her wristwatch again.

Jenny suddenly felt the effects of the giant soda she drank and needed to go to the bathroom. Really bad. "I'm just going to zip into McDonald's and go to the bathroom before we leave."

Her mother reached across the table and squeezed Jenny's hand. She smiled at her, her eyes softening with affection. "Take all the time you need, sweet girl."

Jenny smiled. She loved when her mom called her "sweet girl." That tense moment had passed and her mother was being kind again. Jenny was glad she had come. She had missed her mom. Everything was going to be all right. They were finally going to be a real family. Pretty normal. As close to normal as they could get. "I'll be right back."

In the bathroom, Jenny washed her hands and thought about Chris. By now, Chris might have figured out that she had left town. She hoped he wouldn't be too angry. She hoped he would see what she knew to be true — this time it would be different. Their mom was finally well. She took a paper towel to dry her hands, then carefully used it to open the door handle and avoid germs, the way Fern had taught her. When she stepped outside, she stopped in the bright glare of the winter sun, puzzled. Her breath snagged. A ripple of fear started in her toes and ended in her forehead.

Her mother was gone.

And so was Jenny's backpack.

Since Chris was no longer needed — or wanted — at Windmill Farm, he was back to finding odd jobs at the bulletin board at the hardware store. He had spent the day cleaning the garage of an English couple. He couldn't believe how much junk they had stored away, like chipmunks. He didn't tell them that, though. After work, he stopped by the hardware store again and was disappointed that there were no new jobs posted. The holidays, he figured. Everyone was busy with family. Everyone except those who had no family. He wasn't sure what he and Jenny would do for Christmas. Jimmy Fisher had invited them over for Christmas dinner, but Edith Fisher was a little terrifying. Erma Yutzy had invited them to her granddaughter's house. Maybe they would accept Erma's invitation.

It was Windmill Farm, though, where he and Jenny wanted to be for the day. Fat chance of that.

Chris stopped at the mailbox on his way to the house. He removed his black felt hat and hooked it on the peg by the door. In the kitchen, he tossed the pile of mail on the countertop and washed up at the kitchen sink. He thought Jenny would be home from the schoolhouse by now. He guessed the big project she was working on had something to do with the Christmas program planned for Thursday. Well, that was one good thing about not having any work. He could attend that program. He could hear Jenny's recitation. He could see Mary Kate. His spirits brightened considerably with that thought.

He glanced through the mail — all junk. As he tossed it into the wastebasket, he noticed a small postcard addressed to Jenny. His breathing slowed as he recognized his mother's handwriting. He felt a swirling undercurrent of fear from what might be coming.

Hey Jenny girl! Can't wait to see you on Tuesday! Don't be late, sweet girl! We got lots of catching up to do.

The kitchen clock ticked loud in the silence.

With an overwhelming sense of worry, he ran out the front door and down to the barn, panting by the time he reached Samson's stall.

Help me find Jenny, he prayed. *Keep her safe until I do.*

M.K. looked out the kitchen window and saw a pitch-black horse galloping up the driveway — Samson, with Chris on his back. Something was wrong. She ran outside to meet him as he reached the top of the rise.

"Where's Jenny?" His face was tight with tension. "Was she at school? Has Fern seen her today?"

"No. I thought she was sick."

The kitchen door swung open. "What is it, Chris?" Fern asked, wiping her hands on a rag as she came down the porch steps.

Samson danced on his hooves as Chris held tightly to the reins. "Jenny's missing. She left a note that said Mary Kate needed her at the school early this morning and late tonight — but then I got this postcard in today's mail." He hopped off the horse and handed Fern the postcard.

Fern read it and pinned him with a look. "Chris, where exactly is your mother?"

Chris stared at Fern with a combination of surprise and humiliation. "In Marysville, Ohio. In a drug rehabilitation center."

That was the most M.K. had ever learned about Chris and Jenny's mother.

She was momentarily flustered. Even Fern seemed flustered. She couldn't remember a time when Fern was ever flustered. But it only lasted a moment.

Fern turned to M.K. with a decided look on her face. "Call Rome. He'll know what to do."

Thoughts burst in M.K.'s mind and ricocheted around like corn popping in a kettle. Something had happened and she couldn't tell what. "Rome? Why would he —"

"Do it," Fern ordered.

Flustered, M.K. picked up the scooter that was leaning against the porch and zoomed down to the phone shanty. Chris followed on Samson. A few minutes later, as she approached the shanty, she heard the phone ringing. M.K. jumped off the scooter and lunged for the receiver. "Hello?"

"M.K., is that you?" It was Rome! Rome's deep, bass voice.

"I was just going to call you, Rome. We've got a terrible dilemma and we need your help!"

"Is your terrible dilemma named Jenny?"

"Yes! How did you —"

"I've got your terrible dilemma right here. Jenny's here, M.K. She's safe."

M.K. poked her head out of the shanty

351

and waved at Chris. "She's there! Jenny's with them." His face flooded with relief. She turned back to the phone, astounded. How did Chris and Jenny know Julia and Rome? More importantly, how did she miss that piece of information? Her detective skills were slipping. She blamed the teaching job. Too distracting.

"Ask him how she got there," Chris said.

M.K. repeated the question to Rome and held the phone out between them so Chris could hear Rome's answer. Despite the seriousness of the situation, she found herself extremely conscious of being so close to Chris, squeezed together in the small shanty. He was impossibly close now. She could hardly concentrate on what Rome was saying.

"Apparently," Rome said, "Jenny went to meet her mother just as Grace was getting released from the treatment center. Jenny went into McDonald's to go to the bathroom and Grace took off with her backpack. Jenny went back to the rehab center and someone there found a phone number for Old Deborah's. A neighbor picked up the message and called me. I just so happened to have an errand to do in Marysville, so I was able to pick Jenny up."

M.K. doubted that Rome had an errand

in Marysville. He was just thoughtful that way. Always going out of his way for others and never making it seem like it was an inconvenience.

Chris closed his eyes and slumped. He let out a deep sigh of relief. "Can you put Jenny on?"

"Let me ask her." In the background, they heard Rome ask Jenny if she would come to the phone, then Rome covered the mouthpiece and they could only hear mumbling until he came back on. "She's not quite ready to talk to you, Chris. She's shook up. She feels pretty bad. But I'm hoping you'll come out to get her."

Fern suddenly appeared at the door of the phone shanty. "Tell Rome we'll all come. Tell Julia to expect four more for Christmas. Wait — make that eight if Sadie and Gid and the twins want to come."

"MAKE THAT NINE," thundered Uncle Hank, appearing behind Fern. "I AM NOT EATING CHRISTMAS DINNER ALONE!" Edith Fisher was still spurning Uncle Hank.

Fern rolled her eyes. "Nine, then. We'll tell the van driver to move it up a few days and be there tomorrow afternoon. Tell Julia I'll do the turkey because her turkey ends up as dry as the bottom of a canary cage.

353

Oh . . . and no cranberry sauce from a can. Tell her you can always taste the tin. Tell her I've got most of it made already. Including the dressing for the turkey."

That was true enough. In the kitchen, wherever pies weren't, were big bowls of bread crumbs and bunches of sage, drying, waiting to be made into dressing.

M.K. turned her attention to report all of this to Rome, but he had overheard and was chuckling into the phone. "Tell Fern that I'm just going to inform Julia that Fern is planning to take over the entire Christmas meal. Then I plan to duck!"

Fern wasn't finished with her demands. "And tell Julia —"

M.K. handed the phone to Fern. "You tell him." She eased out of the phone shanty and walked over to Chris, who was untying Samson's reins from the tree branch. When she looked at him, she was overwhelmed by how little she knew him, really knew him. Who would have ever thought his mother was in a drug rehabilitation center? No wonder he didn't discuss his parents. How did it happen, getting to know someone? It took time. It took days spent together, weeks, months.

He glanced at her. "Your whole family doesn't need to go to Ohio."

354

"We were going, anyway." M.K. put a hand on his arm. "It's just a few days earlier than planned. Chris, you and Jenny . . . you're important to us. To all of us."

Their eyes met and held. Suddenly, Amos materialized out of nowhere, interrupting the moment. "What's going on?"

"AMOS!" Hank shouted from the phone shanty. "You won't believe the co-ink-a-dinky around here!" He patched together the story of Jenny-gone-missing-and-turning-up-at-Rome-and-Julia's for Amos, who took in the news with a stunned look. "So Fern's making plans for all of us to head out to Berlin a little early for Christmas to fetch Jenny."

Amos stood beside Chris and M.K., speechless.

"Amos, you don't have to go early," Chris said. "You don't have to change any plans. I can get there, fetch Jenny, and get back again by myself."

Fern stuck her head out of the phone shanty. "Nonsense! We were going anyway. What's a few days?" Then she popped back to resume her conversation with Rome before Uncle Hank could wrestle the phone from her.

"Really, Amos," Chris said. "There's no need —"

Amos raised an eyebrow. "You heard Fern." He looked at Fern in the phone shanty, chattering away with Rome. "Trying to shift my wife's plans is like trying to persuade a hurricane to change course."

Fern popped her head back out of the phone shanty. "M.K., skin on over to Jimmy Fisher's and tell him we need him to feed the stock for a few days. He needs to mist Chris's lettuce seedlings three times a day. Three times. Emphasize that for Jimmy. Write it down so he doesn't forget. He'll forget if you don't make it crystal clear. And then go to Sadie's and see if she wants to come along to Ohio. And then go sweet-talk Alice Smucker into substituting for you tomorrow and Thursday." She pointed to Chris. "You bring Samson over here by six in the morning. Jimmy can take care of him with the rest of the stock. The van will leave at six in the morning. Don't be late." She popped back into the shanty and picked right up with Rome where she left off. Never missed a beat.

"Well, you heard her." Amos stared at Chris awkwardly until Chris picked up the cue to leave.

Chris hopped on Samson's back. "Tomorrow at six. I'll be at Windmill Farm." He reined Samson around and trotted off.

What had just happened? M.K. was rarely astonished, but she was.

18

As Chris nudged Samson forward, a wave of exhaustion rolled over him. He wished he had been able to fend Fern off, to slip off and quietly fetch Jenny from Ohio. But there was both an urgency and a firmness in Fern's voice as she made plans, and against his better judgment, Chris found himself stepping back and letting her take charge. Worry and fear for Jenny weighed him down like a sack of rocks and it did feel good to share the load.

He felt grateful to Rome Troyer for being the one to rescue Jenny. But now the entire Lapp family knew about his mother. And how long would it be before the entire town of Stoney Ridge knew? He felt a deep shame — what must Mary Kate think of him?

The story of his mother was nothing he could ever share with someone as naïve and innocent as Mary Kate Lapp. He could hardly imagine the look on her face if he tried to describe the mean streak his mother had developed after she started to use drugs. She was a different person. He felt tainted — a feeling he had lived with his entire life. Stained by his mother's choices.

What kind of a woman would lure her thirteen-year-old daughter hundreds of miles away, only to steal her backpack and leave her stranded? And he couldn't blame that choice on drugs. His mother was clean, for now. He thought about that postcard — he knew she wanted him to see it. He had no doubt of that. It didn't surprise him that she had figured out where they were living. She was shrewd like that.

He was tired of carrying the burden of his unpredictable mother all alone. He was suddenly too sad for tears. His sadness took on a sharp, shining edge.

As M.K. rounded the bend toward Jimmy Fisher's house, she saw him heading to the hatchery with a bucket of feed and called to him. "Dad wants you to take care of the stock for a few days." She explained the need for the trip to Ohio, only lightly touching on the part about retrieving Jenny. She was still trying to process the news.

Jimmy howled like a lovesick basset hound. "I knew it. Chris Yoder steals my girl right out from under me."

As usual, Jimmy made little sense. "What? What are you talking about?"

Jimmy looked bothered. "Just what does Chris mean to you?"

M.K. blinked hard. "Have you been drinking again?"

"Does Chris Yoder make you laugh?" Jimmy asked.

"No," M.K. said honestly. "But you're not very funny right now, either."

"I can't believe you're doing this to me."

"I'm not doing anything to you. I'm going to Ohio with my family for a few days."

Jimmy shook his head. "The weasel. He's trying to snake his way into your family's hearts. And here I told him my intentions! I thought we were friends!"

"What intentions are you talking about?" M.K. shivered. She had grabbed her coat when she went out to meet Chris at Windmill Farm, but forgot mittens. "Look, the sun is starting to set and I need to get to Sadie's before it gets too dark."

He flashed her a brilliant smile. "The intention to make you my missus," he said softly, cupping her face with his hands. He leaned over and kissed her gently on the mouth. "That's my heartfelt intent. I've already spoken to your father."

Shocked, M.K. pushed him away. Jimmy Fisher was certifiably crazy. She didn't want to know any more right now. In a swift and sudden decision, she picked up the scooter and zoomed away.

"You just remember the thunder and lightning of that kiss while Chris Yoder is trying to woo you in Ohio!" Jimmy called after her.

M.K. was sure she had felt as astonished as a person could be back at the phone shanty. Now, she felt thoroughly flabbergasted. It was a very strange, new feeling.

Since Sadie thought they should stay home and keep Alice company for Christmas, Gid offered to fill in as a sub for M.K. Amos was a little disappointed — he had hoped that M.K. would have no option but to stay behind and teach, thus giving distance to Chris. He still hadn't gotten a handle on how churned up he felt after realizing who Chris's mother was and what she had done. Today's story only confirmed to him that this woman had a truly dark spirit.

Amos knew that he should be able to mentally separate Chris and Jenny from their mother. It wasn't their fault. He should be praying for God's mercy on that woman's soul. Yet all he could think about lately was how much he wanted Grace Mitchell to hurt like he had hurt. It shamed him. He had been taught to love his enemies for his entire life, and here, when it mattered most, he not only didn't love his enemy, he hated her and everything — everyone — connected with her. He would confess this hatred to God and ask for forgiveness. How could he ever expect God to forgive him for his many sins if he couldn't forgive someone else? Hadn't those words of Jesus been etched on his soul from the time of his childhood?

But there was one thing he wouldn't bend on. One thing he couldn't stomach: his darling youngest daughter must not, *must not,* get involved with *that* boy and his family.

Where was Jimmy Fisher and his charm when Amos needed him?

Jenny helped Julia finish setting the table for dinner and stared out the window, knowing her brother and the Lapps should be arriving any minute. She didn't know how she would face Chris after what she had done. Julia and Rome were so kind to her. Rome had hired a driver to take him to Marysville to fetch her and get home again — $35.00 — and his only remark about it was that seeing her was worth every penny. Julia had drawn a hot bath for her to help her get warm. Jenny's jacket had been with her backpack too. Her jacket, her money, her book. How could her mother do such a thing? Where had she gone? Was she doing drugs? Probably. Jenny remembered the look in her mother's eyes when she had seen the cash in Jenny's wallet. It was a strange look, a hungry look.

Jenny still couldn't believe it. After all of those promises.

It was just like Chris had said: for their mother, drugs came first.

A sound caught her attention — it was the big van, turning up into the driveway. Julia's four boys flew outside to meet their grandparents. Rome came out of the barn and joined his sons.

Jenny looked to Julia. "My brother must be furious with me."

Julia put a reassuring hand on Jenny's shoulder. "We'll go out together."

Chris jumped out of the van before it came to a full stop. He bolted up to the house, taking the porch steps two at a time. The moment she saw him, Jenny was on her feet and running, out the door before Chris reached it. She launched herself into his arms, full body weight, and he caught her close to him, hugging her, and both of them were crying.

"I'm so sorry!" Jenny said through her tears. "I went to see Mom, and she stole all my stuff and left me at McDonald's, and I didn't know where to go or what to do. She stole everything from me. Everything! All of the money I made working for Fern."

"It doesn't matter," Chris said. "All that matters is that you're safe."

Chris spun her around and around until she started to laugh with relief. Everything was going to be okay.

In the morning, Fern shooed the men out of the house, saying she and the womenfolk were as busy as bird dogs trying to get ready for Christmas dinner tomorrow. Rome wanted to work on a project in the barn, but Hank talked Amos and those four little boys, like stair steps, into going fishing at Black Bottom Pond. Amos tried to insist that Chris come too, but Rome interrupted and said he was counting on his help with building a tree house for the boys for Christmas morning.

Chris was relieved to get a little space from Amos. He felt as if Amos was practically Velcro-ed to him — he sat next to him in the van, at the fast food restaurants on the road, at supper last night, and again at breakfast this morning. It was as if Amos was doing his best to keep Chris as far from Mary Kate as possible. Chris was pretty sure Amos was savvy to that kiss by the schoolhouse. Why else would he be acting so twitchy? It was as if Amos could read Chris's thoughts and knew Chris was trying hard not to think about kissing Mary Kate again. There wasn't much chance of that happening on this trip — he was never alone with her. He was never alone, period. This house was filled with people. Strangely enough, despite everything — the reason they were there — Chris loved every minute of it. He knew it wouldn't last.

He set up two sawhorses for Rome to place a two-by-four on top. The two worked side by side, talking now and then, but not about anything important. Until Rome looked up and said, "Chris, what is it you really want in life?"

Such a deep question startled the truth out of Chris and he blurted out, "I want a home of my own. Something no one can take away from me."

Rome sawed the lumber into two pieces, then picked up another two-by-four. "I can understand that. It's sort of like a homesickness for a place you haven't come to yet. Being with other families only makes that longing ache deeper."

Chris nodded. That was it exactly. As long as he could remember, he was well aware of a hollow place inside of him, like an air bubble caught in a pane of glass. It was always there hanging about, an ache. It wasn't until he went to live with Old Deborah that he was given a taste of the joys of a normal childhood. It was the main reason he chose to be baptized in the Amish church last summer. He felt as close to that feeling among the Amish as he ever could. But to his dismay — he had since found that the ache was still there, a longing for something that he couldn't seem to identify. "I don't think it's going to happen for me."

"Why not?"

"Let's face it. I've been raised differently. I'm not like all of you. Loving someone, being loved . . . it's too hard."

"You're wrong about love. Love isn't hard. *Life* is hard. But when two people love each other, they create a haven." Rome sawed the other board in half and set it against the wall. "That feeling of longing isn't going to go away when you marry and have children."

Chris looked at him sharply. "What do you mean? Why wouldn't it?"

"Because the problem is in here." He

thumped his chest. "Because that feeling — wanting to belong, wanting to be valued — that can only get filled by God. You can't expect anyone to do that for you. That's God's work."

Chris was silent.

"I know you've had to face some hard things in your life. Ideally, you'll be able to bring everything together — and find God's purpose for your life in the process. He allows hard things like the one that involves your mother in order to shape us into better people. It's not his will that we suffer, but he can bring good from it if you'll let him."

Chris gave a little laugh that sounded more like a cough. "I can't see any good in having a mother who is a drug addict. Look at what just happened to Jenny. Hopes rise, our mother disappoints. Over and over again. It never ends. It never will end."

Rome picked up another piece of lumber and set it on the sawhorses. "Your mother's addiction brought you to Old Deborah. She brought you to church. Church brought you to us, and now to the Lapp family." He handed a saw to Chris to hold. "You're sweet on Mary Kate, aren't you?"

Chris looked away. Was it that obvious? "I didn't expect this," he said, finding his voice again. "I wasn't planning on this. But when

I met her, she was the exact person I'd been waiting for. I'd thought I wasn't looking, but really I'd been just waiting for her without knowing that I was waiting, without knowing that I'd been missing her before we met."

Rome grinned and tossed him a pair of leather gloves to use. "Chris, all the loose ends start coming together when you trust God both with your past and your future. That's what I have found to be true in my life. I pray that you'll do the same."

Chris wished he could borrow some of Rome's confidence, some of his faith, the way he could borrow the leather gloves to keep his hands safe. If only he could be as sure as Rome. Sometimes, just being around Rome, he did feel more confidence, like Rome rubbed off on him. Made him a stronger man. But faith, Old Deborah had taught him, wasn't something you could borrow from anyone.

The kitchen smelled of cinnamon and coffee. Fern scattered a layer of fine white flour across the surface of the counter. She and Jenny worked side by side, elbow to elbow, kneading, turning, punching the dough. In that clairvoyant way she had, Fern sensed Jenny had something to work out. Julia slipped upstairs to lie down for a few moments while the house was quiet.

Last night, while Jenny and M.K. were getting ready for bed, M.K. had confided that Julia was in the family way and that she was having morning sickness all day long. Julia felt confident that this time she was going to have a girl. "Julia has thought she was having a girl four times now," M.K. had whispered. "Julia always thinks she knows everything, but Sadie and I don't put much stock in her sixth sense."

It almost made Jenny cry. Tears would actually have spilled if she hadn't swallowed fast. There was just something so . . . so sisterly about the whispered confidences. Somewhere along the way, despite her best efforts, Jenny had begun to grow fond of Teacher M.K.

She knew her brother was sweet on her teacher — she had known ever since that first dinner at Windmill Farm when she caught him watching her with that goofy look on his face. She knew there was a selfish part of her that didn't want to share Chris. For months, Jenny had felt suspicious about Teacher M.K., waiting to see if she started to treat her differently than the other scholars. Trying to gain Chris's favor through Jenny. It had happened in Ohio with other girls, more than a few times. But Teacher M.K. didn't seem to be changing in any way. She expected the best out of each scholar, even Eugene Miller. Jenny's wary caution was starting to ease up around Teacher M.K. Just a little.

Jenny bent over and inhaled the tangy scent of the yeast in the dough. Fern sprinkled another dusting of flour over the ball of dough. Their elbows bumped as they worked. It was like Fern carried a force field of quietness, and when she came close, it wrapped around Jenny. Tears prickled her eyes. Would she ever stop crying over her mother, ever stop feeling so fragile?

When the dough was finished, Fern put it in an oiled bowl, covered it with a damp dishrag, and set it on the windowsill to catch the winter rays of sun.

Then Fern took Jenny's hands in both of hers and gently squeezed. Jenny remembered when she had first noticed Fern's hands, months ago, and thought they were rough and worn and reddened from too much work. Today they looked beautiful to her.

"You know, Jenny, you live long enough in this world and you're going to get rained on. It's as simple as that."

Jenny took a deep heaving breath. "My

mother is not ever going to be well, is she? God can't fix her."

"Just because God can heal her and that is what you want, it doesn't mean it will happen. Faith means we trust God will act in love."

"I hate her," Jenny sobbed. "But I love her."

Fern opened her arms and Jenny fell into them. "Remember, though, that sometimes you can love and forgive somebody, but you might still want to keep your distance."

There was something wonderful about that moment. She savored it and promised herself never to forget. Whenever she fell into Fern's arms — twice now — it was just like falling into the arms of a mother. A real mother. This terrible thing had sent her into the arms of something called Family.

Two kisses. In less than two weeks, M.K. had been kissed twice by two different men. Two entirely different men. She was surprised by how warm and soft Jimmy Fisher's lips felt against her skin. She was thoroughly confused by that kiss. Even more so by his professions of love and commitment. Where did such an outpouring of emotion come from? She never would have thought Jimmy had such deep feelings for her. For anyone!

She always thought he was mostly in love with himself.

Nor would she have thought Jimmy Fisher could be such an accomplished kisser. But he was. She couldn't deny that his kiss was rather . . . noteworthy. Afterward, it had taken her a moment to regain her balance. But it was curiosity that she felt, not desire.

Now that she thought about it, Jimmy had been hanging around Windmill Farm more often than usual. And he hadn't even talked about Emily Esh since . . . hmmm . . . she couldn't even remember. How had she missed the signals? The obvious clues? She was completely losing her remarkable ability to sniff out news. She blamed teaching. Too consuming.

It was just this one time. That's what Jimmy Fisher told himself as he led Samson down to the horse track where Domino Joe waited for him. The amount of money he owed Domino Joe had grown into a staggering sum. Domino Joe had lost his friendly countenance toward Jimmy and was turning surly. Jimmy needed one big win to pay Domino Joe off, then he would quit pony racing — quit it cold turkey — and start courting M.K. He already mentioned his intentions to Amos last week, and Amos looked pleased. Jimmy would get serious about his future. It was time. He didn't want to end up like his brother Paul, who dallied through life.

When Jimmy had first seen Samson, he knew this was the horse that could get him out of debt, permanently, with Domino Joe. He drove Samson down to the track and put him in crossties to check him over again. Cleaned his hooves, brushed him down, talked to him about the racetrack. Jimmy thought it helped the horse to know what to expect. Or maybe it helped the rider.

Thirty minutes later, he walked Samson directly past Domino Joe to go to the starting gate. He might have slowed a little as he passed him. Domino Joe looked Samson up and down, appreciating the animal's fine form. He whistled. "Hey, Fisher — since it's the day before Christmas and I'm in a charitable mood, I'm willing to offer you a bonus. All or none."

Jimmy narrowed his eyes. "If I win, my debt is wiped out? All of it?"

"That's right," Domino Joe said. "And if I win, I get that horse. Deal?" He held out his hand.

Jimmy looked at Samson. He had tremendous confidence in this exceptional horse.

Today's win would give him a fresh start, a clean slate. He stuck his hand out to shake Domino Joe's. "Deal."

Jimmy lined up Samson at the starting gate. He could feel Samson's tension build: his ears pinned flat against his head. His tail swished. The whites of his eyes were showing. The horse was practically prancing in the box, eager for the race of his life.

Perfect. The moment was perfect.

That afternoon, after the talk with Rome, Chris waited for Amos to return from fishing with his grandsons and cornered him in the barn as the little boys ran into the house with Uncle Hank.

"Amos," Chris said, boldly and firmly, though he didn't feel bold or firm, "there's a hardness between us. Have I done something to offend you?"

Amos's face tightened. "Something like, say, kissing my daughter in front of the schoolhouse? In broad daylight?"

Chris rubbed his face with the palms of his hands. "I thought that was maybe the reason you fired me. Maybe I should have talked to you first, to let you know I care about Mary Kate. I'm sorry about that. But I'm going to own my grandfather's house as soon as I turn twenty-one. Just four weeks

374

from now. I've been fixing the house up so it's livable. I have plans. I want to buy some mares soon and start breeding Samson. I want to settle down in Stoney Ridge." He took a deep breath. "Amos, I'd like your blessing to court Mary Kate."

Amos's face was still tight. "You'll never have it. Never."

This wasn't going well at all. "Do you mind telling me why?"

Amos looked at him. "Your given name is Mitchell."

A feeling of dread rolled through Chris's stomach, but there was no turning back now. "How did you know?" He had been so careful.

"I knew your grandfather, Colonel Mitchell. So did my first wife, Maggie."

Chris tilted his head, confused. "But I thought your first wife's name was Margaret. I saw her grave at the cemetery." Chris felt the air whoosh out of his lungs. "Oh. *Oh.*" Maggie was a nickname for Margaret. He knew that. How had he not connected the dots? Chris had to sit down. The room started to spin and he thought he might get sick. He put his head in his hands. Maggie Lapp was the neighbor lady who came to help them. Maggie Lapp was the woman his mother had pushed down the porch stairs, the reason they fled Stoney Ridge. Maggie Lapp's death was the reason the Colonel went to jail.

Amos's hands tensed into fists. "I realize you were only a child. But I just can't let you court my daughter. I just . . . can't."

"I'm not good enough." Chris wasn't asking. He knew that was true. It always, always came back to that. He was tainted. He glanced up at Amos. He didn't blame him.

Amos's frown of worry eased from his forehead, but he didn't acknowledge Chris's comment. "M.K. doesn't know how her mother died. Neither does Sadie or Julia. They just think their mother tripped and fell and hit her head on a rock, that it was just an innocent accident. There's no need for them to know anything else. It's all too . . . complicated." He rubbed his face. "Jimmy Fisher spoke to me about courting Mary Kate last week, and I told him he has my blessing." He walked past Chris, stopping briefly. "If you truly care about M.K., you'll let her go."

M.K. said she was going to bed early, and that wasn't a lie. She did go upstairs and she did go to bed. But she kept one eye on the window, watching the barn. She knew Rome and Chris were in the barn, feeding the animals. Tomorrow morning, early, the van was coming to pick them up to return to Stoney Ridge. They had gone today to visit Annie and little Joe-Jo, who looked so much like her brother Menno as a little boy that everyone left Annie's home quiet and reflective, remembering Menno. Missing him. Annie was married now to a nice enough fellow, and they had two children of their own. Joe-Jo was happy, secure, growing up in a healthy family. What more could they want for him?

They had done everything they had come to do. Mary Kate didn't want the trip to be over, but in another way, she did. Chris was acting so distant that she couldn't stand another minute of being near him, yet so far from him. She had to do something. Now. Tonight.

Patience, schmatience. It was highly overrated.

She heard her father and Fern go up to their room, listened to the hum of their voices through the wall, and then there was quiet. Jenny, sleeping in the twin bed in M.K.'s room, was snoring a light whiffling sound. The coast was clear.

M.K. waited awhile, quietly dressed, tiptoed downstairs, grabbed her big sweater, tiptoed past Uncle Hank snoring so loudly in the rocking chair by the fire that it rattled the windows, and slipped out the back door without Julia or Sadie spotting her. She had always been particularly adept at sneaking past her sisters. It was one of her best skills.

M.K. hurried across the yard to the barn and pulled the door open. Rome and Chris were just about to leave and looked startled by her appearance. "Rome, would you mind if I had a few minutes alone to talk with Chris? Dad and Fern went to bed, and I got past Julia and Sadie without them seeing me."

Rome grinned. "I'm glad to see you've still got your sneaky side, M.K. I surely am. You've been so quiet this visit that I've worried teaching has plumb worn you down."

"Oh, it definitely has," M.K. said. "But there's something I need to talk to Chris about. Without a crowd listening in."

"Like, a crowd that resembles Amos Lapp?" Rome walked past her and whispered, "I'll cover you for a while. But don't stay out too late. If Julia catches wind of my letting her little sister out in the barn, unchaperoned, with a young man, I'll be sleeping out here for the rest of the winter." He looked back at Chris and added, "Talking only, young man." He grinned, winked, slipped out the barn door, then shut it.

■ ■ ■ ■

Chris's cheeks flamed. He looked at his feet. "Make it fast because I'm freezing."

M.K. blew out a puff of air. "Why are you acting like such a jerk?"

Chris snapped his head up. "How so?"

"Ever since you kissed me at the schoolhouse, you've treated me like I've got the bubonic plague."

Chris turned away, but M.K. pulled his arm, forcing him to turn back toward her. "Just tell me why you've turned so cold and distant. I deserve that much."

He looked right at her. "You do. You do deserve that. You deserve that and much more." He put his hands on her arms. "Mary Kate, you deserve better than me."

"Why can't I make that decision, Chris? Why does everyone think they know what — or who — is best for me?"

He dropped his arms and paced around the center aisle. She was so innocent, so naïve to the cruelty people were capable of. "You don't know me. You don't know anything about me or my crazy family. You don't know what I'm capable of."

"I might not know everything about you, but I do have a pretty good idea of the kind of man you are, Chris."

"No. You don't. You have no idea. My life's not worth . . . anything."

She straightened up as tall as she could and pointed at his chest with her finger. "Don't ever say that again," she told him, sounding like she was talking to one of her scholars. "Don't ever, ever say that again. Don't think it either. That's a lie you should never believe." She took a step closer and reached out for his hand. Her hand tightened around his fingers, and only then did he realize how much was at stake.

"Why me, Mary Kate? What could you possibly see in someone like me?"

"The thing about you, Chris Yoder, is . . . you make me want to be a better person." She reached out and touched his cheek. He turned his face so that he could kiss the palm of her hand. His lips brushed her hand, then again, and he took a half step closer to bring their bodies into light contact.

Then, abruptly, he stepped back, pressing her hands into a prayer, palm to palm. "I'm sorry, Mary Kate," Chris whispered. "I can't do this."

When Chris looked up, M.K.'s eyes brimmed with unshed tears. One finally fell and traced a path down her cheek. She backed up a step and crossed her arms over her chest. Then she turned and pulled the barn door open. She started to walk back to the house alone.

And he stood there and watched her go.

Was he going to let her walk out of his life?

No. No he wouldn't.

He ran to the barn door and whispered as loud as he dared, "Mary Kate!"

19

The van pulled into Stoney Ridge as the sun was starting to set. Amos directed the driver to drop Jenny and Chris off first. Naturally, M.K. thought, still exasperated with her father. As the van went down the long driveway, M.K. noticed someone's car parked out front, but no sign of anyone.

Chris groaned. "That's the realtor's car, Rodney Gladstone. He keeps after me to buy the house." He slid the van door open and let Jenny climb out. "Thank you for everything," Chris told Fern, before turning to Amos. "I'll get Samson in the morning, if that's all right." He gave M.K. a brief glance as he closed the van door.

The van turned around in the driveway as Chris tried to open the front door with his key. M.K. saw him look at Jenny with a puzzled face. "Hold up a moment, Ervin," she told the driver. "I think something's wrong." She unrolled the window.

A man in a business suit came around the side of the house. "Locks were changed, just this morning. Did you forget something?"

"What are you talking about?" Chris asked, coming down the porch steps. "Why would the locks be changed?"

Chris seemed to know this man, so M.K. guessed he was the realtor. She jumped out of the van, and Amos and Fern followed.

"That's what the new owners wanted done, first thing," the realtor said. "My brother-in-law is a locksmith."

"New owners?" Jenny asked.

Rodney Gladstone looked at Chris, baffled. "Didn't your mother tell you?" He scratched his head. "I hope I didn't spoil her surprise."

"Tell me what?" Chris said, his voice filled with alarm.

Jenny's eyes went wide.

"I contacted her a month or so ago to let her know I had a buyer for the house, to see if she might be interested in selling."

Chris fixed him with a hard stare. "How did you know where she lived?"

Rodney glanced at Jenny.

"He did it!" Jenny pointed at him, glaring. "He brought the mail to the house one morning and looked through it! He saw Mom's address on an envelope."

Chris looked at her as if she were speaking in Chinese. "What envelope?"

Jenny looked at him with wild eyes. "Mom and I . . . we've been writing back and forth, all fall. She figured out where we were living by the postmark."

Chris squeezed his eyes shut, opened them. He turned to Rodney Gladstone. "You had no right to meddle in our business. No right at all."

"But I did!" Rodney said. "I absolutely did. I was just doing my job. Grace Mitchell held the title to the house. She was the legal owner. It was all there, down in the title office. I had a buyer. It was the right thing to do. It was my duty to present an offer to the rightful owner. It's my job." His Adam's apple bobbed up and down. "Grace Mitchell called me right away. The same day she got my letter. She said she wanted to sell. I sent her the offer and she sent it back, accepted without contingencies. It went into escrow and she told me to get the paperwork ready for the notary public. She would be in Stoney Ridge to sign the papers on December 23rd."

"She was here?" Chris said. "My mother was here? In Stoney Ridge?"

Rodney nodded, paling. "December 23rd, just like she said she would be. Right before

384

closing time. She said to keep the sale a secret from you and your sister — she wanted to surprise you and buy you a bigger spread. For your horse business."

"You sold our house?" Chris looked and sounded as if he couldn't get his head around this news. "You sold our house out from under us?"

Rodney started to sputter. "It was all legal! The title was in her name. She inherited the house from her father. It was all . . . legal. We had all the paperwork. I was just doing my job . . ."

"You gave her the money for the house?"

Rodney gulped. "A cashier's check." He licked his lips. "I figured she was doing you a favor. I mean, she's your mother."

"You figured wrong . . ." Chris's voice trailed off. He looked shaken, pale and dazed, as if he might pass out. "How could she have done this? How could she have masterminded this?"

Jenny started to sob and M.K. pulled her into her arms.

M.K. sucked in air, held it in her lungs. She wanted to shout, *That's terrible, terrible! . . . What kind of woman would lure her daughter and son to Ohio so that she could sneak back to Pennsylvania and sell their home out from under them? She's a monster.*

Instead, she only murmured, "Everything will be all right."

Fern stepped up to Chris and put a hand on his shoulder. "It's late. We'll get this sorted out in the morning."

Rodney shook his head. "Not possible. The possession date was on closing. The new owners arrive with their moving truck at 8 a.m." He looked cautiously at Chris. "Your mother said she wants to buy you a bigger place. A better place."

M.K. couldn't tell if that was the wrong thing to say to Chris. Or the right thing. Whichever it was, it snapped him out of his shock. Chris's hands were clenching and unclenching rhythmically, his powerful chest shook. He gave Rodney a look as if he wanted to tear him apart. "My mother is halfway to somewhere else right now. She took that house money to feed her drug habit. She'll blow through that money within the month."

Rodney Gladstone's pale face went two shades paler. He looked horrified. "But she looked so normal, and seemed like a nice lady . . . and it was all . . . legal . . ." His voice drizzled off as he realized that he wasn't helping the situation, so he quietly got in the car and drove off.

M.K. watched Chris's arms fall to his

sides, and something seemed to collapse inside of him. She couldn't bear him being hurt any more. She simply couldn't bear it. She looked to her father to say something, do something. But Amos Lapp did nothing. He seemed at a complete loss for words. So she turned to Fern, who seemed just as nonplussed. M.K. was going to have to take charge. "They should come to Windmill Farm."

Fern blinked a few times, then snapped into action. "Of course. Of course they should." She put an arm around Jenny, who was still crying. She led her into the van.

"Chris," M.K. said softly, "come to our house."

Chris didn't budge. He had a strange look, as if he were somewhere else. "Chris, you need to come with us," M.K. repeated. "You can't stay here. Jenny needs you."

With that, Chris seemed to jolt back to the present circumstances. Then his face opened for an instant: grief and loss. He nodded and followed M.K. meekly into the van.

They sat down to a silent dinner of cold turkey sandwiches from leftovers Julia had sent back with Fern. No one was very hungry, but Fern insisted everyone sit down and eat.

"Today, despite everything, is a gift," she said, right before they bowed their heads, "and we should return thanks."

And she was right. Remembering God put everything in its rightful place, even terrible things. Chris's face, Amos noticed, had lost that awful white color from when he heard the news of his mother's actions.

Amos felt disgusted by the treachery Grace Mitchell had pulled over her children. Even animals cared for their young better than that woman.

But there was a tiny glimmer of happiness inside of Amos. It shamed him to admit it, but he couldn't stop the thought from taking shape: Now, surely, Chris Yoder would leave Stoney Ridge. There was nothing to keep him here.

And then he silently upbraided himself for his selfishness.

A knock at the door interrupted his conflicted thoughts. He got up and opened the door to find Jimmy Fisher standing there.

"Come in, Jimmy." Amos pulled him in and closed the door. Ah, finally. Finally, Jimmy Fisher showed up when he was needed. Jimmy stood awkwardly in front of the family.

"Have you eaten?" Fern asked.

"Yes. No." Jimmy scratched his neck. "I have a couple of things to tell you." He looked at M.K. "First, Eugene Miller wanted me to give this to you." He handed her a note and waited while she read it aloud.

Deer Teecher M.K.
 I am running off fer good. Don't worry about mee. I will bee fine. Yurs trooly, Eugene Miller

 P.S. I am not leaving cuz of your teeching. Yur not half-bad.

M.K.'s dark brown eyes, so much like Amos's own, widened. "He's gone. Eugene Miller left home. He's run away." She passed the note to her father.

Amos's heart went out to his daughter. She had been encouraged by the progress Eugene had been making. He was just about to say something to comfort her when Jimmy blew out a big puff of air.

"There's something else." Jimmy moved from foot to foot, ill at ease. "Something I need to say, and I need to say it right away, while I still have the strength." He cast a furtive glance in Chris's direction.

"Did something happen to Samson? Is he

hurt?" Chris jumped up from the table.

Jimmy looked at M.K., then took a deep breath. "He's not hurt. He's fine. More than fine. But . . . something has happened." Jimmy folded his arms against his chest. "I raced him. Over at the track."

"Domino Joe's gambling field, you mean," Fern uttered under her breath.

"Samson's not much of a racehorse, I discovered." Jimmy rubbed his hands together. "I underestimated his —" he glanced at Fern — "manliness."

Chris groaned. "His instincts would make him try to prove to the other colts that he's the boss. He's the keeper of the fillies."

Jimmy rubbed a hand through his hair. "Apparently." He cleared his throat. "But I was just so sure he would be a crackerjack racehorse." His eyes nervously took in the room. Quietly, he added, "So I bet on him." Jimmy carefully studied a crack in the ceiling. "And I lost."

There was a terrible silence that no words could fill. All eyes were on Jimmy.

Chris came around the table. "What exactly did you bet?"

"Samson," Jimmy said, barely a whisper. He cleared his throat. "I bet Samson. And I lost. I lost Samson to Domino Joe."

It took a moment for Jimmy's confession

390

to sink in. A solitary feather would have knocked everyone down. It hit Chris first, full force. He opened his mouth as if forming an answer, then clenched his jaw and closed his eyes in despair. "The only thing that was mine . . . the *only* thing left . . . and you lost him in a pathetic pony race . . ." When he opened them again, he turned to M.K., then to Amos, with wounded eyes. He snatched up his hat and coat and left the house without a word, closing the door gently behind him.

Jimmy wrinkled his face in confusion. "What does that mean — the only thing left?"

M.K. looked at Jimmy with disgust. "Why don't you ever do what you're supposed to?"

He shrugged. "Because I can never figure out what that is."

Mary Kate leapt up to grab her coat off the wall peg.

"You're not going after him," Amos said.

She ignored him and put her coat on.

"Did you hear me?" Amos repeated. "There's more to the story than you know."

"What's the whole story?" Jimmy asked, eyes bouncing from Amos to M.K. and back to Amos.

M.K. glared at Jimmy, then turned to her father. "I know more than you think I do,

391

Dad." M.K. pointed to Jimmy. "I know you'd rather I go out with him — a liar and a cheat and a gambler —"

"Hey," Jimmy said. "That's a little harsh."

"All true," M.K. snapped. "I know you're the one who has been dipping into everyone's coffee cans to pay off your gambling debt to Domino Joe."

Jimmy raised his eyebrows. "How would you . . ." He opened his mouth. Closed it. Opened it, closed it, as if he thought better than to deny it. "I'm not proud of that," he mumbled. "And I have plans to pay it all back."

"Out there is a man — not a *boy* —" she gave a glance in Jimmy's direction — "who keeps his word. Who is fiercely protective of his little sister. Who has plans and dreams for a future. And that future keeps getting ripped from him — through no fault of his own." She threw another dark glance in Jimmy's direction.

"This has nothing to do with Jimmy," Amos said. "This is about Chris. Chris and his mother."

"What about Chris and my mother?" Jenny asked. Everyone looked at her as if they had forgotten she was there.

A pained look crossed Amos's face.

"Dad, I know about Mom's fall. I know

there's more to it than just an accident. Chris told me all about it in Ohio last night. He told me every detail." She walked up to Amos and took his large work-roughened hand in hers. "I realize this is complicated, but hasn't he paid enough?"

"I want to save you heartache, M.K. I want to stop you before it's too late. Before you think you're in love with him."

"With who?" Jimmy piped up.

Amos saw his daughter's face change before his eyes, from a young girl to a young woman. Before his very eyes. There was no mistaking. She wasn't his little girl anymore.

"Dad," she said gently. "It's already too late. You can't fall out of love with someone." She squeezed his hands one last time and went outside.

As she was closing the door, Jimmy pulled a chair out and said, "Think Chris is gonna finish that sandwich?"

"Immer dreizehn," Fern sighed. *Forever thirteen.*

Chris leaned his head against the door of Samson's empty stall. He had led Samson in there just a few mornings ago, gave him water and fresh hay, and told him he'd be back for him. Samson was gone. He couldn't believe it. He wondered if this was what Job of the Bible felt like, as messenger upon messenger brought him news of horrendous proportions. *Bam, bam, bam.* One blow after another. How much could a person bear?

Chris was rendered as motionless as stone, his brow furrowed. In his head, he heard Jimmy speaking about betting on Samson, he heard Rodney Gladstone talking about selling the house, but the sounds came to him as through a long tunnel, over the rush of a freight train roaring in his head. He fought to breathe, to maintain his footing. All he could picture was his mother.

How much would God give a person to bear? How many times had he asked God for guidance and help? To cure his mother of her addiction? To give him wisdom to take good care of Jenny? But apparently God didn't listen to prayers of that sort. Or maybe he just didn't listen to his.

"Where are you, God?" he shouted, pounding the rails of Samson's stall. "Old Deborah said we should trust you. She said to leave everything in God's hands. Now look at this mess! Where are you?!"

"Fern always says that when God seems most absent, he is most there."

Chris whirled around to face Mary Kate. He wiped his eyes with the back of his hand.

"It just gets better and better, doesn't it?" He put his hands on his hips, gazing at the empty stall. His eyes were bleak. "You shouldn't be near me. Your father's right. My family is like poison."

She gave him a gentle smile. "I don't believe that."

"Of course not. How could you? You don't understand, Mary Kate. You couldn't possibly." His face contorted. "This is what it's like with my mother. This is what my life is like. Every time Jenny and I would get settled in somewhere, she'd swoop in and disrupt it all. Today is no different than the way my entire life has gone. This is what it will always be like. She will always find a way to take what doesn't belong to her." He snapped his fingers. "Everything gone in the amount of time it takes to fill your lungs with air one time. Gone." He snatched up an empty bucket and hurled it down the barn aisle. The sound of clinging and clanging down the cement path startled the horses so much that they shuffled in their stalls.

Mary Kate was unruffled. "She might. Or she might not. It doesn't matter. She can't take what's truly important."

The horses went back to their quiet munching of hay.

Could she be right?

Chris went very still, and for a long minute he frowned as he stared at Samson's empty stall, but little by little, tension drained from his shoulders.

He looked over at Mary Kate and he saw her tears through his own. And before Chris realized what was happening, she flung herself at him, clinging tightly to him, sobbing against his chest, telling him that she thought he was wonderful, crazy mother and all. He wrapped his arms around her, hugging her in return — the first embrace he had given or received for a very long time.

Right then, something happened inside his chest. Not a lightning bolt zinging him, but a soft and breathtaking peace that one day, someday, everything would be alright.

As Fern got Jenny settled into Sadie's old room for the night, Amos stood in front of the fireplace, watching the flames dance. He was hardly aware of the clinking and clanking of dishes as Fern cleared the table and put them in the sink to soak. Suddenly, he realized she was standing right next to him.

"Don't you think it's time you told me what's been eating at you?"

Amos put his face in his hands, then slowly dropped them. His voice shook with the effort of getting the words out. "I don't know how to tell you this. It's about Maggie."

Fern's look changed, softened. She reached up and brushed back the hair from his right temple. "Why don't you start at the beginning?"

They sat in front of the fire as Amos told her how Maggie had befriended Colonel Mitchell's daughter. He was able to keep his emotions at bay while he spoke, until he got to the part on that spring day when Maggie was long overdue from a quick visit to take goat's milk over to Grace Mitchell to help her colicky baby. Then, his voice choked up and he had trouble getting the words out.

Fern waited patiently as the scene of that afternoon played through his mind, as vividly as yesterday, and he tried to gather the words to tell her . . .

By the time Julia and Sadie had returned from school, Amos knew something was wrong. Maggie should have been home hours ago. He put Julia in charge of Sadie, Menno, and M.K., and crossed the field to go to the Colonel's house. As soon as he crested a hill, he saw the red flash of police car lights. He ran the rest of the way. There was an ambulance and three police cars. Amos knew something horrendous had happened. He charged through the backyard and was blocked by a policeman.

"My wife is there," Amos said, with a voice he didn't recognize as his own. He shoved the police officer away and went around the side of the house. And there he saw his Maggie, his darling, beautiful Maggie, motionless on the ground with a paramedic by her side. Colonel Mitchell sat in the back of a police car, his head hung low.

"She's gone," the paramedic had told Amos gently. "It looks like she was pushed down the porch steps. She hit her head on that rock and fractured her skull." He gave Amos a sympathetic look. "She must have died instantly. I doubt she ever knew what happened."

The police had pressed him with questions. Did he know why Maggie had gone over to Colonel Mitchell's house? Yes. Did Maggie have any kind of conflict or dispute with the inhabitant? Of course not! Did he know of any reason why Colonel Mitchell might have argued with her? No.

In the end, the coroner ruled the death as accidental manslaughter. The Colonel confessed that he was responsible for the accidental death of Margaret Zook Lapp, though he would not say anything else. Not how it happened. Not why.

It never made any sense to Amos. It never did. The Colonel was a hard man, but he was reasonable. And despite being a career military man, he was not violent.

It wasn't hard to figure out that the Colonel was protecting his daughter, Grace Mitchell. But the problem was that Amos knew who was truly responsible for Maggie's death. He knew, and he didn't do anything about it. Not a thing. It didn't even occur to the police to ask if the Colonel had someone else living at his house. Amos could have volunteered that information, but he didn't. If the Colonel didn't admit it, he wouldn't either.

There was a little part of Amos that felt justified. Vindicated. Someone should be held responsible. If not Grace, then the father who raised her. Weren't parents responsible, to some degree, for the moral outcome of their children?

And then swept in a wrestle with his conscience: who was he to make such an accusation against another child of God? God did not call him to judge another. He was given one soul to account for — his own.

But he knew. And he did nothing. The Colonel was sent to a minimum-security prison and died while serving his sentence, from some kind of swiftly moving cancer.

"So that's the whole story," Amos finally said, after relaying everything to Fern in fits and starts and sobs. "I just can't look at Chris without thinking of Maggie's death. Everything about it — the Colonel's look on his face while he was in the police car. The guilt I feel because I remained silent when I knew it was Grace Mitchell who had caused Maggie's death. I'm not saying she tried to kill Maggie. It might have been an accident, but she never owned up to her responsibility. As far as I know, she never came back to Stoney Ridge. Not even for her father's funeral. Maybe it's not fair or right or logical, but I can't get past it."

Fern didn't say anything for a long while. "Maybe you're not supposed to get past it."

He looked at her. "What does that mean?"

"God brought Chris and Jenny into our lives for a reason. They began here, then ended up with Old Deborah, giving them the opportunity to get to know Rome and Julia. Then back they come to Stoney Ridge. You told Bud at the Hardware Store that you needed someone to help you cut hay on the same day that Chris came in, looking for work. Who would have believed that Mary Kate would be teaching school this term? And that one of those pupils is Jenny. Coincidence after coincidence after coincidence. A sure sign of God's silent sovereignty. I don't think he wants you to get past this. I think he wants you to get *through* it."

"Fern, I don't know how."

"Every single day, you pray to God to help you forgive Chris and Jenny's mother. Pray for mercy for her soul."

Amos wiped his face with both of his hands. How long had he held on to this information, rolling it over and over in his mind? Always simmering, always in the back of his mind, like a wound that couldn't heal. He was exhausted. "I'm afraid I can't find the strength in myself to do that, Fern."

Fern leaned forward, smiling tenderly. "Good," she said. "Now we're getting somewhere."

But Fern wasn't done yet. "Amos, you need to reach out to Chris. To show him how to live with a problem that doesn't go away. Because something tells me we haven't heard the last of that mother of his." She rubbed her hands together like a little girl. "But I have just the idea to start redeeming this big mess."

Amos looked at his wife, amazed that she still loved him after what he had just confessed to her. "I don't deserve it." Grace, Amos meant. And mercy.

"None of us do," Fern answered, understanding.

On Monday afternoon, the pupils stayed late to finish up an art project. It was Uncle Hank's idea: he had a few way-past-their-prime rainbow trout in the freezer that Fern insisted he toss out, and M.K. had extra paint, so the pupils made fish prints. The schoolhouse smelled horrible but the pictures were wonderful. She thought about Eugene Miller, missing whatever his creative mind would have conjured up for a fish print. His empty desk grieved her today. It grieved everyone. Where was he? Was he going to be all right? She knew she would worry about him for the rest of her life. All she could do was to pray for him.

Mary Kate hung the last picture on the wall and stood back to look at the room. It was surprisingly cheerful. Everything about her life surprised her. Not only that she was a teacher, but that she liked it. In fact, there were moments, like today, when she was starting to love it.

She heard a knock at the door and Chris

402

popped his head in. A big smile creased his handsome face. "Can you come outside for a minute?"

She hurried out to meet him. Chris stood beside a pitch-black stallion. "Samson!" She crossed the porch and put her hand out to Samson's velvet nose. "How in the world did you get him back?"

"I didn't," Chris said, grinning. "Your dad and Fern went to an auction this morning and bought him back from Domino Joe. Cost a pretty penny. I told your dad that I wanted to pay him back, but he said no, that it was a down payment."

"Down payment on what?" M.K. stroked his long neck.

"He said something odd — something like 'refreshing the sponge.' Fern explained that was bread baker's code for a fresh start." Samson dipped his big head up and down, making Chris take a step back. "I finished up minor repairs on the bishop's buggy today. The bishop was happy about that. He seems pretty determined that I should help your uncle in the buggy shop. But I don't want to step on your uncle's toes."

"Don't worry about that. Uncle Hank wants to retire from buggy repair. Just last night he said he's going full time into finding water. Much more lucrative, he thinks, especially after Edith Fisher corrected him about the puppies' mother. Turns out she isn't a poodle at all. She's a Portuguese water dog. So now he has a theory that he can train the puppies to find the water for him. All four."

Chris laughed.

"I knew he would never give those puppies up."

"Mary Kate, there's something else I want you to think about. Your father and Fern offered to have Jenny and me stay at the honey cabin." The air had gone quiet, falling into the purple hush of dusk as the winter sun slipped behind the trees. He glanced down at his shoes, suddenly shy. She understood that he was every bit as nervous as she was. "I wondered how you might feel about that, seeing as how it's your workplace for your bees."

But where would she keep her honey equipment? she thought, and then, Chris would stay in Stoney Ridge! Swirling in the back of her mind had been a nagging worry that he might return to Ohio since he no longer had a home to live in. Suddenly, she was filled with a wild sense of happiness. It seemed incredible. Miraculous, even. She wouldn't mind moving her honey equipment out of the honey cabin. Not one little bit! A smile uncurled. She didn't quite trust her voice. "I think it sounds just fine. Better than fine."

He watched her, a small smile turning up the corners of his lips. "We're alike, Hank and I."

"How's that?" M.K. said. She'd just noticed he had a large envelope behind his back and she craned her neck to see whose name was on the address label — better still, who had sent it — but he kept it away from her and slipped his other arm around her, pulling her close to him.

"Hank and I both know a good thing when we see it."

M.K. hid a smile.

He leaned closer to her. "And we won't let go of that good thing."

"Really?" The word came out as a soft gasp. "Not ever? Not even when your mother reappears and makes you feel like you're worthless? You won't believe her and retreat into your turtle shell?"

He looked at her as if he thought she had spoken in another language. Then his face slipped into a smile. "Not even then," he said, and just like that, she couldn't breathe.

Their eyes met — those familiar blue eyes that crinkled at the corners when he smiled. She stood without moving as he bent over to kiss her. Then she slipped her arms around his neck and he kissed her until she was too breathless to think straight.

He let her go and waved the large white envelope. "Fern wanted me to hand deliver this to you."

M.K. grabbed it from him and opened it up. In it was her passport. It had finally arrived in the mail. She looked up at Chris and smiled. She could go anywhere in the world.

But she didn't want to be anywhere else.

QUESTIONS FOR DISCUSSION

1. Mary Kate started this story with an immature perspective on her life. She didn't appreciate what she had or what she might be giving up if she left her family and church. Which relationship had the most effect to help her turn the corner toward adulthood: Erma Yutzy? Chris Yoder? Fern Lapp? Eugene Miller?

2. Chris and Jenny's mother is aggravating. I even felt it as I wrote her character! It would have been nice to have a happy ending for Grace Mitchell, but it just doesn't always happen that way in life. Whether Grace chose addiction or it chose her, she was stuck. Do you have someone in your life who seems stuck in a cycle of selfish sin?

3. Loving someone who continues a pattern of harmful sin is very complicated. Here's an example of how Jenny struggled with hope and reality over her mother: "Despite

everything, despite how confused she felt, it was her mother whom Jenny couldn't stop thinking about. Her mother needed her. She should be there when her mother was released from rehab." Have you ever been betrayed by a person you trusted? How did you react? How does it affect you today?

4. Jenny wondered why Chris didn't argue back to their mother. Old Deborah explained, "Years ago, your brother read something from the Bible that spoke to him and settled deep. Jesus said we should be as wise as serpents and as harmless as doves." What a puzzling phrase! Yet filled with practical wisdom. How would you explain Jesus's words to someone?

5. Old Deborah explained that Chris was wise enough to know that words were like tools. "Your mother uses her tools to tear down. Chris uses his tools to repair and fix up." Have you ever thought of your words like that?

6. Trace the effects of love in this story on Chris and Jenny: Old Deborah's, Fern's, Mary Kate's. What do you think this story tells you about the impact of love?

ACKNOWLEDGMENTS

Last year, I read a short comment at the end of a scribe's letter in *The Budget*. It was written from an Amish woman who participated in an informal program with a women's prison. This woman fostered a prisoner's child and took her to visit her mother once a month. I started to do a little digging and found a similar program with the Mennonite Caregivers Program. This program's aim isn't to recruit children for the Mennonite Church or to be adopted. "And whoso shall receive one such little child in my name receiveth me" (Matt. 18:5) is the only motivation for these thirty Mennonite families who live in Southeast Pennsylvania. Studies have shown that incarcerated women who mother their babies have a lower recidivism rate. How remarkable! I felt so impressed by these quiet heroes, trying to strengthen family ties.

So that's how the story of Chris and Jenny

Yoder began, with Old Deborah — another quiet hero. Remember, though, it is a work of fiction. Chris and Jenny's mother, Grace Mitchell, was caught in a cycle of drug addiction. It would have been nice and tidy to have Grace "see the light," but that just doesn't always happen in life.

There are many types of addiction — some that are obvious, like drugs, and some that are more sinister. Fern's comments to Jenny toward the end of the book had so much wisdom in them: "Remember, though, that sometimes you can love and forgive somebody, but you might still want to keep your distance." Sadly, some problems are just not going to be solved in this lifetime.

A special thank-you to my first draft readers, Lindsey Ciraulo and Wendrea How. You're the best!

A big shout-out to my insightful editor, Andrea Doering, named Editor of the Year at ACFW in 2011. And to my agent, Joyce Hart, who is always my Agent of the Year. Thank you to the support team at Revell: Michele Misiak, Janelle Mahlmann, Robin Barnett, Deonne Lindsey, Twila Bennett Brothers, Claudia Marsh, Donna Hausler, and so many others who help get my books from the warehouse to the shelves and into readers' hands.

As always, my gratitude goes to my dear family. And finally, I would like to give a heartfelt thank-you to the Lord who has been blessing this endeavor of mine. I hope I'm doing him proud.

ABOUT THE AUTHOR

Suzanne Woods Fisher is the author of *The Choice, The Waiting,* and *The Search* — the bestselling Lancaster County Secrets series. *The Waiting* was a finalist for the 2011 Christy Award. Suzanne's grandfather was raised in the Old Order German Baptist Brethren Church in Franklin County, Pennsylvania. Her interest in living a simple, faith-filled life began with her Dunkard cousins. Suzanne is also the author of the bestselling *Amish Peace: Simple Wisdom for a Complicated World* and *Amish Proverbs: Words of Wisdom from the Simple Life,* both finalists for the ECPA Book of the Year award, and *Amish Values for Your Family: What We Can Learn from the Simple Life.* She is the host of *Amish Wisdom,* a weekly radio program on toginet.com. She lives with her family in the San Francisco Bay Area.